W9-CFQ-681

EDEN'S REVELATION

BOOK II *of*
THE ORDER SERIES

Printed by CreateSpace
Charleston, South Carolina

Eden's Revelation

by

John Butziger

Copyright © 2016 John Butziger

Library of Congress
Control Number 2016902232

This novel is a work of fiction. Names, characters, places and incidents are either the product of the author's imagination, or, if real, used fictitiously. Any resemblance to any person or persons, living or dead, events or locales is entirely coincidental.

ALL RIGHTS RESERVED. No part of this work may be reproduced, transmitted, stored, or used in any form or by any means graphic, electronic, or mechanical without the written consent of the author.

First Edition 2016
ISBN: 978-1523781706
Editor: Karen Frisch
Cover Design: Giovanni Auriemma
Formatting: Nina Pierce of Seaside Publications

Synopsis of THE SECOND TREE
(The Order Series Book I)

On a shoot in Uganda for the Culinary Network Channel, Martin stumbles into a hidden valley in the Rwenzori Mountains and finds a strange fruit. He brings it back to New York and gives it to his friend and co-worker, Andrew, who recognizes its unique flavor and wants to sell it to restaurants in Manhattan.

Andrew has difficulty growing it in his Long Island greenhouse at first, but after learning that the valley's high walls allow only brief sunlight to reach the plant in its native setting, he tries limiting the seedlings' exposure. It works, and he is astonished at the resulting plant growth. The fruit is delicious, and restaurants clamor for the rights. It becomes an overnight sensation, and the Culinary Network Channel features a program on the fruit that airs internationally. In it Martin and Andrew are shown holding the fruit, and Martin divulges that he found the fruit in the Rwenzori Mountains of Uganda.

Andrew, who has been eating the fruit continuously, later discovers through a freak accident that regular ingestion imbues the consumer with near-instant healing. He tells Martin and his sister, Laurie, of the amazing find. They all agree to keep it a secret.

Greedy Martin, however, now wants to make millions by commercializing it with the pharmaceutical industry, and he begins gorging himself on the fruit in an attempt to gain healing powers rapidly. At first none of the pharmas will meet with Martin, thinking him crazy. One of them even reports him to Ed Lambard, the NSA Cyber Crimes Section Chief and Corporate Liaison, believing Martin's antics to be related to recent cyber-attacks.

After several failures Martin finally convinces Andrew to help him, and together they secure a meeting with Regentex, a leading pharmaceutical company in the tristate area. Meg Hennessy, type-A business executive at Regentex, is astonished by the opportunity and immediately begins negotiations. But after meeting with Meg, Martin and Andrew return to the farm to find that they've lost all of their fruit in a fire in the greenhouse. Desperate to continue gaining power and maddened by his rapid consumption Martin begins to lose his sanity while Andrew flies to Uganda to seek the fruit's source.

In Uganda, the Economic Development Ministry is trying to stimulate financial growth by selling the rights to mine copper from the Kilembe Valley, which lies near the Rwenzori Mountains where Martin once found the fruit. They reopen the mines with local workers to demonstrate its viability for the solicitation. Bidders from the US, China, and several other countries express interest, attracting the attention of a Ugandan nationalist terror group. Fearing a US presence in Uganda, they kill several miners in the hopes that the US will be scared away from the Kilembe region forever.

Meanwhile in the US Ed Lambard of the NSA has been investigating the cyber-attack accusations against Martin. He finds that Chinese hackers have indeed infiltrated the servers of several pharmas in the region, including Regentex. He also learns of a "miracle healing drug" from hacked emails. Guessing that Martin's friend Andrew is connected to the cyber-attacks, Lambard contacts his friend Colonel Frank Anderson, Director of US Special Operations Forces in Africa, to tail Andrew in Uganda. But Anderson can't free up any Ugandan resources to help, as they are tied up thwarting further terrorist attacks at the Kilembe mines.

In his search for the fruit, Andrew is approached by a tall Ugandan named Kabilito, who clearly knows of the fruit's powers. Kabilito reveals that the fruit is called "maisha" in their native tongue. He tells Andrew that maisha not only speeds healing, but over time it also increases strength and speed. In fact eventually the consumer ceases to age, and older bodies revert back to their prime. Kabilito tells Andrew that his tribe discovered the fruit in a secret valley over a hundred and fifty years ago, and that a prophecy compels his people to protect the fruit until a sign is revealed. Humanity is not ready for the maisha fruit, he says, and a madness may ensue if too much is consumed too rapidly, as the fruit can amplify character flaws. Kabilito explains that the prophecy describes the sign as a shift in humanity, and as a result the tribe decided that Kabilito would leave the valley and form a business in the busy international shipping port of Mombassa, in Eastern Africa, to watch for the sign. Finally, he reveals that the tribe believes the valley to be Eden, and that the maisha fruit is of the Tree of Life. He tells Andrew that it was he who burned down the greenhouse, ensuring that fruit would be removed from the outside world. Andrew is infuriated but knows he is no match for a tribe of super humans. He agrees to give up on the fruit but wishes to see the valley for himself. Kabilito acquiesces, but requires Andrew to be blindfolded and stripped of any electronic devices before visiting Eden.

Even after the terrorist attacks, international interest in the Kilembe Mines is strong, especially with the US military patrolling the valley. But the presence of the US forces in the Kilembe Valley further infuriates the nationalist terror group. Led by Jelani, a terrorist mastermind, they gear up with a massive, well-equipped force to destroy the US soldiers, kill the miners and dissuade foreign interest in the mines once and for all.

While Andrew is gone, Martin falls deeper into insanity. He finds seeds from a final, remaining fruit and begins to regrow their stock, but he has completely lost his mind. He takes over Andrew's home and attacks his sister, Laurie, when she makes a surprise visit. Laurie escapes and contacts Andrew, who immediately leaves the valley with Kabilito to stop Martin and destroy the remaining fruit.

But their route back to the airport runs through the Kilembe Valley, and their progress is blocked by the terror group's attack on the US troops. Outgunned and outnumbered, the US soldiers are pinned down and taking casualties. Kabilito suggests circumventing the Kilembe battle, but Andrew convinces him to help the US forces. The tribe's combination of enhanced healing, strength and speed allows them to neutralize the attacks, but not before several US soldiers and miners witness their incredible powers. All of the terrorists are killed or captured except for their leader, Jelani, who escapes.

Reaching New York, Kabilito and Andrew cannot locate Martin at first. They search Andrew's farmhouse only to find a macabre scene: Martin has been cutting off body parts and displaying them as specimens in jars. He suddenly appears and attacks them, and a terrible battle ensues in which Andrew's arm is ripped from his shoulder. Kabilito and Andrew try desperately to subdue Martin and save him, but he is too far gone, and he is destroyed. During the fight Andrew's farmhouse is burned to the ground. Having lost his home, his job, his friend, and even his arm, there is nothing left for Andrew in New York. Convinced of his selflessness and willingness to protect the secret of the fruit, Kabilito offers Andrew a place with the tribe in Uganda.

Meanwhile, Lambard at the NSA and Col. Frank Anderson in the US military cover up the stories of the incredible healing witnessed in the Kilembe Mine battle. The data recovered from the Regentex cyber-hacking incidents, the sightings from the mine battle and the information revealed in the Culinary Network Channel program Martin and Andrew had produced are too compelling to ignore, and they begin plotting to secure the fruit to synthesize a drug for use as a weapon.

At Regentex Meg Hennessy's team also finds the culinary video program and realizes that the drug resides in a fruit from Uganda. Meg assembles a team and begins a desperate search for the lost opportunity in the Rwenzori Mountains.

Characters from *Eden's Revelation*
Returning from *The Second Tree*

The Tribe:

Andrew farmed fruit that was given to him by his friend, Martin, and eventually discovered its powers. He lost his arm in the final battle with Martin in Book I. Kabilito invited him back to the tribe after Andrew proved his worth by sacrificing everything to stop Martin and protect the secret of the fruit.

Kabilito is the man chosen by the tribe to watch the world for the prophesized sign. As a boy he fell into the pit during the missionary battle many decades ago. He operates the Mombasa Port international shipping operations inherited from Bea, the Lake Captain's daughter.

Subira is the leader of the tribe and motivated the group to overthrow French missionaries who had gone insane consuming the fruit, ruling the tribe cruelly.

Akiiki is the religious leader of the tribe. He helped young Kabilito out of the pit during the missionary battle. The prophecy came to him in the form of a dream, that one day a shift in the people of the world would be realized, signaling mankind's need for the fruit's power.

Other Characters:

Meg Hennessy is the Type-A Business Development executive from Regentex, the pharmaceutical company pursuing the fruit deal with Martin and Andrew. They know the fruit is somewhere in Uganda based on a cable network show that featured Martin, Andrew and the Manhattan restaurant that exploited it. At the end of Book I she was on her way to Uganda to find the fruit.

Ed Lambard is the NSA Cyber Crimes Section Chief and Corporate Liaison. He interfaces as a corporate liaison with Regentex and discovered the Chinese hacking activities, through which they learned about the fruit. He is friends with Colonel Frank Anderson.

Colonel Frank Anderson is in charge of African and Middle East Special Operations. He forced his underling, Major Graham Mackenzie, to dismiss the notion of supernatural powers reported by the US soldiers from the Ugandan mine battle. Frank is friends with Ed Lambard of the NSA. Frank is working with the tech warfare division in secret to pursue and develop the fruit into a weapon.

Major Graham Mackenzie runs the Special Operations Forces in Uganda under Col. Frank Anderson.

Chapter One

Arzu unrolled his Turkish prayer rug and smoothed it over the rocky mine floor. The reed mat sewn on the underside protected his knees during the Salat al-dhuhr afternoon prayer, but an errant stone pushed through a bare spot, and a sudden jolt of pain shot up Arzu's leg. Shifting his position, he embraced the pain – it was a sacrifice he made for his faith. He continued his prayer amidst his brethren, each facing Mecca, or at least the best approximation they could make from deep in the Kilembe mine shaft.

Light from the dim lanterns splayed across the roughly-hewn cavern walls and danced across the dusty faces of the supine men as they practiced the Salat. Their Chinese employers frowned upon the frequent Muslim prayer rituals, but fifty meters down in the old Ugandan copper mine they were far from disapproving eyes, and they would not be denied.

As Salat ceased and the prayer rugs were rolled, Arzu smiled thinking of the small fortune he was able to send back to his family. It had been a rushed departure, and he regretted his children's tears as he had hurriedly packed his bags. But at three times the going rate he couldn't turn away from the opportunity. Work was scarce in their homeland of Urumqi, in the Xinjiang region of western China. Largely controlled by the Chinese Han population, Urumqi had become less tolerant of the Uyghur people's ancient claims to the land. Each year fewer projects were won by their small Turkish construction company, forcing the owner to accept work farther from home.

Nearby, Arzu heard his friend grunt as he plucked a stone from his boot. Yusup stood and spat on the mine floor. "These Chinese – always looking for ways to rid themselves of us. They ship us out here to this empty mine, they make us sleep in tents and feed us nothing but chicken stew."

Arzu frowned as Yusup threw the stone against the rock wall and brushed the dust from his robes. It was easy to become depressed and frustrated deep in the mines and far from family, especially when the work was as unproductive as it had been.

Yusup continued complaining in his native Turkish. "Not a single vein of copper found in the month we've toiled here. It's as if they don't care. They keep us digging in this empty shaft just to keep us out of Urumqi. They'd rather see us dead than return home."

Arzu patted his friend on the back comfortingly and smiled. "Easy, Yusup, these same Chinese imported contractors from all over China and the Middle East, too. And they pay us handsomely – they're just desperate to dig because they overbid on the mine rights. So stop with the conspiracy theories. Besides, at the rate you work, you're not likely to die from overexertion anytime soon."

The others laughed as they stirred and gathered their equipment to continue their shift. Even Yusup smiled wryly at the jest. Chuckling, he picked up his air hammer and rested the tip against the nearest rock face.

"What's the point in working fast when there's no quota to fill?" he replied. As Yusup pulled the trigger the air hammer sprung to life with a familiar, metallic clanging. Dust rose from the point as the hammer worked, and soon a crack formed in the rock wall.

But as the hammering continued Arzu squinted suspiciously at the rock face. Something about the crack felt *wrong*. It *sounded* wrong. He watched nervously as the fissure suddenly propagated up the wall toward the ceiling, then ran horizontally along the cavern roof.

Yusup sensed the danger as well. Frowning, he halted and dropped the air hammer, stepping away cautiously. Men gaped as the crack continued to splinter down to the floor, and they began to stagger backward.

"Get out!" Arzu cried as he turned, pulling Yusup away from the wall. He pushed past several of the miners gawking at the massive slab of rock now outlined by the crack. Others started following him toward the main shaft.

Arzu risked a look back as he slid past the workers, dragging Yusup by the arm. A deafening crackle filled the air, and Arzu watched in horror as the rock slab suddenly slid from the wall, revealing an enormous cavity. He heard a loud hissing noise – the sudden release of trapped gas – and a rotting, acerbic smell filled the mine shaft.

Men were shouting and screaming now. The miners began desperately shoving each other forward to escape, following the path Arzu had started. Some fell to the floor, while others were pressed against the rough rock of the mine walls as their countrymen pushed past.

Stuck against wooden shoring as a tide of flesh swelled against him, Arzu looked back at the rock face once more, just in time to witness the final act of his own demise.

A loud snap reverberated through the mine shaft, followed by a rumbling thud. He watched helplessly as the huge slab completed its descent onto Yusup's air hammer, sparking angrily along the hardened metal as it slid down to crush the tool as if it were a soda can. Sparks instantly turned the venting gas to flame, and shouts became screams as fire erupted throughout the cavern.

The men closest to the slab were engulfed in flame and fell to the floor, writhing in agony. Arzu's cries joined those of the dying as the ceiling suddenly collapsed, ending their misery and entombing the Uyghur under the crushing weight of the falling stone.

Chapter Two

Yeh Xin glided silently over the packed earth, matching his target's pace. He peered through the vines spilling from the rocky overhang above him and drew a slow, practiced breath. Brilliant Ugandan sunlight reflected from the young American woman's blonde hair as she trampled noisily through the overgrown mountain path.

Reaching the end of his vine cover, Yeh Xin paused to allow her some headway. He froze as she turned in his direction and shouted out the unfamiliar names again.

"Jack!" she yelled. "Beth? Dammit!"

She snapped her head back, her golden hair splaying in a wide arc. Yeh Xin scowled and shifted his weight to the balls of his feet as the strange woman his dossier had named "Meg Hennessy" began swearing again.

"Goddam slugs – can't even keep up. Jack, damn you, I'm over here!" She squinted and listened intently, then continued along the path toward the crest of the nearby hill.

Yeh Xin smiled, recalling her profile. She was a type-A, American executive for a large pharmaceutical company – *of course* she was used to getting her way.

"Beth!" she yelled once more as she disappeared over the crest and down to the small valley below.

After several moments, Yeh Xin left the cover of the vine curtain and sprinted lightly along the same path. He slowed and crouched as he approached the hilltop, then stopped to peer over the crest. She was jogging now, but moving erratically and breathing heavily. Yeh Xin could tell she was beginning to panic. He quietly counted out his estimate of her growing distance in Mandarin, though he was fluent in five other languages as well. *"Twenty meters…thirty meters…forty…"*

When he reached fifty he began sprinting again as Meg neared a copse of trees covered in thick, mossy heather. He stayed low to the ground, fixated on her frantic gait as she drove a wake through the sea of brilliant blue lobelia flowers covering the valley floor.

Yeh Xin winced as she suddenly fell to the ground and disappeared into the lobelias, tripping over an unseen obstacle. He instantly dropped and flattened his body against the ground amidst the scant grass cover near the top of the ridge.

An ungodly wail rose from the bright blue flowers, and Yeh Xin frowned. *She couldn't have made that sound.* He raised his head and risked a glance in her direction. The shrieking wail continued, sounding a lot like an infant, like a…

"Oh, no," he whispered under his breath as she rose slowly from the flowers.

"Oh!" she exclaimed loudly, crouching to reach

tentatively into the lobelias. "It's okay – I won't hurt you!" The wailing subsided as a tiny, furry arm shot up from the sea of blue to swat at her dangling hair. "It's okay!" she cooed again sympathetically.

A deafening roar cut through the thick mountain air. Yeh Xin desperately scanned the underbrush near the foot of the trees, searching for the source as Meg jerked upright, clearly terrified. The scrubby brush thrashed violently, disturbing a flock of African black swifts that flew up and away, squawking.

Suddenly a furious ball of angry black fur burst from the undergrowth, bounding directly toward Meg, pouncing from curled fists to hind legs.

Yeh Xin watched in horror as she screamed. His African wildlife training sprang to mind. *When a mountain gorilla charges...*

"Drop!" he whispered urgently. "Drop – submit!" But instead Meg ran, and the angry gorilla gave chase. Yeh Xin stood slowly, oblivious to his exposure, morbidly drawn to the scene.

Meg ran away from the copse of trees in the only direction possible – directly along the foot of the hill she had descended earlier. Unfortunately the hillside steepened and joined with the opposite valley wall ahead of her, forming a natural funnel with no exit. Yet she continued sprinting desperately into the trap, and the maddened gorilla roared as it closed the gap.

From his vantage point Yeh Xin watched in frustration as his charge was cornered. Meg stretched out her arms to arrest her wild dash but slammed into the back wall of the cliff anyway. She spun around, her hair lashing out in an arc of sweat-drenched gold. Panic washed over her features as the massive ball of angry gorilla rumbled to a stop and confronted her.

A primal roar erupted from the gorilla as he bore his fangs and beat his chest. Meg feinted toward the gorilla's right flank, then darted to the other side. Yeh Xin inhaled sharply as the gorilla easily snatched up her leg and sent her spinning through the air. In an instant the gorilla was on her, monstrous teeth sinking deep into her upper thigh. She let out a shriek that sent a chill through Yeh Xin's bones.

But the gorilla wasn't finished. Maddened by the taste of blood, the animal pummeled Meg's head into the packed earth and pounced on her back. Yeh Xin tensed as the frightful scene tore at his soul. His mind raced. He could expose himself by scaring the gorilla away with his pistol, but the training ingrained in him compelled him to find cover and abandon his target.

Yet his morality won, and he tugged the pistol from his belt. Quickly he raised it in the air to shoot, but movement from the ridge above the gory scene arrested his trigger finger.

A young African man, tall and lean, dropped from the ridge above the attack – a fall of at least ten meters. The man easily absorbed the shock of the fall with his legs, rolled and sprang lightly to his feet directly in front of the attacking gorilla. Startled, the gorilla roared at the newcomer from its perch atop Meg's supine form.

Taking advantage of the surprise entrance, the African man launched himself at the animal, extending a leg in the split second before impact and delivering a solid kick to its leathery chest. Yeh Xin squinted in astonishment as the gorilla was thrown back several meters, tumbling head over heels. His gun forgotten, he let his hand drop to his side in disbelief.

The gorilla was enraged now, and Yeh Xin knew that the newcomer didn't stand a chance. The animal screamed and rushed his attacker, tackling him and sending him sprawling to the ground. In a blur of motion the gorilla pounced on its victim's thighs, pinning him. The man let out a grunt as the gorilla pounded his head with its hairy fists, then cried out as the creature bent down and ripped flesh from his shoulder with its teeth. Incredibly, the man lifted the gorilla from his chest and threw the animal to the side as he rolled in the other direction, rising swiftly to his feet.

Yeh Xin squinted intently at the scene and held his breath. *Could the reports be true?* Once gushing with blood, the wound in the man's shoulder had ceased bleeding altogether, and the man flexed his arm in an arc, seemingly unaffected.

But a moment later the gorilla recovered and lashed out at the man with a massive fist. The man caught the hand easily, twisted gracefully around the beast and kicked it squarely in the back, sending the animal sprawling to the ground once more. Yeh Xin's jaw dropped. Now the man was on the attack, fully healed, *against a wild gorilla three times his mass.*

The African grabbed the gorilla around the torso and lifted it from the ground. He tossed the animal into the air, flipping it around and catching it by the wrists. The man spun faster and faster in a circle as the animal flailed its legs helplessly. Finally the man released the gorilla, launching it toward the copse of trees. The living projectile arced toward the small forest in a black, furry streak, screaming in fear as it disappeared into the tree canopy with a thunderous crash.

Although he had been briefed, although he had read the

dossier thoroughly, Yeh Xin simply couldn't believe his eyes. But clearly he had found evidence of the source. He was one step closer to his goal.

Track the girl. Find the tribe, find the fruit. His last mission...

The tall, young African stooped to study Meg's limp form. Blood ran freely from the bites on her thigh. As the man scooped up her body her head rolled, revealing crimson rivulets running freely from a gash on her temple. The African slung her over his shoulder and started away from the cliff face, down the path leading away from the hillside where Yeh Xin stood, stunned.

Shaking his head, Yeh Xin gathered his senses and assessed the situation. The newcomer was a clear threat, but obviously of a higher value than his original target. The amazing nectar most definitely ran in his veins, and if he didn't lead Yeh Xin directly to the fruit, there were other options for which he was well trained. Bullets might not truly harm the man, but they would slow him.

Yeh Xin fingered his gun absently, hoping he wouldn't need to use it. He descended, his form melting behind a large rock. From there he glided over to the cover of the underbrush, all the while keeping a careful eye on the stranger carrying Meg's body.

Over hills and rock outcroppings he continued, keeping pace with his new charge but remaining undetected. He deftly navigated a path from boulder to brush, pausing at each hiding place, taking advantage of the lengthening shadows. At one point he marveled as the African man climbed effortlessly up a steep rocky slope, one-handed, with Meg's seemingly lifeless form draped over his shoulder. Incredulous, Yeh Xin scrambled after him, breathing heavily as he reached the crest of the rock face.

He followed the pair in this manner for a few miles before the land flattened and the cover of brush and boulder became scarce. Yeh Xin scowled as he was forced to halt, his progress slowed by the threat of discovery in the grassy plains.

Waiting until the African man and his burden were far ahead, Yeh Xin decided to risk it and emerged. He ran stealthily on the balls of his feet, crouching to stay low. In the distance ahead the grasslands rose slightly, and he sprinted as he saw the man carry Meg swiftly over the crest of the hill and out of sight.

Several minutes later he climbed the same rise and found that the plains continued only a short distance beyond the hill before suddenly dropping off, continuing ahead as a narrow strip of land – a thin ridge with steep sides that led away from the plains.

And his prize was nowhere in sight.

Yeh Xin paused. *Had the stranger continued ahead to the narrow ridge,* he wondered*? Or had he turned after he crested the top and escaped along the hill below the rise? And if so, in which direction?*

Faint tracks crisscrossed the packed earth, and the grass was bent in all directions. Some tracks were new, others old. He saw human, animal, and possibly even tire tracks – but it was impossible to discern the stranger's from the rest. *Who else would be way out here in the middle of the mountains? Hikers?*

Taking his best guess, he ran the short distance to the ridge and onto the high, rocky path. Each footfall was calculated to avoid slipping over the edge. *They couldn't have left the path – it's too steep,* he thought. *Well, too steep for any* normal *human.* Yeh Xin swallowed nervously and continued.

The narrow ridge rose sharply in the middle, blocking the path ahead from view. Beyond the ridge crest a sheer mountain face was visible, covered in vines that sprouted wildly from a ledge jutting out halfway up the face. Reaching the top of the crest, Yeh Xin stopped. The ridge sloped downward then stopped, terminating at the foot of the steep cliff, buried in a thick cascade of vines that spilled haphazardly over the entire face of the mountain.

Yeh Xin exhaled sharply. He spun around, whipping his head from side to side. He peered over the edge and down the steep slope, considering the possibility once more. *No - there's simply no way he scaled down, not even* him...

He explored the stone ridge all the way to the cliff face, searching desperately for any sign of footprints, but the rocky crest was unyielding, leaving no trace of the man and his burden.

He doubled back to the plains. *Maybe the man had veered off along the hill after all...*

Yeh Xin searched the plains for the better part of an hour until the sun began to dip behind the Rwenzori Mountains to the west. With the glaciers of Margherita Peak lit from behind like a brilliant jewel, the Chinese operative sighed and shook his head. Exhausted and dejected, he headed back to the Kilembe Mine valley to inform his superiors. Despite his discovery, they would be most unhappy with him for losing the trail.

Chapter Three

Andrew breathed deeply of the rich, earthy orchard air and reached for a fruit on a branch near him. He was still amazed at its shape – an hourglass, two spheres joined at the center with a bright green skin crisscrossed with angry red veins. It was impressively exotic, but the powers held within were even more incredible. He plucked the maisha fruit from the delicate branch and marveled over it for a moment, then dropped it into his woven grass basket. His hand brushed against the fruit he'd already picked, and his fingers absently caressed the ridges of the fruit veins. The sensation in his fingers awoke another memory, and he looked down at his hand.

It was fully healed. His arm had been severed in the fight with Martin in New York, but within two weeks had grown back completely. And the healing had accelerated in the last few days. Andrew swore he could even watch the regrowth.

He certainly *felt* it – tissue knitting over bone, tendons and ligaments connecting, muscle filling in. He rotated his hand back and forth, amazed at its restoration. The nerves, bones, muscles, tissue and skin all now perfectly in place – it was nothing short of a miracle.

His shattered soul had begun to recover as well. Having lost his family home, his best friend, and his job, there had been nothing left for him in New York. Although it had been difficult saying goodbye to his sister Laurie, she had understood, and he knew they would make plans soon enough to get together again.

He just needed a little more time to restore the parts of him that the fruit couldn't heal. The tribe members were helping with that. All seemingly in their mid-twenties, Andrew knew that the fruit kept their true ages hidden. Every one of them was five or six times his age, and each had experienced several lifetimes of knowledge, relationships and learning. Their calm approach and steadfast teachings had opened Andrew's eyes. Although not particularly religious, Andrew found their mix of spirituality comforting – a blend of the various Christian denominations. They had adapted, grown, and traveled a long way spiritually from the days when missionaries taught them organized religion from books.

His basket full, Andrew climbed down the ladder and dumped the maisha fruit into the cart. There was no need to worry about bruising it – its regenerative powers extended to its own fruity flesh, and it never rotted, never decayed, and needed no refrigeration. Andrew had an affinity for this particular property as he was responsible for cooking it.

Ever since coming to the valley Andrew was expected to pull his own weight, which was fine by him. His training in the culinary arts and love of cooking meant he was perfectly suited to take over as the chef for the tribe, a job he embraced willingly and enthusiastically.

And how could he not? Looking around the gorgeous valley, he drank in the colors of the vegetation on the high slopes – the same lush walls that limited the day's sunlight to only a brief visit, allowing for the exact conditions needed for the miracle fruit to thrive.

Vines cascaded over the tall tree limbs and covered the slopes, running down and around the bamboo groves like a living green river. A stream fed the valley, its waters clear and cool – glacial melt from the Rwenzori Mountain peaks that surrounded the valley. The leaves of the kifabakazi "fire trees" swayed gently in the breeze, igniting the forest canopy with a brilliant display of red and orange flame.

Andrew was certainly not lacking ingredients within his new valley home, either. Game was plentiful, especially for the superhuman members of the tribe's hunting party. The duiker antelope, bush pig, and guinea fowl were just a sampling of the fare brought back from the wilds of the Rwenzoris to supplement the domesticated goats, chickens, and long-horned Ankole-Watusi cattle the tribe kept as livestock.

Some members of the tribe maintained a gorgeous farm, growing beans, yams, sweet potatoes, and a variety of tasty African vegetables Andrew had never seen or heard of before – the small-leafed, purple flowered amaranth, the eggplant-meets-tomato fruit of the nakati plant, and the leaves and roots of the cassava tree.

The valley's wild vegetation supported the tribe as well – tasty bamboo shoots, succulent green berries from ensali trees, and milky white nectar from the trunks of euphorbia trees.

And then of course there was the maisha fruit – the most delicious of all the vegetation available in the valley. Stewed, fried, baked, grilled, broiled – no matter how it was prepared it paired well with almost any other food and was, itself, incredibly delicious. Savory umami flavors burst from the tender flesh, ignited by the heat of the nectar in the deep red veins that burrowed from the skin all the way to the core of the fruit.

To his delight Andrew had ample cooking facilities to experiment with new culinary dishes. Though the location was remote, the tribe had inhabited the valley for well over a century, and during that time they had created an efficient, comfortable, yet clandestine habitat. All the creature comforts were carefully considered in the planning of the village – generators, satellite Internet, four-wheelers to transport heavier materials into the valley. But of course there was no need for medicine or first aid. Not while the fruit remained a major staple of their diet.

The settlement was camouflaged with netting suspended above the tops of the huts to prevent discovery. Though the valley itself was well hidden, accessible only by the vine-covered lava tube on one end and a concealed path on the other, the tribe was careful to protect its secret. Revealed to them in a vision long ago, their mission was to protect against the premature unveiling of the fruit's power – until a foretold sign appeared.

Andrew effortlessly wheeled the massive fruit cart over roots and ruts toward the cooking pots as the sun began to dip below the high walls of the western ridge. As he approached the outdoor grilling area, he smiled as he gazed at the bounty he would prepare for the tribe tonight. Fresh goat meat, bamboo shoots, imported spices and a new variation of chapati flat bread made from ground amaranth was on the menu, as well as stuffed game fowl from the day's hunt. It was a dream for Andrew to finally escape from his Manhattan Culinary Network Channel cubical and use his training to create dishes that were appreciated. His work as chef was spectacular, and the tribe applauded his efforts.

He began chopping the greens but stopped as a commotion across the encampment caught his eye. Squinting, his eyes followed the activity, then widened. He dropped the knife and stumbled toward the confusion.

Then he jogged. *Then he ran.*

Kabilito was returning, but not alone. Over his shoulder Andrew could see a limp form – a woman with long blonde hair, matted with sweat and blood. Several of the tribe had already reached Kabilito and were surrounding him.

It barely registered how fast Andrew was running, how fast he *could* run now. The settlement was merely a blur as he raced past at an inhuman speed. Slowing as he approached, he saw Kabilito lay the woman on the ground as other tribe members gathered around. Akiiki, the tribe's spiritual leader, and Subira, the tribal chief, hunched over her supine form as Andrew pushed through the crowd. He looked down at the woman's face, and his jaw dropped.

"Meg?" he exclaimed.

Kabilito's head snapped around to regard Andrew with his ancient, penetrating gaze.

"You know this woman?" he asked, his rich voice accented in a mixture of British and French. Kabilito held her head up gently, and Andrew caught a glimpse of the tattoo on his forearm – a flaming sword in a circle of fire – through the curtain of Meg's golden hair.

"I – *yes,*" he gasped, staring dumbly at her ruined leg and bleeding head. "This is Meg Hennessy from Regentex in New York. She..." Andrew trailed off as Kabilito held up a hand to stop him.

"First things first. Please make the draught I showed you, and be quick. She's lost a lot of blood."

Andrew nodded, turned and bolted for the kitchen area and his fruit. His mind raced as he ran. *What the hell was* she *doing here?*

Luckily he had already started a pot boiling for dinner. He diced some fruit, threw it into the water, and began stirring. The last time he had seen Meg was in the Regentex Pharmaceutical meetings in New York with Martin. He remembered her as aggressive, driven, *and damn cute*.

He shook his head to clear it as he continued stirring furiously. She must have come here in pursuit of the fruit. But how had she made the connection between their few, cautious meetings and the location of Martin's discovery in Uganda, back when he had been on a shoot for the Culinary Network Channel...?

He stopped stirring. The Culinary Network Channel. *The video*. She must have gotten hold of the program they filmed to promote the restaurant – the first restaurant that had bought Andrew's fruit. That was before he knew of its wondrous properties. In the cable network piece Martin spoke of Uganda, the Rwenzoris, falling into a valley...

And now he had unwittingly endangered the tribe's location. How many others were descending on the valley because of his foolishness? Andrew cursed and peered into the pot. The maisha was fully boiled, so he removed it, strained and mashed it, and prepared the draught as Kabilito had taught him – a miraculous draught that saved lives. Little

Bea's life for one – the Port Bell captain's daughter, almost a century ago. The same draught that they had planned on administering to his best friend, Martin, to help him recover from the madness...

The last memories of his friend were painful. Martin's character flaws had been magnified by the madness when he turned, his fears, greed and aggression twisting him into something inhuman, something deadly...

...and so they had been forced to kill him. Horribly. Andrew was still haunted by images of his severed head, his face contorted by rage, the smell of his burning flesh...

I'm sorry, Martin. We tried...

Swallowing hard, he poured the completed draught into a cup and sprinted, impossibly fast, back to Kabilito and Meg. Kabilito took the cup, raised Meg's head and dribbled some on her lips. She coughed and sputtered, eyes still closed, but her full lips parted and she hungrily gobbled the healing potion.

With her thirst quenched, she slipped back into unconsciousness. Kabilito lay her back down and poured the remainder on her open wounds.

"Will she survive?" Andrew asked.

Quiet, broad-faced Akiiki answered him. "The maisha draught has never failed, though admittedly we've only needed it a few times."

Kabilito stood, brushed the dust from his clothes and addressed Andrew. "Now I'll be hearing that story from you," he asked sternly.

"But what if she wakes? She'll have truly discovered the valley then," Andrew replied.

Kabilito shook his head. "They sleep for many hours, even days sometimes after drinking the draught. We'll return her to the hiking paths outside the valley long before she wakes. So now, tell me how you know of her."

Andrew relayed the entire story of Regentex, their meetings, Meg's position at the company as Director of New Business Development and his own theory of how Meg made the connection between their healing powers and the fruit revealed in the video.

Kabilito considered Andrew's words soberly. "Ahh, the video. The one that I saw – it was shown even in this country. I've thought on this for a long time, and I feared something like this might happen. I've been taking time away from our shipping operations in Mombasa lately to patrol the area myself – to watch for outsiders in the region. First I saw the US forces from the mine battle leave, but new ones came back to relieve them. Then the Chinese came to the Kilembe Valley with their own special operations troops, then the mining contractors arrived."

Kabilito paused before continuing, his expression solemn. "Of course there's always been the threat from the occasional hiker, but suddenly this woman appeared with her crew from the US. They were clearly searching for something, scouring the Rwenzoris for days on end with hired hands from Kasese. I was tracking this one when she was separated from her group. She's gotten the closest to the lava tube entrance of any of them, but I fear you and Martin have put us on the map, quite literally."

"Should you have even brought her here?" Andrew asked. "What if she turns? What if the madness sets in? In New York she worked for a greedy pharmaceutical company, and she was one of their top dogs..."

"Such a small, concentrated draught isn't enough to drive anyone mad, even with severe character flaws.

Regardless, working for a profit-driven firm doesn't make her a bad person. I understand your cynicism and mistrust, given what you've been through, but eventually you'll need to restore faith in humanity *outside* the valley."

Andrew thought on this as he helped them clean Meg's wounds. They made her as comfortable as possible, and he returned to making dinner.

The central fire blazed as the tribe enjoyed the meal he had prepared. They peppered Andrew with compliments as they ate in a circle around the fire pit. He absently nodded his thanks, consumed by the implications of Meg's appearance. The fire lent small comfort, and he took little pride in the praise.

With his eyes fixated on the fire and his meal untouched, Andrew tensed when he felt a strong hand on his shoulder. Turning, he saw the solemn face of Subira, the tribal leader. A silence grew over the tribe as conversation died, and Andrew rested his full plate on the ground. As one, Kabilito, Akiiki and the others in the circle stood. Andrew slowly rose to his feet, scanning the youthful visages of the tribe.

He looked back at Subira, who spoke to him in a deep, rich voice. "Andrew, you have recovered quickly – physically, and to a lesser extent, spiritually. For one who had so little residual maisha in your blood upon arrival, it has been quite startling how you've healed so quickly."

Andrew considered this. He raised his healed arm and flexed the fingers of his hand as Subira continued.

"We've also observed that your strength has near tripled. You may not have noticed, but you carry several times the weight a normal man could *without effort*. I myself watched as you moved that massive cooking pot, simply out of convenience, when it was completely filled with stew.

Others observed you casually relocating the generator by yourself, with one arm, as a matter of fact."

Andrew looked at the ground and frowned as he recalled those events. Were those things really *that* heavy? It didn't seem so at the time...

Of course they were. Andrew rubbed the back of his neck, then his expression sank. Slowly he raised his eyes to meet Subira's.

"Does that...do you mean that...does it mean that I'm developing the madness?" he stammered, shocked.

Subira drew a deep breath. "You know our history. The missionaries who almost destroyed us so long ago – Levesque and Roux – were deeply flawed. Greed, ambition and power drove them. They were not here to guide us spiritually. They were here to count us among the number of their converted, so they could gain the political favor of their bishops back in Europe. Any of your own flaws pale in comparison to theirs." He paused.

"And you haven't eaten undue portions of maisha over the short time you've been with us. So in answer to your question, we do not believe that you are turning."

"You don't *believe* I'm turning?" Andrew asked, incredulous. "How does that help me? You've been around this fruit for, what, close to a hundred and fifty years? How is it that you don't *know*?"

Subira continued calmly. "That's the point. We don't know. We've never seen such rapid strength and healing gain in someone so new to the fruit, and we need to understand its extent."

"*How*?" Andrew asked, stunned.

"You cannot truly be physically hurt now, Andrew, not for long. And, of course, the same applies to me..." Subira turned and raised his voice. "Clear a space!" he commanded.

The men and women of the tribe began dragging the heavy log benches away from the central fire pit effortlessly. Subira removed his shirt, revealing his young, heavily-muscled chest and arms.

"What are we doing, Subira?" Andrew asked slowly.

"Fighting," came the reply.

Chapter Four

It was night when Yeh Xin heard the low-pitched hum of the generators as he neared the mining valley. Moments later the familiar crunch of crushed stone underfoot told him he had reached the edge of the mine tailings that littered the valley floor.

Spotlights blazed on the far side of the sprawling work site, illuminating the entrance to one of the mines as bright as day. As he approached he saw men toiling to extract rubble from the shaft. Stretchers lay strewn haphazardly in the island of light, some with sheets covering shapeless forms. It was in this mine that the Uyghur crew from Xinjiang had perished earlier that week in a terrible explosion. Most of the Muslim Ugyhur had left in anger over the accident, and Yeh Xin suspected that soon many of the Turks and Uzbeks would, too. But work crews continued to pour into the valley, and despite the tragic accident, mining operations continued.

The clank of metal plates was deafening as he walked past conveyor belts driving boulders toward the massive crushing drums that processed rock mined from the bowels of the Kilembe valley. Billowing clouds of stone dust were belched up into the cool night air. Gasping, Yeh Xin covered his mouth and nose with the collar of his shirt.

The workers operating the machines labored in earnest far from home, but they were grateful for the employment. Crews subcontracted from all over the world gave life to the valley. Rushed to the site from all over Asia and the Middle East, the workers were sure the Chinese government was hell-bent on wresting every remaining scrap of copper from the deep subterranean veins.

But Yeh Xin knew differently.

His cover was that of a liaison between the mine operations management and the nearby town of Kasese. That was how the workers knew him. But in reality he answered to a very different set of leaders, with a very different set of goals – to find the source of a miracle drug that could establish China as the world's sole superpower.

Yeh Xin had been briefed on all of the data they possessed surrounding the fruit. Mere months ago, routine government-funded hacking of US corporations had unearthed cyber gold. Three big pharma companies in the New York area had been infiltrated by Chinese hackers, and servers from two of them revealed emails about a wonder drug with near instant-healing. The names of two former Culinary Network Channel employees, Martin Riley and Andrew Durant, appeared in several Regentex non-disclosure agreement files. After that the Chinese intelligence agency was quick to uncover the CNC video program featuring the two friends and the culinary wonder they had brought to New York. In it Martin had even named the Ugandan mountain range, the Rwenzoris, where he had found the fruit. Like Regentex, the Chinese quickly made the connection between the video and the miracle drug.

And they wanted it – *desperately*. All they needed was a foothold in Uganda near the Rwenzori Mountains. That opportunity had presented itself in the international solicitation for the Kilembe Valley mining rights. China had quickly formed a public-private shell of which the government owned fifty-one percent – a corporation they named the "Yincang Chinese Mining Cooperative." They had offered more than twice their estimate of what the highest bidder would submit, and the Ugandan Economic Development Ministry had ecstatically awarded the rights to Yincang.

Led by their majority owner, Yincang was eager to establish a base of operations. They snatched up every available worker and mining subcontractor east of Europe by paying a fortune in expedite fees, often at two to three times the going rate. Heavy equipment had been hastily shipped to Africa via air, barge and rail from all over Eurasia, and within a month contractors from Russia, India, Turkey and China were breaking ground in the Kilembe Valley.

But Yeh Xin knew it was nothing but a front. As soon as the mine deal closed he had been deployed with a Chinese Special Operations unit to "secure the site." The Ugandan Government had not been pleased to entertain such a military presence, but given the recent terror attacks on the mine, Yincang was more than justified.

The mine attacks had provided even more evidence of the fruit's existence, as well as a means to find it. Impossibly, a small US force had defeated a vastly superior terror group hell-bent on scaring the US away from bidding on the mine rights. Outmanned and outgunned, the US soldiers had managed to defeat the terrorists, killing only a handful while capturing the rest. Only the terrorist leader, Jelani, had escaped the valley.

From the accounts of the few miners who had survived the attacks, the US troops were not the only ones fighting the terrorists. Two workers who hid in a mine railcar during the battle had told incredible tales of a group of strangers who were torn apart by terrorist gunfire, only to rise and kill their attacker before disappearing.

The stories were dismissed as delusional by all but Yeh Xin and his commanders. To them the fantastic tale was proof that some group was consuming the fruit, and that they were likely hiding in the mountains where Martin had first found it. This also meant that rather than look for a fruit in the mountains, they could instead search the Rwenzoris for a settlement.

Unfortunately for the Chinese, the US maintained a presence in the Kilembe Valley region after the mine battle. The Ugandan Ministry assured them that the American troops were simply searching for Jelani, the terrorist leader that had escaped. But the Chinese guessed that the US was looking for the fruit as well, though that wasn't an argument they could use with the Ugandans.

Yeh Xin paused for a moment as a movement caught his eye across the valley floor. Through the gaps in the worker's encampments he saw the Chinese Special Ops unit loading gear into several off-road trucks. Frowning, he changed course and jogged in that direction. Any detour from reporting to his superiors was most welcome.

He approached one of the men loading a crate into the back of a camouflaged truck bed. He tapped the man's shoulder, and the soldier spun around, a tightly-wound ball of aggression.

"Oh, it's you," the soldier exclaimed in Mandarin, turning back to his work.

There was no love lost between the Chinese troops and Yeh Xin. Neither was accountable to the other, as they reported to different commanders. But the troops knew Yeh Xin was supplying the advanced information that shaped their missions, and it was obvious that they resented him for it. He knew they weren't briefed on the fruit, but he could tell that they sensed there was more to their endless searches in the Rwenzori wilderness than what Yeh Xin divulged.

He tried to appear casual. "Where are you guys headed?" he asked as disarmingly as possible.

"I don't have to tell you shit," the soldier replied.

"You know our commanders want us to work together. I have to report to them in a few minutes anyway, and I'm sure you don't want your name thrown around as being uncooperative..." He trailed off.

Scowling, the soldier dropped the heavy crate into the back of the truck and shook his head. He knew Yeh Xin's higher security level meant he could find out where they were headed anyway. He pulled a worn map from his breast pocket and spread it out on a crate as he sighed.

"Here – a valley in Sector twenty-three, about ten kilometers northwest of here. Got it? Now can I finish?"

"What are you guys looking for there?" Yeh Xin pressed.

"Settlements, signs of life, anything other than tourist activity that seems like a semi-permanent encampment. That's all I know. Now if you don't mind, I've got work to do."

Yeh Xin swallowed his pride, thanked him, and headed toward the makeshift headquarters. Sector twenty-three was more than nine kilometers north-by-northeast of his phenomenal encounter earlier that day. At least they wouldn't be mucking up his newest trail any time soon. But surely his superiors would re-deploy them once they heard Yeh Xin's report from today. Perhaps he could buy a little more time – a chance to redeem himself, by feeding them only select information. Perhaps he could keep the special ops guys away from his site just long enough for him to get another look, before they destroyed the trail with their clod-hopping military boots...

He winced, reliving a painful memory.

Hard, black, unyielding military boots...Boots kicking him over and over. Boots walking away as he lay bleeding on the floor of his home, boots belonging to the men that dragged his mother away...

Hate the crime, not the men. Yeh Xin whispered a chant – a forbidden prayer. He wouldn't allow himself to hate the soldiers from that day – to hate the commanders that forced him into service with threats and coercion. But it wasn't easy. He patted his cargo pants and breathed deeply of the cool night air, reassured by the small, familiar lump in the secret pocket on his thigh.

Find the fruit – the promise of freedom. His last mission. Her release.

The trauma from the event flooded his mind once more – flashbacks of the day they took his mother from their small house. They had beat him to keep him down while they dragged his mother out and threw her into a waiting police car. He was a minor then, but they had beat him anyway, until he no longer resisted. Then they forced him into a van full of other scared boys and brought him to a military camp.

A dissident activist – that's what they had called his mother – a dangerous, disruptive force. Yeh Xin had known she was outspoken. She had organized the public protest of the government's callous treatment of the explosion at the state-run chemical plant. With no safety measures in place to protect the workers the plant had burned to the ground, and his father was one of hundreds to perish in the flames. Families across the community were devastated, and it didn't take much to rally them. The secret late-night meetings with the neighbors and the boxes of printed flyers hidden at their home didn't seem like a big deal back then.

But then they took his mother away, and that was the last he had seen of her. That was, until *that* day – the day his commanders did some of their best work on him.

He had trained hard at the camp, determined to make something of himself – to restore some honor to his family name. His effort, athleticism and intelligence were not overlooked, and he had been singled out early. They wanted him to be an operative – a spy. But Yeh Xin was through with secrets. Secrets tore families apart, and he wanted no part of destroying the lives of others. He refused, demanding instead to continue with his military training.

They didn't argue with him. They didn't yell at him like the drill sergeants did at the military camp. Instead they forced him to comply with a chilling coercion.

They drove him out from camp in a jeep, with two armed military police and a strange man he had never met. They drove for hours in silence, then pulled onto a dirt road. He had been terrified as the jeep pulled into the gates of a prison complex, but what they showed him next changed his life forever.

They marched him down a long corridor, cells on either side, until they reached the maximum security solitary-confinement area. Then the strange man reached for the handle of the steel door and opened it.

And that was the last time Yeh Xin had seen his mother. Huddled in a corner, she was a shell of her former self. Her prison uniform hung loosely from her gaunt frame. He rushed in, both of them crying and hugging, holding desperately onto each other for a brief and terrible moment before they came for him again. And once more he had found himself being dragged away by military police, screaming, as he watched his mother fade from view – this time behind the heavy steel door of solitary confinement.

He had agreed to their demands after that, and his operative training began in earnest – stealth, hand-to-hand combat, covert operations, reconnaissance, and every type of weapon imaginable. And he had excelled. The training was endless, but they recognized that motivation could not exist without hope. They threatened him with his mother's execution, but had promised her eventual release if he played along.

Throughout his training he abhorred them. His hatred consumed him, but it drove him to succeed. He had been wise enough to know that his performance depended on acceptance. He knew he must submit to serving his mother's captors – the very government that had destroyed their lives.

He had gained some freedom from prying eyes once he was first deployed, but he continued to struggle with his hatred. Ironically the answer surfaced from his own defiance – the acceptance of religion, something strictly forbidden for operatives.

He began studying Mahayana Buddhism in secret to

reconcile serving his own enemies, and he learned to suppress hatred of his commanders through meditation. He gravitated toward the Buddhist tenet that life was inevitably filled with suffering caused by desire, with enlightenment obtained only through release of those desires. This realization, along with the practice of meditation, helped him to function and to become a better spy. Then a good spy, then a great spy – one of China's best.

His highly-decorated career had been bloodless – an accomplishment that astonished his commanders, secretly made all the more impressive because it was driven by his spirituality and faith and not by a desire for clean, traceless execution. Still, he appreciated the terrible irony of a Buddhist spy – if commanded to kill, he would have a dreadful choice to make. Refusal would necessitate desertion, and his mother would most likely die. And yet the complexity of his ironic position extended even further. In direct conflict with his religion, his mother's release was the one desire he could not shed.

Yeh Xin shook his head to clear the memories. Walking across the valley floor, he began to rehearse his story. No lies, simply omissions. He needed to account for Meg's disappearance but give his commanders an excuse for him to investigate the area once more.

He decided to reveal the presence of the stranger – the tall Ugandan man, and the fact that the man took Meg away into the mountains. But he'd mention nothing of the man's encounter with the gorilla. Not yet, at least.

Finally the headquarters loomed ahead – a sprawling complex of tents and sheet metal structures hastily erected in anticipation of more permanent structures. The "war room," as they liked to call it, was located in the smallest of the tents in the middle of the other shelters. He walked across the crushed stone, watching the ever-present shadows of the men inside the tent. As always, they were hunched over a map, tablets in hand, evaluating the latest field data and arguing over communications with Beijing. Yeh Xin swallowed hard and pulled back the flap to his superior's tent. It was going to be a long night.

Chapter Five

Shirtless, Subira raised his fists as the tribe stepped back to make room. The light from the fire pit danced across his lean, muscular torso as he began to circle his opponent.

Andrew stared back at Subira in bewilderment. "Why do you want us to fight? It makes no sense. I'm not even trained in fighting," Andrew protested, "and I'm nowhere near as strong and fast as you! What could this possibly demonstrate? You're just going to beat the crap out of me!"

Wordlessly, Subira stepped forward and engaged Andrew. He grabbed Andrew's shoulders and pushed hard against him.

Andrew fell back and twisted to the side. "Stop – wait! What the hell is *this* proving?" he exclaimed.

"Nothing, if you do not engage," Subira replied, circling.

Andrew reached out an arm to keep Subira at bay, but Subira merely swatted it aside. "Are you afraid, Andrew?"

Andrew crouched and backed away, circling in the opposite direction warily. "No...I mean yes, but not because of injury. I mean it hurts, of course, but...I don't know how to fight, and you've had a hundred and fifty years to train!"

"It won't matter – now *engage*," Subira responded, advancing.

Again Andrew stepped back. He was dimly aware that he was approaching the edge of the circle formed by the surrounding tribe members. "What is this, some kind of test?" he asked, ducking under Subira's well-thrown punch. Even *he* was surprised at his own reaction speed.

Impressed, Subira raised an eyebrow. "If you must know, then yes – it is a test." He raised his fists and balanced on the balls of his feet, watching Andrew intently. "We designed it long ago to determine if someone was turning."

Andrew raised his own fists in defense. "But there's been no one new to the tribe except me! What did you need the test for?" He felt a presence behind him – the edge of the circle. An unseen, gentle hand in the small of his back nudged him back toward Subira.

"For the children," Subira replied. In a move too fast to follow, Subira planted his right foot against Andrew's. Lightning-fast, Subira's arms shot out, his right hand grabbing high on the inside of Andrew's upper arm, his left grabbing the outside. Twisting and falling, he flung Andrew back to the middle of the circle. Andrew flew through the air, landed hard on the ground with a grunt and rolled.

The children?

He raised himself to his hands and knees and turned his head toward Subira. "*What children*?" he cried in astonishment.

Subira studied him somberly, his fists raised. "Yes,

Andrew, there were children. Several, in the beginning. We are *human*, after all." Subira took a step forward, maintaining his stance, his face pained. "At birth they were the pride of the valley – new life in Eden herself. But some behaved strangely once they began eating the fruit, and it was clear that we needed to test *all* children when they reached maturity, before they became a real threat. Most passed the test. Three did not."

With his hands still raised, Subira motioned for Andrew to rise. Andrew sighed and hung his head in frustration. Climbing slowly to his feet, he asked, "And the three who failed?"

"They were forbidden the gift of the fruit," Subira replied curtly, "yet we couldn't let them leave, either. The prophecy compelled us to protect our secret, and so we stopped having children here in the valley."

Andrew scanned the faces of the tribe and saw a great sorrow reflected there. "Where are they now?" he whispered, absently raising his hands in defense once more.

Subira's voice shook. "The pain of living here while cut off from the blessings of the fruit was too much for *anyone* to bear. Two of them lived their lives in a deep depression, later dying of old age. The third tried to escape. He failed, but he could no longer live without the fruit." Subira's eyes locked on Andrew's as he finished the story. "He was my own son, and he killed himself."

Crushed, Andrew dropped his arms to his side. "I'm so sorry," he breathed.

Subira took a deep breath, then stepped forward. "But that was long ago, and now we find that we need the test once more. Get ready, Andrew."

Again Subira advanced. In a flash he was on Andrew,

grabbing at his shoulders. Andrew leaned in, flattening his palms against Subira's chest and pushed back. As they began to grapple Andrew quickly found that Subira intentionally eliminated the advantage of his own fighting skill by focusing on strength and speed alone.

The strange dance progressed slowly as they struggled, circling around the fire while the others stood witness. As hard as Subira pushed, Andrew pushed back equally, the two of them locked in a sumo-style contest, hands fighting for position against the other. Finally Subira disengaged and smiled wryly at Andrew.

"You're holding back, Andrew. I know you're stronger than this. You're not doing anyone a favor hiding your strength. You'll either pass the test or you won't, but we'll know either way."

And with that, Subira's fist streaked toward his friend's face. Startled, Andrew pulled back, but he was too late. Bone crunched and he reeled from the impact, spinning as he was driven to the ground.

Wide-eyed, he spat out several teeth in a bloody puddle on the ground. His nose was bent over so far it almost touched the bloody skin of his cheek.

How could this be happening? These are my friends...

"Get up!" Subira yelled, kicking him across the clearing so hard that he felt several ribs crack. But by the time Andrew stopped rolling across the ground his face had healed. His nose had pulled itself back into place with a sickening crackle, and teeth grew from his gums to replace the missing ones.

Wiping his mouth on his sleeve, Andrew rose and squinted at Subira as his ribs realigned and reset into position. "So this is the test, huh? You beating me into a pulp?"

"Fight," Subira answered, "and learn the truth."

In an instant Subira was on him again, striking out with his open palm. Andrew braced against it and felt the impact against his chest – a punch that would have sent most men sprawling across the encampment. But this time he was merely driven back slightly, his feet gouging channels in the earth as he slid backward from the force of the blow.

Andrew caught a glimpse of surprise in Subira's eyes before he began his own attack. He pounced at Subira, lowering his shoulder and tackling the tribe's leader around the waist. His full weight and the power of his legs drove his body into his friend. Together they toppled to the ground, Andrew on top.

But Subira was not so easily overcome. He shoved upward with his muscular arms, tossing Andrew over the fire pit and into the corner of the goat pen. The wooden fence splintered apart upon impact. As Andrew fell he uprooted two posts and shattered several of the railings. He sprung up in anger, fists clenched.

Pain shot through his leg, and he looked down at his thigh. A long, pointed shard from the broken wooden railing stuck out from his quadriceps, blood pulsing from the ghastly wound. Agony rushed in, but Andrew recognized it and blocked it from his mind. Taking a deep breath, he grasped the jagged spear and ripped it from his leg. His face twisted in pain, but his muscles knitted together within moments and the torn skin closed, sealing the bloody gash. Shaking with rage, he exhaled sharply and glowered at Subira, but he restrained himself. Recognition briefly spread across Subira's face.

"You're only committing disservice to yourself by hiding the truth, Andrew. Don't you want to know for certain whether you're turning? Whether the fruit is for you?"

Andrew reached down and hefted a splintered railing. In a flash he spun it around, pointed the sharp end at Subira and hurled it as hard as he could.

Subira lifted his hand just in time to arrest the railing's flight, catching the splintered end of the six-foot long shaft in his palm. The spear point drove through the sinewy tissue, splattering blood over Subira's face, then tilted upward as the shaft pivoted in his hand and the butt dropped to the ground. Subira drew his hand from the railing and let it fall as the wound healed.

Subira flexed his healed fingers and chided Andrew. "Come on – you can do better than that! Don't you want to know if you'll go mad – if you'll end up like your friend, *Martin*?"

Subira attacked again. He dove at Andrew, a flurry of fists and open-palm blows faster than the eye could follow. Andrew tried desperately to defend himself, blocking those that he could, letting others hit their mark. One punch bloodied his eye badly, crushing the socket, but he fought on knowing that it was already healing, already reforming.

But still Subira was not satisfied. "Harder!" he bellowed. "Fight for your place in the tribe! Your farm burned down, you lost your job, and you lost your friend! Are you going to lose the fruit, too?"

Andrew redoubled his efforts, punching and kicking wildly with incredible strength. To his surprise one of his kicks broke through Subira's guard, shattering his femur. His leg buckled instantly and Subira crumpled to the ground. But he kicked against the earth with his good leg as he fell, rolling away from Andrew. By the time Subira sprung upright the bone had recovered and he was on Andrew again.

My God, Andrew thought, *he heals quickly!*

The grisly dance continued, and Andrew struggled to keep up. His opponent's attacks became more powerful, and the superior strength and speed began overwhelming Andrew. Abandoning finesse, he finally grappled with Subira to neutralize the fury of his fluid blows.

In a final effort, Andrew drew Subira in close, then grabbed him in a bear hug, squeezing as hard as possible. Ribs cracked, and Subira tried to push away. With a frown of surprise he retaliated, wrapping his arms around Andrew's torso, returning the embrace. To Andrew's dismay, Subira's grip was the stronger, and he felt himself losing consciousness. He had no idea if he had passed this bizarre test and proven himself, or if he had failed and would be shamed. Or worse yet, cast out.

Where would he go? He had nothing left but the tribe...

His head was bursting from the pressure of Subira's embrace, and his eyeballs were squeezing out of their sockets. A terrible desperation welled up, consuming him. He would lose the test, he would lose the fruit, *and he would go mad*.

But something from deep inside suddenly called out, soothing him, strengthening him, and he was able to suppress his panic. Maybe there was no way he could win this contest on his own, but he sensed an immense power welling up, demanding to be released. He feared for his sanity, but Subira was right. *Better to find out now if I'm turning*.

So, teetering on the edge of consciousness, Andrew let the subconscious take control. Suddenly a commanding voice erupted from his mouth – a string of unintelligible but powerful words. The air vibrated around him, and he saw the tribe members covering their ears at the deafening sound.

Is this what it feels like to go mad?

As sound flowed from his mouth he began to fear for himself, for his friends. He felt himself shaping the words, and what once started as a commanding voice became...protective – a warning of sorts – or more like a shield against something alien and unseen. The voice continued flowing from him as he struggled in Subira's combative embrace. The words seemed to reverberate around the amphitheater formed by the lush valley walls – layer upon layer of lilting, resonant, fluid sound that vibrated the charged air, simultaneously rattling his skull while enveloping his mind.

It was a voice of raw and utter compulsion.

Finally Subira let go of Andrew and knelt on the ground, hanging his head in a submissive bow. A stunned silence fell over the tribe as Andrew stared downward, dumbfounded at the man he had just subdued. He felt his spine realign and heal as he stood and stretched, his head still in a fog.

Akiiki was first to react. Stumbling forward, he reached the scene and laid a hand on Andrew's shoulder.

"*What have I done?*" Andrew asked, shocked.

Akiiki responded slowly, seemingly wary of Andrew. "I was about to ask you the same."

"I was just...trying to pass the test. I didn't want...I didn't want the tribe to reject me, so I..." Andrew trailed off, noticing Akiiki's reaction to his ramblings.

Frowning, Akiiki answered Andrew solemnly in the stillness, the two of them surrounded by a sea of silent, bewildered observers. "Do you even realize what you are saying, Andrew?"

"Of course I do," he answered, frustrated. "I'm telling you that I have no idea how I..."

Because you're speaking in perfect Swahili," Akiiki interrupted.

Andrew jolted in awe as he realized Akiiki was correct. His hand rose absently to his mouth as he stared stupidly at the tribe's spiritual leader.

Still crouched on the ground in submission, Subira finally shook his head, blinked, and stood to join them. His voice was shaky at first but gained strength as he continued. "It's clear there is something powerful at work here. You suddenly speak Swahili as if you were born to it. How is this possible?"

Andrew shook his head. "I don't know," he whispered. "I've never learned another language."

But his confusion was cast aside as he noticed Subira's expression slowly change to dread. He stared past Andrew, focused beyond even the circle of observers. Andrew turned to follow his gaze.

An icy grip seized him. Outside the tribal circle stood a figure – a female form, with blond hair and an all-too-familiar face. Her jaw was slack, her mouth hanging open. And though her clothes and hair were blood-stained, *she was completely healed*.

And it was immediately clear to Andrew that Meg's mind was completely blown by what she had seen.

"Oh, *shit*," was all he could manage, perfectly expressing the emotions of the entire tribe.

But yet another danger loomed in the valley, hidden beyond the tribal circle. Dark eyes blinked slowly from the brush at the encampment's perimeter, eyes that waited and watched. They belonged to one trained in stealth and experienced in espionage.

He lowered his hands from his ears. The beginning of the American's shout had been painful, but he had blocked the latter part with his hands. Quietly he picked up the fruit he had dropped and raised it to his mouth for another bite, careful to swallow noiselessly.

Wistfully he pondered how this latest development with the power would manifest, but in truth he didn't care. His eyes rolled back in his head as ate the last of the succulent fruit, then paused to savor the mouthful, his eyes closed in rapture. He still hungered after consuming both halves, but he knew where to find more.

He had been living in secret in the valley, his skills put to the test in avoiding the prying eyes of the tribe as he survived on fruit stolen from the very orchard they harvested daily. Those who tended the fruit trees worked the same time each day, allowing him more than ample time to plunder their stores at the orchard's edge.

Chuckling quietly, the man eased back into the brush to steal more. It was all he ate now. In fact, it was all he could *think of* now – it consumed him as he himself consumed it. He cackled and scratched his ribs absently. He was lonely living by himself in secret in the valley, and the recent death of his friend, Kipanga, still haunted him – his brother in arms, a man he had trained since childhood. A man once known as the Hawk, a deadly sniper of great skill feared across all of central Africa.

But soon he ceased to dwell on Kipanga, for he had greater ambitions now. And though he could use a man of the Hawk's talent, he needed more than just one man.

He needed an army.

Soon, he thought to himself. Soon he would leave the valley, stealing away in the blackness of night, taking what he needed with him to rebuild his forces. But this time, with the power of the fruit, he'd be invincible.

Drunk with power and plans, Jelani glided silently through the brush on the balls of his feet. He headed back toward the dark orchard to feast once more, cackling softly to himself.

Chapter Six

Yeh Xin breathed heavily in the humid mountain air but continued pushing toward the lost trail of the superhuman Ugandan. The path ahead was faint but clear, flattened by some type of hooved herd animal. Brush blurred by as he ran, but he was compelled to keep his pace despite the uneven footing and wild growth.

They were coming...

His radio crackled to life with short, clipped Mandarin. "Pixiu to Bifang, Pixiu to Bifang – come in."

He stopped and caught his breath before responding. "Bifang here – come in, Pixiu."

"Transmit your coordinates, Bifang – we're back and gearing up for re-deployment."

Too soon – they got back to base too quickly from their last deployment. He'd need to hurry.

Yeh Xin transmitted coordinates and signed off. Then he

ran. He tore through the jungle growth now, *faster...still faster.* His commander's face lingered in his mind, almost impassive as he threatened to pull Yeh Xin off the mission. *And he knew all too well what that meant...*

Two days – all he had bought with his initial deception was two days of fruitless searching around the plains that led to the high ridge. He cursed himself for losing the man. He felt sure the Ugandan had been headed toward the ridge, but there was no sign of him on the rocky trail that ended at the sheer vine-covered cliff, and he had been forced to return to camp empty-handed.

So with his commander's threat still hanging in the air he had been compelled to tell the rest of the story – of the man who fought off the gorilla, and of a trail lost. But they hadn't scolded him. They knew the pressure they were putting on him. They just wanted results. *And he just wanted what they had promised.*

They had immediately called the special ops forces back from their deployment and sent Yeh Xin to set the target position in advance of the troops – the same troops that would trample the grass and trod any remaining signs of the man's trail into the moist earth. *Just one last look at the site – that's all he wanted...*

He hurdled a fallen log then was forced to duck under a low branch, scrambling to regain his footing. Something unseen caught the toe of his boot – *a vine*, he thought, as he was sent sprawling through the air. The ground rose up quickly, and his head slammed into the slippery, packed soil of the trail with a jolt.

Yeh Xin pushed himself up and sat on the ground, his head spinning. He stood, brushing the moist earth from his pants, then peered through the trees to the open plains beyond. He was almost back at the lost trail. *One last look – his best remaining chance to find the fruit.* His last mission, they had told him. Then his mother was free, and so was he.

With shaking fingers he fumbled in the secret pocket of his cargo pants and pulled out his worn copy of Buddhist sutras. The pages fell open to his favorite, and he paused to read, to chant, to rejuvenate, to refocus. He closed his eyes, breathed deeply of the clean mountain air, and slid the book back into place. Then his eyes snapped open, refocused.

And then he ran.

He bolted from the forest at full speed and flew across the plains. He ran over the grasses and open fields, over the crest and past the game tracks that crisscrossed the earth and obfuscated the stranger's trail. He let his spirit guide his body and his subconscious control his actions, and soon he found himself sprinting toward the rocky ridge. Then he stopped and closed his eyes again, letting his mind reach out beyond the path.

He tried envisioning the stranger, with Meg slung over his back, scampering down the steep slopes on either side of the ridge. *No* – there was no way anyone could have managed the loose trap rock without sliding to the bottom and leaving a trail. The man was super strong with inhuman healing, but he couldn't fly.

Yeh Xin took a step forward onto the rocky ridge. He opened his eyes, then took another step, determined. He walked slowly along the path as the terrain fell away to either side, his eyes fixed on the steep cliff ahead, vines cascading from an outcropping halfway up.

Did he scale the cliff? Did he climb the vines?

He continued walking toward the vine-covered cliff, faster now. His eyes lifted above the outcropping halfway up

– the source of the vine growth. He squinted farther up the cliff to the bald, rocky top. *What was up there? How would the stranger have scaled the remainder of the cliff with no vines to climb?*

Still pondering this mystery, he finally reached the cliff face and stopped. He craned his neck and studied the cliff. *There was simply no way – the man couldn't have jumped the remaining distance from the outcropping to the top...*

His hand absently caressed the dangling vines in front of him. They moved freely, dancing side to side from the motion of his hand, the leaves shimmering in the cool draft from behind the vines...

...from behind *the vines?*

Excited, he thrust his arm through the thick, cascading vegetation. *There was no cliff here!* He parted the dense curtain and stared into a gaping black hole – the entrance to a tunnel.

He breathed in sharply. *So this was where the man disappeared.* Yeh Xin wriggled through the vine curtain and felt it envelop him, closing around his back as he stepped into the darkness. As his eyes adjusted, he became aware of a faint light at the end of the tunnel that rose from below. A few moments later he was able to discern wheeled tracks on the dusty tunnel floor, and he smiled. Abruptly his radio crackled to life.

"Pixiu to Bifang, Pixiu to Bifang – come in."

Yeh Xin jumped and clamped his palm over the radio speaker, scowling. The call from the special ops troops echoed loudly from the smooth walls of the lava tube. *Too loudly.* Agitated, he angrily twisted a dial and shut the radio off before he began to descend.

Chapter Seven

US Special Operations Sergeant David Harel sat with techno-nerd Corporal Kate Dun. He peered down at the circuit boards inside the drone, poking a finger at the electronics. "What's that one?" he asked.

Kate slapped his hand aside. "You idiot, the shielding's removed – you'll short it out."

"But what *is* it?"

Kate grinned and shook her head as she continued to work. "You're such a dork. It's the main transmission circuit, if you must know. Now can I get this thing running? Geez!"

He watched as Kate touched connections with her multi-meter, alternating touch points and gazing back and forth from the drone to the circuit diagram on her tablet. "Can't I just..."

"No!" Kate exclaimed. "Don't you have something to

do?"

A cool breeze enveloped them, bending the long grasses around the clearing. David looked up, past the Kilembe valley and toward the Rwenzori Mountain range to the west. *Such a gorgeous place*, he thought.

He recalled their deployment only a few months ago. They were here to replace the troops that had fought the mine battle against Jelani and his terrorist group. It would have been helpful for at least a few of the veterans of that skirmish to have stayed behind to show them the terrain and the most strategic positions. Strangely, not a single one remained – all had been reassigned, and so everything they learned they had to glean from the reports. *Maybe not so strange, given the infinite wisdom of the US military,* Harel surmised.

He rose when he heard the crackle of static from the satellite communications bench behind him. His Superior Officer Captain Devon Maxwell was speaking into the radio now, standing over by the makeshift encampment they had erected in the Nyamwamba River valley. Situated between the Kilembe mines to the west and Kasese to the east, the valley was prone to flash floods during the rainy season, but that was months away. And since they had been kicked out of the valley when the Chinese complained to the Ugandan Economic Development Ministry, it was the best remaining location for their base – quick access to the road that led to the valley for their Humvees and a wide, open clearing for takeoff and landing of Kate's drones as well as for their Bell UH-1Y Venom helicopter.

Theirs was largely a reconnaissance mission, so the chopper didn't have rockets mounted, but instead was equipped with twin M240D machine guns. The guns were there in case of another terrorist attack, but the drones and the helicopter were there to help in the search for any signs of Jelani and a hidden mountain tribe that might be harboring him. The military birds also helped keep tabs on the Chinese troops who, in addition to maintaining a balance of force in the region, reportedly had a mission similar to their own. At least that's what the Ugandan government told the US military, according to the briefings.

The radio static sounded once more in response to the captain, and Kate flashed her winning smile at him again. "Looks like I'll finally get some peace around here," she taunted.

"Yeah, well, I'll be back to bug you again soon," he replied, "but next time you gotta let me fly this thing."

"Not a chance, grunt."

He chuckled and started in the direction of Captain Maxwell as yet another breeze stirred. Here in the Rwenzori foothills the heat wasn't too bad. The cooler mountain air flowed from the snow-capped mountains down through the Nyamwamba River valley, but the terrain and vegetation was completely foreign to Harel. The car horns and traffic of his native Brooklyn were replaced by the endless babbling of the river, the chirps and cries of local birds, and the wind rustling the trees and grasses.

He and several others from his unit approached the captain as the conversation was wrapping up. "Will do, Major," Captain Devon Maxwell said loudly into the radio. "Over and out."

The radio blared a final order before going silent. "See to it, Devon. Mackenzie, over and out."

The rest of the troops assembled around the captain, knowing a call from command meant they were likely to be deployed into the field.

"What is it, Captain?" one of the soldiers asked.

"That was Major Graham Mackenzie, from the Pentagon. I told him the Chinese troops returned and that they're gearing up to deploy again right away, from the looks of our drone recon." He turned his head slightly towards the drones. "Thank you, Corporal Dun!" he yelled across the clearing.

"Don't mention it, Sir!" Kate called back without looking up from her work. The men chuckled.

"Anyway, we're gonna take a small team – five men – to keep an eye on our Asian friends, wherever they're headed. Maybe they found something – I don't know. So I'm taking four of you with me, but we're doing this all stealth-like, see? So gear up light. Stephenson, Greco, Messina and Harel – saddle up."

Harel felt a slap on his back and turned to see Greco grinning like a fool. "We got the toughest little Jew in the army comin' with us, boys!"

"Oh, my God – it spoke!" Harel retorted, smiling back.

The Humvee hauled them to within a quarter mile of the mine before they bailed and watched their ride disappear back down the valley road toward camp. They continued up the road on foot. High above them the drone was circling while Kate fed them data from the Chinese troop movements via radio.

"Okay, boys, they're headed out the southwest entrance, through the main gate, and circling around to the west – about a quarter-klick to your west."

Harel and the team kept out of sight but close to the Chinese troops with the help of Kate's radioed data. They followed the river for about seven kilometers to the northwest, but then the Chinese turned farther to the west and began ascending a steep path that Harel thought might have been created by hooved mountain animals. He grunted as he struggled through the brush alongside the path, staying out of sight.

The steep path eventually flattened, opening up to a grassy plain. Harel and the team were forced to drop back, with only the occasional stand of brush available for cover. But soon the Chinese were out of sight over a ridge across the plains, allowing the US troops to cross the plains without being seen.

They advanced to a ridge at the edge of the plains. The grasslands fell away to a steep ravine, leaving only a rocky path that rose out of sight then dropped off, seemingly terminating at a vine-covered cliff. The Chinese continued along the path, so Harel and the other men followed, advancing just below the top of the ridge. Harel scrambled to keep his footing in the loose trap rock, pausing only occasionally to peer above the ridge top and locate the Chinese Special Ops forces. He watched as one of the Chinese soldiers repeatedly raised a radio to his mouth as they hiked along the path, apparently calling someone over and over. Soon they were out of sight below the rise in the ridge, and Captain Maxwell motioned for his group to continue, cautioning them against the treacherous footing.

Captain Gao cursed and scowled at his radio man. "Try him again, Sergeant," he grumbled in Mandarin. *That bastard Yeh Xin better not have ditched us again*, he thought. He wiped the sweat from his brow, slung his rifle over his shoulder and surveyed the setting. His men were stuck here on this ridge with no sign of the spy, apparently at a dead end. The path ended at a cliff face covered in vines with no way to climb up and certainly no way down the loose rock of the ridge slopes. The sides of the bald ridge top were slick from recent rains, and the rocky soil was almost certainly undercut beyond the edge, forming dangerous overhangs. Yet still his men insisted on getting too close to the sides...*like Sergeant Wu Yue just now...*

"Dammit, Wu Yue! Get away from the..." Too late, Captain Gao watched as the slope disappeared from under Wu Yue's feet. The sergeant flailed his arms wildly, falling toward a large boulder just over the ridge top. His rifle swung in a wide arc as he fell backward, and the butt of the gun slammed into the boulder, setting off the charge.

The rifle shot echoed across the valley as Wu Yue slid down the slope, tumbling through the vegetation below and out of sight. But before Captain Gao could even react, a voice cried out from behind them on the path, out of sight and over the ridge crest.

A human voice...not one of those damn mountain gorillas...

"Defensive positions!" Gao barked out to his men, all too aware that there was no cover here on the ridge. He crouched and scanned the crest of the path behind them.

Who would be out here? Insurgents? Hikers? Someone from the missing tribe they were looking for?

It was then that the first shot from the unseen strangers tore into the ridge top near his foot, causing Gao to leap over the edge to the loose, rocky slope below.

"Get down!" Captain Devon Maxwell commanded his

men as the shot from the Chinese troops echoed across the valley.

Then he heard the scream.

Sergeant David Harel, who had been peering over the ridge a moment before, fell backward clutching at his shoulder. Maxwell watched in horror as Harel fell, sliding down the loose slope and tumbling through the tree canopy below.

"Goddammit!" yelled Sergeant Messina, leaping up and onto the ridge. He crouched and returned fire as Maxwell, Stephenson and Greco scrambled up the loose rock and onto the bald path. Together they lay down bursts of cover fire as they backed down the ridge toward the plains, but one shot tore into Greco's thigh and he crumpled to the ground.

One man down, another wounded and missing, and they began *this mission outnumbered – this was not going well…*

"Fall back!" Captain Maxwell barked as Messina and Stephenson each scooped up one of Greco's arms and pulled him away from the edge of the slope. Captain Maxwell continued firing at the Chinese troops as gunfire pinged off the bald, rocky ridge top. While the Captain covered them Stephenson nodded at Messina, who slung Greco over his back and continued carrying him alone. Stephenson tore the radio from his pack and punched the transmission button.

"Eagle One, Eagle One – come in, Eagle One! We are under fire from the Chinese and need back-up and extraction. Repeat – we need backup and extraction NOW, over."

"Copy that, Eagle One," the radio spat back, "we're on our way."

Moments later Captain Maxwell and his remaining soldiers had made it to the plains, sporadic gunfire still chasing them from the ridge. He heard the chopper from a distance, the rhythmic beating growing louder every second.

Finally the chopper arrived, flying over their position and dropping smoke bombs to provide some cover before it landed a safe distance from them. Stephenson and Messina dragged Greco into the open door of the chopper, followed by Maxwell. As the helicopter lifted into the sky Maxwell pulled out his satellite radio, dialed up Major Graham Mackenzie in Washington and filled him in on the unexpected attack and the loss of Sergeant Harel.

"They just opened fire on us, Sir," he yelled into the receiver, his voice competing with the whirring chopper blades. "Not sure how the bastards knew we were even there."

Captain Devon Maxwell had to strain to hear Major Mackenzie's reply over the radio. "...any way to retrieve Harel?" he gleaned from the speaker.

"We'll do a flyby, see if we can locate him and try and clear them out. But they're dug in pretty good, Sir. It's just too hot for boots on the ground. The chopper can't get through the tree canopy, and with the Chinese firing at us it would be suicide to try and drop a man down on the hoist. Plus we've got wounded we gotta bring back. We'll need to regroup and come back for him."

Captain Maxwell tapped the pilot on the shoulder and spun his index finger around in the air, ending up pointing toward the ridge. Then he pointed at the gunners on each of the Venom's twin M240D machine guns, pointed at his eyes, then down at the ridge as it came into view.

The gunners took aim, fingers on triggers...

Firing furiously back toward the plains, Captain Gao

heard the chopper before he saw the rising smoke.

"Take cover!" he bellowed. "Incoming fire!"

Just then the helicopter blasted through the cover, smoke tendrils curling up and over the blades as it roared toward them. Gao suddenly recognized the chopper, and he saw the symbols painted boldly on the side.

It's a Venom, he thought, *a fucking US chopper...*

He hit the deck as the Americans opened fire from the chopper, twin M240D's blasting from the mounts, and two men shooting their rifles from the open doors. Bullets shattered the rock all around him as casings fell from the sky. But the Venom swung around in a wide arc, sweeping past the ridge to hover over the slope and tree canopy below.

It was as if they were searching for something...

Now that the chopper wasn't directly overhead his own troops opened fire on the Venom. The gunners in the helo returned fire, seemingly laying down cover as they searched for...*what?*

After a few moments the Venom circled the ridge once more, then headed off in the direction of Kasese. A few of his men continued firing after the retreating chopper, but as the gunfire subsided, Captain Gao radioed back to his commanders. They would be most interested to learn who had attacked them – *totally unprovoked*.

Chapter Eight

The air was warming as the sun rose over Istanbul, but the massive stone slabs still cooled the mosque as the pre-dawn Fajr prayer came to an end. Echoes reverberated from the chamber walls as the mosque emptied while Nur Sabir, the Xinjiang Uhygur Business Association representative, was being ushered to an audience with the Imam.

Nur suppressed a yawn and blinked sleep from his eyes as he was led to the Imam's office. He never slept on airplanes, and his rushed flight from Xinjiang had left him restless. He was left to sit in a chair in a spartan office, staring listlessly at the books and paper strewn on the desk as he awaited the Imam. Finally the door opened and Nur stood respectfully. The religious leader greeted him warmly as they sat and exchanged pleasantries before turning to business.

"I have learned of this mine accident – it is most troubling," the Imam spoke in Turkish.

Nur opened his bag, pulled out pictures of the Uyghur killed in the blast and showed them to the Imam. "We're not so sure it was an accident, Imam. My entire crew – lost. Their families in Urumqi are devastated, and all of Uyghur Xinjiang is rife with talk of scandal."

The Imam accepted the pictures and slowly shuffled them, staring at each face before he spoke. "The region is a stew of mistrust, and China's refusal to recognize Uyghur claims to the land stir the pot. It is only natural to suspect treachery."

Nur shifted in his chair. "My construction business was slow – it isn't easy in a Han-dominated city. But we have mining equipment, and when they offered us triple the going rate, well, it kept our business alive. They even shipped the equipment at no charge. But something felt wrong – it was too good to be true...and I...*I ignored it.*" Nur's voice shook and he leaned over the desk, whispering in a broken voice. "I ignored it – *for the money.*"

Nur sobbed as the Imam reached out to comfort him. "You couldn't have known..."

"I *should* have known. I shouldn't have been blinded by the money, but I was. And now they are dead – all of them." Nur wiped his eyes and composed himself before continuing. "Our Uyghur brothers, competitors in the construction business but friends in our homes, were lured to Uganda as well. It is known – this thing is not suspected, it is *known*. Our crews were put at the most risk, our men are killed on purpose – it is *genocide*. And still they do not stop. They are bringing in more Uyghur from all over Xinjiang to work the Kilembe mines. For what possible reason would they need men so quickly and at such expense to dig a dead mine, with so little copper yield that they haven't even bothered to ship it from the site?"

The Imam continued to listen, studying Nur's intense features as the story unfolded, his own face darkening with each word. After a long pause the Imam finally spoke.

"This is not the first report of the escalating efforts to cleanse the Uyghur from the homeland. We will pray for the families of the dead." He stood and held out his hand to Nur, who rose and embraced the Imam. As he led Nur to the door, the Imam spoke reassuringly. "I will seek council with the Allamah and the rest of the clerisy. These atrocities will not be ignored."

Nur fell to his knees crying and thanked the Imam.

Chapter Nine

Colonel Frank Anderson, African and Middle East Special Operations Chief, shifted in his leather chair uncomfortably and tugged at his uniform. It was too small for him these days, and he associated it with problems since he only wore it on certain occasions – situations like this that were big enough to summon him to this stuffy Pentagon chamber to meet with people he didn't particularly like.

He glanced at the officers and politicians around the table. They were all listening intently to his Ugandan Special Operations Force leader, Major Graham Mackenzie, who updated them on the Ugandan issue. It was hard for him to focus on Mackenzie's brief, having already gone over it with him several times. Instead, he studied the faces of the men around him, trying to predict their responses.

Frank tensed as Mackenzie concluded. "So in short, the attack from the Chinese Special Operations forces was unprovoked. Recovery efforts have failed, and Sergeant David Harel is MIA, presumed a hostage or KIA."

The men in the chamber stirred and chatter broke out. Frank saw a hand rise above the heads of the men to his right. He leaned forward, catching a glimpse of the bespectacled face of the US ambassador to China, who addressed Mackenzie while still looking down at his notes.

"Major, the Chinese are claiming the same thing – that the attack on their troops was unprovoked, and that your team fired first. Similarly, they claim one of their own men is missing – captured, they presume, by *your* forces. How is it that these stories are so...*similar*?"

Frank rolled his eyes. The ambassador was one of the men he didn't particularly like.

"I'm not sure what you are insinuating, Sir," Mackenzie replied. "As I stated in the brief..."

A hand slammed down on the table with a resounding thud. Frank scowled and turned toward the outburst. The fat fingers of one of the Representatives on the House Armed Services Committee were splayed across the polished mahogany surface. Frank followed the hand up to the man's corpulent, red face – another one he didn't like.

"And why in *hell* are we still poking our nose around in the mountains of Uganda anyway? This Jelani character is long gone. You've had your time to find him, Major, and all we've got is a pile of military expenditures and yet another mess with the Chinese. I want those men out of there!"

Frank calmly waited for the representative to wipe the spittle from his mouth before responding on Mackenzie's behalf. "That's not possible, Sir. We have actionable intelligence that requires us to stay in the region."

"*What* actionable intelligence?" the fat face demanded.

"I'm sorry, Sir, but that's classified," Frank responded dryly.

Before the apoplectic representative's face could explode, the chairman of the committee interjected. "Major, could you go over your defensive positions on the ridge again? I'd like to understand the line of fire a bit better..."

Frank sat back in his chair as the meeting droned on, but motion caught his eye as yet another staffer leaned in to an official to hear a whispered command. Just like the others, the staffer nodded and scurried out of the chamber, no doubt to report details from the briefing to someone upstairs. Frank visualized phones ringing off the hook all over Washington and sighed. It was going to be a long night.

An hour later he emerged from the chamber into one of the endless Pentagon corridors and waited for his man. Several others filed past until finally he saw a weary Mackenzie exit.

"Graham...," he called to the Major.

Mackenzie looked up and found Frank in the crowd. He handed a stack of papers to one of his aides, gave him a few commands, and then wove through the stream of exiting officials to meet up with Frank.

"About what we thought, eh, Colonel?" Mackenzie asked.

"About. Walk with me." He led the Major down another corridor, and they lost themselves in anonymity among the shifting tide of Pentagon workers as they spoke.

"It'll be days before any decisions are made, Major, but they'll pull the plug soon. I want your men back at that ridge. Find Harel and scan the entire region – the ridge, the valley around it, even the plains. There was a reason the Chinese hightailed it to that location."

Mackenzie paused. "This is about the incident in the mines – the 'group hallucination', as you called it, isn't it, Sir? Men healing instantly, impossible strength and speed..."

Frank stopped short and spun to confront Mackenzie. "Just drop it, Major. You have your orders – report back if you find anything." He leaned in to drive the point home. "And I mean *anything* – you got that?"

Mackenzie retreated, leaning the back of his head against the corridor wall. "Yes, Sir," he conceded.

After a long, hard stare Frank spun and walked away, letting his command hang in the air. He hated being so short with Graham – the man was doing a solid job. But he had his own orders. Finding the lost soldier might lead them to the Ugandans from the mine battle and their miraculous fruit. Somewhere there was a group of friendly superhuman Ugandans in those mountains, eating a super fruit he needed to find, and he had damn well better get to them before the Chinese did.

He let his feet carry him back to his offices as his mind churned, finding himself in front of his door sooner than he anticipated. He wrenched it open, startling his secretary as he strode through the receiving room.

"Jenna – get me Ed Lambard right away, and cancel my four o'clock," he barked as he closed the door to his office and fumbled with the buttons on his shirt. He was already back in fatigues when his phone rang with Ed Lambard, NSA Cyber Crimes Section Chief on the line. He punched the speakerphone button as he zipped up his pants.

"How are you doing, Ed?" he began with his old friend.

"Hey, Frank – not bad. You?"

"Shitty. This Ugandan situation is a bucket of suck. And don't play ignorant with me – I know the NSA's all over the intel."

"Great to talk to you, too, Frank."

Frank sighed and picked up the phone from its cradle. "Sorry. You know what a shit show this is."

Frank heard Ed take him off-speaker, too. "No worries. What can I do for you, buddy?"

"The Chinese must be getting close. Either they've found something, or they have a lead. Has there been any more hacker activity from China?"

"No – sorry, Frank. We were gonna feed in a little misinformation once we locked down the compromised servers at Regentex, but it got a little hot when e-mails started flying about their own trip to Uganda – you know, the Meg Hennessy girl – so we shut it down. We didn't need the pharmaceutical company feeding the Chinese intel on their own efforts to find the fruit."

"Well, what about Andrew – the kid who bailed after the farm burned down? Any word on his whereabouts? Did you talk to his sister – what was her name?"

"Laurie – and yes, we spoke to her, but all she knew was that he was working for a shipping company in Mombasa, which checked out. A few calls to the Mombasa office told us nothing – apparently he travels on business around Africa and could be in any one of a number of places. Hey – I *told* you we should have tracked him the first time he went over there, remember?"

Frank winced. "Yeah, yeah – my guys were a bit distracted at the time with a little terrorist skirmish at Kilembe Mines, as you well know. Anyway, what about his buddy, Martin – did he ever surface?"

"Nowhere to be found, Frank. Martin hasn't been to his apartment, hasn't paid his bills – he just disappeared. Last we knew he was living at the farm before it burned down, but there's no trace of him."

Frank chewed his lip and frowned. This was going nowhere. "Well, what about Meg Hennessy? What has Regentex found so far in Uganda?"

Ed paused before answering. "She disappeared, too. She was with a few other people from Regentex, hiking around in the Rwenzoris, when she was separated from her group. We got a call from the pharma company – they were pretty desperate – but there wasn't much we could do. The State Department is looking into it with the help of the Ugandan government, but after a cursory investigation the Ugandans were chalking it up as a hiking accident. And we weren't about to tell them why she was there. The State Department has hit a brick wall. They don't have any boots on the ground to search."

"But I do," Frank replied. "Gimme everything you got on Hennessy and I'll see what I can do."

Ed paused again, then Frank heard him whisper intently into the phone. "Look, Frank, you know I'd help you if I could, but our agendas are a little different. I'm NSA, man – we see this as a security threat if the Chinese get hold of this thing, but you and your sicko buddies at Techno-Warfare are trying to *weaponize* this shit."

"Now who would be feeding you *that* line of crap, Ed?" Frank demanded.

"NSA, remember? We got ears everywhere."

"Fuck you, Ed. You do your job and I'll do mine. You know we have joint orders to cooperate on this. I need those files *today* – send 'em over."

He slammed the receiver into the cradle and glowered at the phone. *Some friend.* He composed himself before picking up the receiver again. Now Mackenzie's team had three people to find – Sergeant Harel, Jelani, *and* Meg Hennessy. Oh, and a group of Ugandans, and hopefully a fruit...

Chapter Ten

"Let's start from the beginning again, Andrew," Kabilito said calmly, sitting near him on a rough wooden bench.

Andrew threw the twig on the ground that he had been sticking into the earth aimlessly. "We've gone over this a hundred times, Kabilito. I don't know how I invoked this power. Subira told me to fight harder, so I did – I was just fighting to keep my place with the tribe. But no matter how many times you ask me, I can't replicate it. I'm not even sure I *want* to. What if this means I'm going mad – that I'm *turning*? I wasn't in control at all when it happened – it took control of *me*. What if this time the madness is simply taking a new form – a more *dangerous* form, with new powers?"

Akiiki tried to console him. "Andrew, there's no evidence that you are turning. Just because we have never encountered this manifestation of the power doesn't mean..."

"The fact is that you don't know what it means," Andrew interrupted. "You said it yourself – the rate at which I've gained healing and strength is much faster than normal. We saw that happen with Martin, too. And the reality is that the only experience you've really had with anyone turning is with Roux and Levesque over a hundred and fifty years ago, then later with Martin."

"That's not true," Kabilito interjected. "As Subira told you, several of our adolescents began to turn before we cut them off from the fruit. And we learned of the turning through testing them."

Subira continued where Kabilito left off. "Look, Andrew, although the subject believes the test is designed to evaluate strength and healing speed, in truth it is primarily to determine if the subject's aggression levels soar irrationally when under duress. In our experience – albeit limited – the madness manifests most when the subject is stressed both physically and mentally, which is why I was goading you. We know that you have suffered great loss – your job, your home, your best friend, and the business opportunities you started with the maisha fruit. Knowing how precious your new life with the tribe was to you, as well as your sensitivity to turning given Martin's recent madness, I threatened you during the test with what's most precious to you – your place with the tribe."

Andrew's face fell. *Are my vulnerabilities that transparent?*

Subira continued. "The test subjects that were truly turning tended to attack the circled tribe members during the trials, or they began acting irrationally and destroying objects. Accelerated strength and healing is a possible indication of the madness, but behavior under duress has been more telling in our experience. But something altogether different manifested when your stress levels rose, something of which we have no experience, as you have so adroitly pointed out."

Andrew remained silent, his face impassive. "That's not exactly comforting, Subira. The truth is you don't really know whether I'm turning or not." He stood and gazed across the encampment. Meg was there, sitting alone at a table under the watchful eye of several of the tribe members.

"And what about Meg?" Andrew continued. "You're just going to keep her here against her will? You're going to let her continue eating the fruit knowing that she's a corporate beast – a type-A, greedy capitalist driven to bring the fruit back for fame, fortune and advancement? You don't know people like her. I saw her in action at the meetings at Regentex."

Kabilito stood and joined Andrew in watching Meg. "You forget that I've been managing one of the largest international shipping companies for decades, and I most certainly have encountered people like her. But their personalities don't mean that they're bad. Their dedication and actions may outwardly seem to focus solely on the business, but more often than not they are driven by something else – a perceived shortcoming or a great loss in their past. They are often driven to impress, seeking validation in the rewards they receive for their hard work." He paused and turned to Andrew. "At any rate, she's seen too much. She must be assimilated, like the tribe members born to us long ago."

"That makes no sense," Andrew replied angrily. "She'll never agree to stay – she'll run away, or at least she'll try. And why are you feeding her the fruit? What if *she* turns, like

Martin did?"

"She'll be tested, too, in time," Subira answered, "once she's consumed it long enough."

Andrew's face dropped in exasperation. "Don't you think someone will come looking for her? Do you really think she'll just accept leaving her job and her position in life to live here with the tribe, just because you tell her to?"

"Calm yourself, Andrew. There is simply no choice in the matter." Kabilito spoke with grave finality.

Andrew shook his head and swatted the argument away with an open hand. "It's easy being calm when you're not the one turning," he retorted, storming off toward the cooking area.

He was forced to pass Meg on the way to the outdoor kitchen. She was eating something, and staring down into her bowl he saw the plantain mash and maisha fruit that he had made the night before.

Meg lifted her head and their eyes met. His face twisted into a rage, and he spun away.

She'll turn. Just like Martin. Just like me.

As he walked away in anger he didn't know what scared him most – losing the fruit and his place in the tribe, or going mad and hurting those around him.

And they all probably saw that conflict in me long before I did...

Chapter Eleven

Yeh Xin's mind raced as he ducked into the shadows on the outskirts of the ring of huts. Sweat dripped from his brow, and he forced himself to regulate his breathing.

*This is the tribe – I've found the fruit...*and *a group of people that could tear me apart.*

Overhead the sun dipped below the rim of the valley, though it was only early afternoon. Long shadows crept over the tribal home, and Yeh Xin used them to his advantage. He crept away from the huts, circling wide around the common area, blending into the darkened cover of the tall, tended plants of a wide garden.

He spent another hour in that position, observing the tribe as light faded away and torches were lit. The tribe was fascinating – they interacted almost without communication, as if each knew the thoughts of the other. Clearly they had lived together for a long time.

The presence of the American man startled him at first. He was across the clearing, speaking with others from the tribe. Yeh Xin scoured his memory for a moment before recognizing Andrew from the video he had seen in his briefings – the Culinary Network Channel production. He recalled that in it Martin had reported finding the fruit in Uganda, then Andrew had sold it to a restaurant in New York.

Sunlight reflected from golden strands, catching Yeh Xin's attention.

It's Meg – the American girl is here. Her blonde hair was unmistakable. She sat alone at a table, picking at her food. And she was fully healed.

If she's *here, then where is...*

Oh – *the man speaking with Andrew.* He recognized the tall, young Ugandan that had fought off the mountain gorilla. Even from this vantage point he could see the maturity in the man's bearing – the way he carried himself, and the manner in which he commanded attention.

Yeh Xin ducked back under cover as he saw Andrew suddenly bolt up straight, clearly frustrated by something said by one of the men around him. He peered between broad leaves long enough to witness Andrew scowl at Meg, then pass by without a word.

No love lost there, he thought.

Soon after Andrew had stormed off, the gorilla fighter came over to Meg and rested a hand on her shoulder. Yeh Xin backed farther into the vegetation. *Enough of the tribe – time to explore the valley and find the fruit.*

It didn't take long. Adjacent to the vegetable and fruit tree farm were root plants, then berry bushes, and finally, laid out in beautifully maintained rows was the orchard he sought.

It was unmistakable – the fruit was so...*different*, the trees so lovingly cared for. As darkness closed in he wandered amidst the rows of trees, reaching out to caress the leaves and the fabled fruit. He picked one, eyes wide with excitement, admiring the hourglass shape and the fiery, red veins crisscrossing the brilliant green skin.

Instinct told him to move – he'd been in one location too long. He passed through the rows of trees, careful to walk only in the well-worn footsteps of those who tended the fruit. He continued toward the edge of the orchard where the tracks thinned out, and where a chance encounter was less likely. As he walked he shrugged the small pack off shoulder and dropped the lone fruit into it.

He reached for another but stopped, distracted by something that caught his eye – another set of tracks, less deliberate, more...*random*.

He followed them, noting that the tracks hugged the tree roots before disappearing from the orchard edge, only to reappear at the base of a nearby kifabakazi tree. From there the tracks picked up at the base of another tree, always jumping, avoiding detection...invisible to the untrained eye.

The tracks ended at a hollow a good distance away from the orchard. The flat, surrounding brush formed a leafy canopy that covered the depression, obscuring it completely from view – a perfect place to hide, if it hadn't already been claimed. Squinting in the darkness, he crouched, lifting a branch as he scrambled under the broad leaves.

He wrinkled his nose and turned his head while his eyes adjusted. Shapes formed in the darkness – half-eaten fruit and seeds were strewn about the flattened earth, and in one corner of the hollow were several piles of human defecation. He backed out of the hollow and breathed deeply of the fresh air. *Who would be living out here, in secret, apart from the rest of the...*

A twig snapped nearby in the darkness. He stood, fully alert, scanning his surroundings. There was nowhere nearby to hide, just two tall trees standing together, dense with leaves, about ten meters away.

Move...

He bolted for the trees, cursing himself for not harvesting more of the fruit earlier. He'd need to go back to the orchard after this latest danger passed. He flew past the first tree to distance himself as much as possible. Reaching the second tree, he vaulted the roots, planted a foot at the base and launched himself skyward, grabbing at the lowest branch as he heard footsteps approaching the hollow. He hauled himself up and hid among the leaves just in time to catch a glimpse of a shadowy figure as it approached the makeshift shelter. He heard several thuds as objects were emptied onto the ground to roll down into the little hideout.

Fruit – he must have collected some fruit.

Below him the man squatted, muttering to himself as he shuffled around the outside of the hollow, apparently picking up some stray fruit that hadn't cooperated. Yeh Xin sighed softly. He was stuck here until the man moved on or went to sleep. He lifted his eyes and surveyed his view. From his vantage point Yeh Xin could see the torches of the settlement. In fact he could observe the entire clearing quite well. He could make out Meg, still sitting at the table, with the tall Ugandan man sitting with her. They were talking, Meg clearly irritated...

And then a gunshot rang out above the valley. It echoed across the lush amphitheater walls, and Yeh Xin whipped his head around, trying to locate the sound. It seemed to come from the ridge, back up near the lava tube entrance.

He saw Meg and the Ugandan man rise, staring in the general direction of the gunshot. Below him the dark figure also stood and scanned the ridge.

Then another shot tore through the air, and another, followed by a flurry of gunfire from an unseen battle above them all. The tribe was scrambling around the clearing now, and even from his perch he could hear cacophony rise from the Ugandans as they shouted in confusion and alarm.

Oh, no...

The dark figure was advancing on the two trees, chewing noisily on something as he strode fearlessly across the clearing. Thankfully he reached up to a branch in the other tree – the one closer to the hollow, but it was still only five meters from the one hiding Yeh Xin from view.

He held his breath and pressed his back against his tree, unmoving, unblinking, stuck staring directly at the other man as he climbed. After what seemed like an eternity the dark form turned to settle in and get a better look at the disturbance taking place in the tribal clearing.

It was then that Yeh Xin got a clear look at the man's face. The sight almost knocked him from his perch. It was most certainly the face of the man from the brief on the recent mine battle – a known terrorist based in Uganda. He was a man wanted by the authorities for years – elusive, smart, and backed by some of the most hated organizations in the world.

It was the face of the terrorist, Jelani.

Chapter Twelve

Meg Hennessy's hand trembled as she set the spoon down and watched Andrew walk away. She rested her elbows on the rough wooden table and buried her face in her hands, but the protection it provided was fleeting. The sounds of the encampment infiltrated rapidly, and her captivity wrested her thoughts away once more. She shoved the bowl away angrily, sending the spoon careening across the table, leaving a trail of maisha and plantain mash in its wake.

Then she felt a strong hand on her shoulder, and she turned. It was the man named Kabilito – the one who had saved her. Still, she shrugged the hand from her shoulder and leaned away. Kabilito disregarded the aversion and sat on the wooden bench next to her, remaining silent.

So she said nothing. Until she couldn't. "I don't know what's worse – being eaten by a gorilla or being a prisoner," she burst out, twisting her body around to confront him.

Kabilito regarded her calmly with his ancient eyes. "You were attacked – the physical healing is complete, but your mind will take time. This is a safe place – you are in no danger here. Rest and recover." He picked up her spoon and placed it gently back in the bowl. "And gorillas don't eat people. You were simply a threat to the infant."

"Oh, so you were watching me all along?" she challenged.

"We've been watching anyone that comes close to the valley, particularly with the recent culinary propaganda."

"Ah – the video," she responded, staring off into space. "More will come, Kabilito. You can't keep this a secret forever, just like you can't keep me here."

He allowed a long pause before replying. "In time you will come to understand. You will be accepted here, and with a greater purpose than profit." He leaned forward. "Think of it – a chance to never again experience sickness or lasting injury, but more importantly, a chance to become part of something much larger, as the history Subira shared with you plays out. You'll find that it holds more significance than the accomplishments of corporate America."

She dismissed him with a wave of her hand. "They'll come looking – a missing person doesn't go unnoticed. Don't you think my company will search for me? Or my country?"

Kabilito leaned back, a trace of sympathy in his penetrating gaze. "Your company and country – that is who will miss you? No family, no friends?"

Meg turned her head away, avoiding Kabilito's eyes, but he continued. "I have spoken with Andrew. I know your position at the company is an important one – that you are a high-level executive. This is not unfamiliar to me. As Subira has told you, I've managed the shipping company that generates our revenues for many decades. We inherited the operation long ago, but we've kept the sea captain's legacy alive while growing a resource for our people. We've employed thousands for a very long time, and I've been privileged to lead them – every sort of person imaginable – every walk of life. So I understand your world, and I understand corporate structure and executive ambition. Some dedicate their lives to advancement, but without purpose it is an empty endeavor."

Meg shifted on her seat uneasily and kicked at the valley's rich soil under her feet. Kabilito pressed on. "I'm guessing your life is filled with nothing but your work, and that you have had little time for friends or family. Am I close?" he asked.

Meg sighed, staring absently at the earth, silent. Her full lips finally parted, but her voice was barely a whisper. "I'm an only child. My father left us when I was eight, and my mother raised me alone. She put me through college while on a shoestring budget, and I studied hard so the investment wasn't wasted. I remember how proud she was at my graduation." Meg sighed. "But she died soon after, and she never got to see the fruits of that diploma. I vowed to honor her support through success and hard work. I devoted myself to my career, and I rose quickly through the ranks."

Her voice strengthened. "All I've ever had was my work. That's what drives me – it gives me purpose. Yes, I draw my own self-validation from my accomplishments at the firm. Society finds fault with that somehow – they call it shallow. But what's so wrong with the pursuit of success? So what if I'm not close to anyone? I don't need anyone – they need me. That's what happens when you're good at something – the world comes to you. And maybe that's all I need – for people to need me."

Kabilito reached out and lifted Meg's chin, then pointed around the settlement at all the activity. "Look around you – look at the people here, living and working together, happy, content, and with purpose. They all need each other – it's not one-sided. There's no one to impress, no fear of failure, no greed to satisfy. Only simple coexistence and harmony, all working towards a singular, noble goal – to protect the world from this incredible power until its time comes."

Meg snorted, causing Kabilito to raise an eyebrow.

"You don't have to believe in the prophecy," he continued, "but you've seen firsthand the madness the fruit can cause. You said Martin was falling apart when you last saw him. It got worse, as you now know, and he could have killed many people. If you don't believe in the prophecy, you must at least see that this power needs stewardship."

"Science can fix the madness," Meg responded.

It was Kabilito's turn to snort. "Only the purest science is driven by the desire to understand, but corporate science is driven by greed. No company can own the fruit, let alone control what happens when its power is released. It's a fruit, not an invention. Some things are not meant for profiteering. Your science and your laboratories are ultimately controlled by the shareholders, and they simply want a return on their investment, not to mention those who would seek immortality and power alone. And those who would use the fruit to this end would most certainly go mad and destroy others."

Kabilito shifted his attention to the lush walls of the beautiful valley and breathed in the mountain air. "This place is a gift – one that cannot be replicated. The waters of the stream, the plants and animals, the rich earth – they seem so simple at first, but the interaction, the symbiosis, the balance of the entire system – it's all by design. Science can only attempt poor copies of its complexity. Nature is the best laboratory, Meg, and God the ultimate scientist."

Meg surveyed the valley. It was so foreign, so different from grey skyscrapers and dark city streets. *It is incredible – I could almost be happy here*. Her eyes caressed the trees and drank in the high mountain walls, the glacial peaks. Even the settlement and its huts blended in with their natural setting. This very table, rough-hewn and from the earth. Everything was organic and simple, yet functional. From the fire pit with its log benches to the cooking area, even the hand-carved barrels of the incredible maisha fruit...

The fruit... She rubbed the palm of her hand with her thumb, and her pulse quickened as her eyes narrowed.

A gunshot suddenly rang through the valley, then echoed from the far mountain peak. Kabilito bolted upright and stood, eyes scanning the slopes, trying to locate the sound. Meg jumped from the bench and joined him.

"So much for your peaceful valley, Kabilito," she said dryly.

Chapter Thirteen

Sergeant David Harel raised his head weakly and spat blood. Trap rock from the slope lay strewn all about him. Wearily he rested his head back on the ground and let his mind drift…

Gunshots from the ridge above jolted him back into consciousness, and he lifted his head once more. Tall trees filtered only dim light through a dense canopy high above him, but even so Harel could make out a lush valley floor with trees and plants he had never seen before. Giant leaves the size of elephant ears hung from thick, green stalks, and mossy heathers dripped from branches like long, thin beards. His eyes followed the steep, rocky slope upward until his vision was obscured by the treetops hiding the ridge above from view. There was no way up, and no way for anyone on the ridge to see down to him.

I'm screwed.

The flurry of gunshots tapered off as he strained to

listen. A few sporadic shots punctuated the end of the battle.

Why would the Chinese suddenly attack? How did they even spot us? It made no sense.

He sat up, wincing at the pain shooting from his left shoulder. Opening his collar, he pulled back his shirt to look at the wound...and immediately regretted it. There was a clean exit, but his scapula was almost certainly shattered. That meant that there were bone and shrapnel fragments still in there, and possibly material from his fatigues – a recipe for infection if it wasn't treated soon. And he was losing blood – it didn't look bright red, but it wasn't as dark as venous blood, either – had he nicked an artery, too?

He did his best to stop the bleeding and immobilize the arm, then sat back against the slope and rested from the effort, feeling lightheaded. Looking back up the slope, he considered his options. Even without his injury it would have been impossible to scramble back up to the ridge. So the play for now was to stay put and wait for rescue.

Within minutes he heard the far-off beating of helicopter blades. *They're coming for me,* he thought. But scanning the tree canopy once more, he knew that getting a chopper down to his location was an impossibility.

His hopes sank further when he heard the battle resume. The chuffing whine of the guns mounted on the Venom was unmistakable, and soon he could make out rifle fire from the Chinese as they shot back. He heard the chopper make a final pass, then the familiar rhythmic beats faded away. His face fell as it dawned on him that the chopper was there primarily for the team's extraction. They only made one pass looking for him before the ground fire and tree canopy drove them away.

They'll be back. His training told him to stay and await

rescue, but he knew his location was a poor one. An hour passed, then another. No one was coming, and he continued bleeding. The pain was sickening.

Time to move.

He staggered to his feet and immediately stumbled down the slope, finding his ankle badly sprained from the fall. His shoulder pounded with the effort of movement and his breathing was labored. -He had almost assuredly broken a few ribs as well.

He continued downward, hoping for a stream in the valley below that could lead toward a settlement. Grasping at trees with his good hand, he slowly and painfully wove his way to the base of the slope. His M16 weighed him down as it swung wildly on its strap. He slung it on his back and continued down the slope, pausing only to wipe blinding torrents of sweat from his brow and to swat at the black flies that swarmed around him.

Eventually the slope flattened at the base of the ridge. The trees and brush were thicker here, and through the dense vegetation he could hear the babble of a stream. Disoriented and dehydrated, he pushed through the brush, but his thirst was forgotten as he broke through the overgrowth and entered a clearing.

His jaw dropped and he froze. Camouflage netting hung from the treetops over a settlement. Large, grass huts circled a central fire pit surrounded by benches. There was even a cooking area, an animal pen and a small garden. A mixture of modern and ancient, the generators and four wheelers clashed with the rough-hewn table and benches.

And there were people there in the settlement. *And they were looking at him.*

Startled by his sudden entrance, they remained

motionless at first. Time stood still. Although Harel's exhaustion and injuries sapped the last of his strength, he surveyed the tribe as they stood frozen in their actions – some tending the fire, others repairing the broken rail of an animal pen.

Could this be the tribe that was harboring Jelani – the tribe from his briefing? But two others caught his attention – white, seemingly European or American – a man and a woman...

He blinked and staggered, the exertion and blood loss catching up to him. *So tired...so dizzy...*

He was dimly aware that the people around him were moving now, reacting to his presence. Strong hands supported him as his knees collapsed. They held him up and led him into the clearing, helping him as he limped, all the while chatting excitedly in Swahili.

Riding the edge of consciousness, Harel lifted his head just in time to catch motion in the brush across the clearing – motion that the tribe, distracted by his sudden presence, did not yet see. He squinted at the tree line as a figure emerged, staggering from the cover of the dense bush.

It was a uniformed Chinese soldier, wounded, blood dripping from his head and staining his pants. Startled by his surroundings, the man waved his rifle drunkenly as he stumbled forward. Harel opened his mouth to shout, but someone in the tribe beat him to it. The ones nearest the soldier reacted first, rushing toward him like they had with Harel.

It was then that the Chinese man saw him, eyes narrowing in recognition. The soldier raised his rifle, his face contorted in rage.

This was one of the Chinese troops who attacked my

squad, who shot me in the shoulder...

Excited shouts filled the air, and a flurry of Swahili erupted around him. In the ensuing commotion, Harel shook free from the unseen hands holding him upright. Tunnel vision set in, and everything seemed to move in slow motion.

Just as the Chinese soldier took aim Harel raised his own weapon, unleashing a surge of bullets directly at the assailant from his semi-automatic M16.

But several from the tribe were already in motion, rushing toward the Chinese soldier. They moved incredibly fast, their momentum drawing them directly into the line of fire.

The gun recoiled over and over and his shoulder exploded in agony. Harel's bullets flew across the clearing and tore into the Ugandans, ripping open their torsos and spraying blood in crimson arcs.

Horrified, Harel dropped the rifle as the bodies fell to the earth. His head was forced to the ground by those near him as others sped toward the fallen. Strangely, they didn't rush to the aid of the wounded. Instead, they constrained the Chinese soldier and forced him to the ground, kicking his weapon away. But the reason for their distraction became all too clear a moment later.

Ear pressed to the earth, Harel watched in shock as bullets wriggled out of the chest holes of the dead men. Tears in their flesh closed while bloody gashes sealed and skin knitted back together. The men rose, none the worse for wear, and several of them wiped blood from their skin, glowering at him.

His sideways gaze briefly met the Chinese soldier's, and astonishment replaced animosity. Both of them were in awe of the miracle they had witnessed.

These men were dead only a moment ago, by my own hand...

Suddenly an unseen voice called out from above him, speaking English, accented slightly with French and British. "Andrew – make up the draught," the voice intoned richly.

He caught a glimpse of the white man rushing off as dizziness washed over him, and he felt his cheek sink impossibly far into the earth while confusion and helplessness ushered him into blackness.

Dark eyes watched the bizarre scene unfold, peering through the leaves of a tall tree, one of a matched pair that grew near his hollow. Jelani shifted his position in the bough, settling in to watch the tribe nurse the unconscious soldiers back to health from his vantage point.

How long have I been here? An hour? A day? It didn't matter – the events unfolding in the clearing were more entertainment than he'd had in months, since the mine battle for sure.

He scratched his ribs and cackled, muttering to himself in Swahili. *More and more people in the valley now.* First there was the American man, then the girl, then these two soldiers. Who would be next? And with the American gaining these new powers, things were getting out of control.

How had he done that, anyway? He thought briefly. *The American incapacitated the tribal leader with a word...* He filed it away in his mind – something he'd have to revisit later.

They'll be on alert now with all these newcomers. He shook his unkempt hair and scowled at the tribe. He hated the valley people – always displacing him, forcing him to hide. He was just as powerful now, but there were many more of them. *And even more, now – more and more and more – what* will *they do with all of them?* He cackled and scratched his ribs again.

But I have bigger plans in mind, and it's time I set them in motion. He stroked his shaggy beard and grinned. Reaching into his pocket he withdrew a combat knife. He drew the blade across his palm, delighting in the red blood welling up and at how quickly the gash reformed and closed. He cooed and chortled, lapping at the blood dripping from his hand. His eyes rolled back in his head in rapture.

He composed himself after a few moments and began climbing down from his perch silently, his brain churning, plans forming. As he dropped to the ground, he heard a twig snap in the second tree – the twin to the one he had climbed. He froze and scanned the branches, but the only motion came from leaves stirring in the wind.

A monkey, or a chameleon, nothing more.

A few short steps brought him back to his hollow and all the fruit he'd need. He knew the secret of growing it – brief daylight, mimicking the effect of the valley's high walls. Diving into the depression under the shrub cover, he soon emerged with a bulging sack full of the valley's treasure – every single one he had stockpiled.

He sat at the base of his twin trees, caressing the fruit in his bag and rocking back and forth, occasionally chuckling softly to himself. Finally, as night fell, he stood and bid his hollow farewell.

The tribe was already setting up watches around the perimeter of the settlement. It would be difficult to evade them, but if he hurried he would make it. He skirted the orchard, straying far from the men who were now walking among the rows of ancient trees. Careful to remain in the darkest shadows, he swung wide of the settlement and huts, hugging the ground and hiding in the underbrush when anyone came near.

Finally he approached the lava tube exit. A single man sat near the gaping circular rock, whittling a stick and singing softly.

Are they guarding the tube now?

Jelani scowled. *They can't control me.* He balled his fists and leaned forward, preparing to attack the man and escape the valley. Shifting his weight to the balls of his feet, he frowned and winced, feeling something sharp under his toe.

He reached down and picked up the offending rock, then paused and cocked his head. Briefly gauging the weight of the stone in his hand, he sighed, then tossed it far to the left of the tunnel entrance. The rock crashed through the leaves and the man jerked upright and stood, then left to investigate.

Better that than raise alarms, though it would have been fun...

Jelani started up the lava tube entrance with his bag slung over his shoulder, scrambling quickly to gain some distance before the man sat back down at his post. As he climbed he recalled his first journey through the tube – his only other, but in the opposite direction. It seemed so long ago that the mine battle had gone so horribly wrong...

They had been winning – the Ugandan National Troops were killed off, and the Americans were pinned down. But that's when the mysterious Ugandan tribesmen had arrived. Slowly, methodically, the gunfire from his men had been snuffed out, and one by one the mortar and rifle stations around the mine valley went silent. Finally Jelani had left his friend and companion – the deadly assassin "the Hawk" – alone at their station to investigate what was happening at the other attack positions.

What he had found changed him forever. As he crept toward the adjacent attack position a dark figure had leapt from the brush, hurtling toward the rifleman stationed there. The gunman rolled to the side just as his assailant landed, slamming his foot into the ground where the rifleman's head had been. Jelani's man was well-trained, and before the newcomer could react the rifleman had squeezed off several rounds directly into the man's chest. The attacker had fallen to the ground, and the gunman had even put one more bullet in his head for good measure.

But something had felt wrong at that moment, and instead of rushing over to congratulate his man, he paused just long enough to witness the impossible. For as the rifleman turned back to his station, the dead man *had risen*, blood stained but...*unharmed*. Stunned, Jelani had tried to choke out a warning, but before he could open his mouth the walking corpse was on his man, smashing his head against the earth with incredible force, knocking him out cold.

Jelani had squatted behind cover and let the attacker pass as he heard a muffled shout from across the mine valley, and yet another rifle went silent. *These...immortals...are what's taking us out*, he had thought to himself, wide-eyed. *Nothing can withstand such a force...*

By the time he sneaked back to his station, his friend, The Hawk, was gone. His troops, once in a commanding position, had now been neutralized.

He had moved to a safer position behind some boulders where he could locate the American forces. But all hope drained when he saw the Hawk down on the valley floor. The famed assassin had met his fate at the hands of the Ugandan newcomers – the same immortals that had neutralized the rest of his men.

Having lost the battle, he had turned and slunk from the mine slopes. He skirted the valley on the ridge, hiking west until he reached a road guarded by a Ugandan National sentry. Keeping the road in sight, he continued, hiding under the cover of the mountain brush until suddenly he had come upon several four-wheelers hidden off-road. He had paused in the cover of dense brush until he heard men approaching. Several of the Ugandans from the mine battle, their clothes bloodied and torn apart from bullet holes, started the hidden vehicles and sped down an overgrown jeep trail.

He had followed on foot, jogging along the jeep trail until he could no longer hear the motors. After that he tracked the tire imprints in silence. The forest had eventually opened to a flat, grassy plain. He had raced across, following the tracks until they disappeared over a ridge.

The plains dropped off and ended in a cliff, save for a spit of land that pinched off to form a rock bridge that led to...*nowhere*. It terminated on the face of a mountain, with vines spilling down over the natural stone bridge. But faint mud splatters from the tires were still visible along the bare, rocky path, and soon he had found the tube behind the vines – an ancient, lava-draining vessel that bled a volcano millennia ago.

The same tube I now climb, this time with a satchel-full of treasure.

The climb was effortless, and he marveled at his own speed. He was nearing the top. *Three months spent there, infusing my blood with the fruit's powers. But now I'm one of them – even* better *than them.*

The vines ahead signaled the end of the tube. Pushing through them he squinted in the moonlight reflecting from the bald rock of the ridge top. Then something metallic glinted on the ground, and he stooped to retrieve it.

Shell casings. And beside them, blood. A battle had been fought here. The soldiers captured by the tribe must have been involved. They could have easily fallen into the valley during the fight.

He raised his face and stared at the glacial mountaintops to the west. Margherita Peak shimmered like a diamond, bathed in the light of the moon. He fingered the casings absently, blood smearing on his hands. Then he turned northeast and smiled.

He began with a walk, but he was capable of so much more. So he jogged, then he ran, racing through forests and over the mountain terrain, his satchel bobbing and swaying with the weight of the prize within.

Chapter Fourteen

Colonel Frank Anderson balled his fists under the table as the Chinese ambassador to the US calmly wiped his glasses on a silk handkerchief.

This is why I stayed out of politics, he thought.

The representatives of the State Department diplomatically inquired about the missing Chinese soldier.

"I'm afraid he has not turned up as of yet," the ambassador replied dryly, "but I suspect you'd know more about that than me."

Frank slammed his hand on the table and heads turned. "And what about *my* man, *Harel*? What have *you* done with *him*?" he bellowed, no longer able to contain himself.

The ambassador smiled smugly. "What are you suggesting, Colonel Anderson? A prisoner swap? I'm afraid that can't happen, since we don't have your man. But your intentions speak volumes."

Frank's face reddened as the ambassador rose. "We're done here," the impeccably-dressed Chinese man announced. He motioned for his aides to follow and headed toward the door.

Frank continued. "You haven't addressed the cyber hacking – we have proof, Ambassador. Server records, IP addresses – *everything*."

The ambassador stiffened, still facing the door. "I have no idea what you are talking about. This meeting has concluded." And with that the ambassador and his entourage exited the meeting room.

"Nice work, Frank," one of the representatives spat sarcastically.

Frank was about to tear the man's head off when an analyst he recognized, Andrea Blaine, entered the room carrying an armful of reports. She looked weary and red-eyed as she set the stack of papers on the table and addressed the room.

"In the past twenty-four hours we've seen significant activity around the Xinjiang city of Urumqi, in the Eastern Shuimogou District. As you know, the Uyghur – the Muslim Turks with ancient claims to the region – are rioting. They've claimed for years that the Chinese are trying to cleanse them and other ethnic Muslims from the area, and they're using the recent mining incidents in Uganda as a lightning rod. The Chinese army moved into the region yesterday, and they're amassing troops on the Urumqi city limits. The riots are further fueled by Muslim leaders in Turkey speaking out against the treatment of the Uyghur. Imams from Istanbul are spreading the word, and the situation worsens by the hour."

"How so?" the representative asked.

Andrea continued. "The Imams claim that the recent mining deaths underscore their proof of genocide – that the Chinese government views them as expendable or worse, contracting them solely to undertake the most dangerous work. The riots started as a protest, but escalated when the Chinese troops arrived. Many Uyghur were jailed by the Urumqi police, and the Turkish Islamic leaders have denounced their treatment. Other ethnic Muslim groups sympathize with the Uyghur in this matter and are being jailed as well – Kazakhs, Tajiks, Kyrgyzstanis and Mongol Muslims, among others. But the police have been unable to quell the uprising, and China has deployed hundreds of troops to the region. They haven't yet entered the city, probably due to global perception – Xinjiang is an Uyghur Autonomous Region, after all."

"Andrea, can you give us some background on the region?" Frank asked.

Andrea brightened. "Certainly, Colonel. There are approximately nine million Uyghur in Xinjiang, of which only two hundred and fifty thousand live in Urumqi. The Uyghur's claims to what used to be called East Turkestan have been a flashpoint of unrest between the Turks and the Chinese for centuries. Although the Uyghur represent the Muslim majority, significant strife also exists between the Chinese government and the Muslim Kazakhs, Tajiks, Kyrgyz, Mongols, and even the Chinese Muslim Hui living in Xinjiang."

Frank considered this before speaking. "So that means that the Chinese troops amassing near the Urumqi border are..."

"Inciting the wrath of certain Middle Eastern countries?" Andrea eagerly finished his thought. "Absolutely, sir. Of course the Turks are defending the Uyghur in the press and are beginning to saber-rattle. It is only a matter of time before Kazakhstan, Tajikistan, Kyrgyzstan and Mongolian Muslim leaders follow suit based on the treatment of their own in Urumqi."

No one spoke as the statement hung heavily in the air.

Chapter Fifteen

Andrew paced the valley floor in frustration, glowering at the soldiers. Fully healed by the draught after only a few hours, they had been put to work by Subira, helping to build wooden packing crates.

Crates that would soon hold all that the tribe took with them as they left the valley.

He was still in shock. He turned to address Kabilito again, angrily. "You make no sense, Kabilito. You're *all* overreacting. Let's just search them, make sure they have no fruit – then *release* them. What do they really know? So what – so they saw something miraculous when they were delusional from their wounds. Who's going to believe them?"

"It's not that simple, Andrew. You and Martin started a chain of events. First Meg's presence, then the soldiers – it's no coincidence. The location of this valley is no longer a secret, but protecting the fruit is still paramount to us. The less the world knows of its power, the better. And these soldiers have witnessed it firsthand. There's a reason they're here in the first place."

"They know *nothing*, Kabilito, they just fell in here – they'd never find it again, not in these mountains," Andrew spat vehemently. "They know *nothing*!"

Furious, he rushed over to the American soldier, David Harel. Andrew opened his mouth to demand that Harel divulge his mission, but what emerged from his lips was something utterly different. A rolling, sonic boom spilled forth – like thunder echoing from cloud to cloud across the sky. The words of his command were clear, the power they carried irresistible.

Caught mid-swing with hammer in hand, Harel immediately froze with a glassy sheen in his eyes. Then he answered in a flat, near-monotone voice. "We were commanded to track the Chinese. I didn't know anything about the fruit until I got here," he replied.

Andrew looked up at Kabilito wildly. "See? They know nothing, Kabilito!" he yelled. But Kabilito stood wordlessly, clearly taken aback by the demonstration of power. Frustrated, Andrew flew over to the Chinese soldier like a man possessed. Again he issued a command, this time in a voice so intense that the ground shook under their feet.

The Chinese soldier stiffened, and a stream of Mandarin spilled out of his mouth. Andrew responded, words blasting as if from a giant brass instrument, and the Chinese man replied flatly in Mandarin once more, speaking at length before trailing off. Andrew stared hard at the man, considering the response. Moments passed before he finally sighed in defeat and looked up at his friend. Kabilito stood frozen, his face stricken with confusion.

"Well, I guess you were right," Andrew said slowly.

"What do you mean?" Kabilito managed.

"You heard the man," he replied.

Kabilito paused before whispering, "I would have if I could speak Mandarin – *like you just did, Andrew.*"

Eyes wide, Andrew sunk to the ground as if punched in the gut. His chest heaved, but he couldn't catch his breath. A high-pitched whine sounded in the deepest reaches of his mind, and a dull pain wormed its way through his skull. He shook his head to relieve the screeching sound, but it persisted.

Suppressing the cacophony in his mind, he managed to utter, "The man's name is Wu Yue. He's a Chinese special ops soldier, and he says their mission was to find a tribe in the mountains, and that his squad will soon return and search for him. His men were fighting the American soldiers, just up there on the ridge."

Andrew paused to look up at Kabilito, noticing that Subira and Akiiki had joined them.

"That means the Americans were there, too, and will be looking for Harel," he continued. "Two squads, each looking for their respective missing men *and* a hidden tribe, all of them up around the lava tube entrance and in the surrounding valley."

Subira clapped a hand on Andrew's shoulder. "We anticipated this, Andrew. We are not unprepared. We've been expecting a situation like this for years, and we've practiced dismantling and packing so we can leave in only a few hours – just in time to leave before the soldiers arrive. It will work itself out if we follow the plan." Subira helped him to his feet and walked him toward the orchard. Pointing, he showed Andrew that several of the tribe members had already begun stripping the trees and picking up all of the fruit that had fallen. “It is set in motion, Andrew. By mid-morning we will be gone, and the secret will be safe.”

Acceptance set in as Andrew worked tirelessly throughout the night, side by side with the tribe members, the soldiers and Meg. Andrew found the work cathartic; physical labor helped clear his mind of anxiety and his fear of the growing powers. But the headache remained, and the whining sound slowly escalated to a steady buzzing noise.

They toiled in the darkness, packing equipment and loading small trailers to be hauled out of the valley by the four wheelers. The fruit was loaded into crates lined with canvas, and Andrew was amazed at how much the orchard had yielded.

Around four in the morning he was still constructing crates with Kabilito as the final push to evacuate the valley began. They spoke as friends do while working together, and eventually Kabilito asked Andrew if he felt any different when the new powers were manifesting.

“When it’s happening I feel like I’m losing control,” Andrew replied, driving a nail home. He set down the hammer and leaned on the half-finished crate. “It’s scary that no one knows what’s happening to me. It’s as if the maisha is somehow more potent now – accelerating the absorption of the healing and strength powers, but more recently adding completely new ones – at least in me.”

He glanced briefly at Kabilito but no explanation came.

Andrew continued. “We saw Meg and the soldiers heal in, what, an hour or two from when they got the draught? And look at them now – they’re twice as strong as they were. It never happened that fast in me, or even in Martin. But now all of a sudden I’m speaking in tongues, too. And I feel a pressure inside, like a headache that won't go away. What if the others start experiencing this? What if they develop these new powers – this new voice thing? And why hasn't any of this affected the rest of the tribe? What if all of the newcomers are turning, including me?"

Ignoring the questions, Kabilito continued pressing. "So you don't know when this new power is going to manifest? And when it does, you can't control it?"

"It's not like that. When it happens it seems as if I start it – at those times I'm focused on a specific goal, something I desperately want. My mind shapes the initial action, but then the floodgates open and an enormous, uncontrollable power takes over. That's when these commands come out of me. But then it's too much to handle, and I feel overwhelmed. It's like a flood or a wave washing over me, pushing in the direction I started. And then it's too late – the power of the voice is activated somehow. This last time I tried to fight it off – to not let it take control, but it was impossible." He picked up the hammer and started driving another nail.

Kabilito considered this for a moment as Andrew worked. "Have you tried embracing this power? Can you let it flow without fighting it, and try to shape it instead?"

Andrew froze in mid-swing, feeling the blood drain from his cheeks chillingly. "No, Kabilito – you don't understand. This thing – I can't let it continue. I need to find a way to stop it – to contain or absorb it. I watched the power of the fruit twist Martin into something...*else*. It took control of his mind. I can't let that happen to me, especially now that the power has increased and added new...*properties*."

"The maisha magnified Martin's being, Andrew, including his flaws. He succumbed to his own mind, not to the fruit. If you opened up to these new powers..."

"No!" Andrew shouted as his hammer crashed down uncontrollably. The force of his blow crushed the corner of the crate, splintering several planks and driving shards into his forearm. Shaking, he withdrew the long splinters, not even noticing the speed at which his wounds closed and healed.

Frustrated and terrified, he dropped his hammer and turned, holding his head in his hands, wishing the pressure and buzzing would go away. And though his back was to his friend, he could feel Kabilito's penetrating gaze upon him as he walked away.

Chapter Sixteen

Jelani dug through the dumpster outside the church, searching. Here in the northern Ugandan city of Gulu he didn't need much time to find what he was looking for – an empty bottle of waragi banana gin. He lifted it from the dumpster and smiled before he headed into the church. Walking up the steps, he looked down at his trousers and saw dried blood. *That's OK – perfectly in character*, he thought to himself, recalling the events of last night.

After escaping up the lava tube he had run across the mountainside, heading northeast. Like all of those imbued with the power of the fruit, he ran incredibly fast. But maisha didn't do anything for his eyesight in the darkness of night, and so he had stumbled and fallen over the rocky slopes several times. At that speed, falling meant broken bones – each time. One particularly bad tumble resulted in his tibia bursting painfully through his skin, but he had just turned his face to the night sky and laughed hysterically as the bones pulled back together and fused once more.

Running all night, he had finally arrived at the town of Fort Portal as dawn broke. He had bought a ticket for the morning Postal Bus to Gulu, home to radical, Christian militia rebel groups that commit unspeakable acts of terror and violence. That wasn't the description on the Gulu tourism poster in the bus station, however, and Jelani cackled hysterically at the picture of merry folk laughing and dancing in the idyllic Gulu city square.

The bus ride had given him time to plan, and after several hours he finally arrived. He withdrew cash at a bank, located a rental office and leased a small but secure apartment to store his fruit. Temporarily settled, he had explored the town of Gulu. He passed through the marketplace packed with stalls, each separated by hanging bolts of colorful cloth. Vendors sold meats, fruit, clothes, plastic bins, shoes and carved wood – anything and everything. Those who bought larger items carried them off on top of their heads. A bunch of bananas, a gas can, even a carved wooden rocking chair floated above the crowd, bobbing up and down as their new owners walked them home.

Finally he found what he was looking for – a Christian Church with a small symbol carved into the wooden frame to the right of the door. An unrecognizable symbol to most, faint and almost indiscernible, but a calling card of a group he knew of from his time in the training camps long ago. A violent and bloody gang that ruled the town from the shadows.

A group which he now needed.

As he passed a wooden cross on his way up the steps of the small church, he told himself to savor this moment – the moment he started his own little army. Although the power of the group he targeted had waned over the decades, several hundred loyalist soldiers still remained.

It would be a good start.

He tore open the door to the church, disrupting a service already in progress. Heads turned from pews as he stumbled against the doorframe, waving the empty bottle in the air.

"You call yourself good Christians," he yelled, slurring badly, "but all you do is kill and maim! You don't help the people – you rape our women and destroy our society!"

A gasp ran through the crowd as Jelani began to stumble down the aisle. An acolyte at the altar ran to the minister and whispered frantically in his ear as Jelani continued his tirade.

"...and if I ever catch one of you bastards, I'll kill you!" he screamed, falling hard against a pew. He smashed the bottle against the floor to emphasize his point, and someone in the congregation screamed. The minister nodded to the acolyte, who promptly ran from the altar and out the side door of the church. Jelani suppressed a smile and continued his ranting, mixing in religious slurs with name-calling and political criticism. He even challenged the minister to a fight, taking a few swings before several members of the congregation rushed to help.

A sudden yell silenced the church from the main doors. Everyone turned. In the doorway stood three rough men, one carrying a semi-automatic rifle, the others with makeshift clubs. They advanced down the aisle rapidly, and Jelani came at them, swaying.

A quick bash from a club to the side of his head sent Jelani sprawling. But he slowly rose to his feet, laughing hysterically. He dove at the man that had clubbed him, tackling him around the legs. The man with the rifle smashed

Jelani in the back of the head, and he sank to the ground.

"Stay down!" the rifleman yelled as Jelani stirred. He rose to his knees, prompting the men to grab him by the armpits and drag him screaming from the church and toward a waiting car. As he was carried down the steps, Jelani saw the congregation squeeze through the church doors. They gawked at the scene as he was stuffed into the back seat.

The car sped away with its new passenger. Behind him he heard the crowd erupt in cheer. But hidden under his bloody, matted hair, Jelani secretly smiled in satisfaction.

Chapter Seventeen

With no better hiding place, Yeh Xin had slept in the arms of the tree that night. He had watched Jelani fade into darkness with his satchel of fruit. Yet with all the new activity in the valley settlement, he was reluctant to attempt an escape himself. The tribesmen were crawling all over the orchard, picking every last piece of fruit, and still he had but one – not enough to end his mission and free his mother. He was told he'd need several for the experimentation his country would conduct. And now, as dawn broke, he watched with growing desperation as the focal point of his mission was being packed into crates before his very eyes.

Were they...*leaving?* The fact that the soldiers were still there likely meant that search parties were already looking for them. Yeh Xin squinted across the clearing. Sure enough, he recognized the Chinese soldier from the mine camp. His commanders would deploy a recovery team, but the primary mission would be to secure the region, especially with the Americans nearby.

And the tribe must know this, too. He composed himself by closing his eyes and chanting softly for a moment before descending from his perch. The valley was cast in darkness with the morning sun still well below the basin rim, and there were enough shadows for Yeh Xin to use. He skirted around Jelani's makeshift hollow, wrinkling his nose as he passed. *How had the man lived like this, squatting in his own feces for months? Was he insane?*

There were tribesmen still in the orchard, but they had already scoured the portion closest to Yeh Xin. He entered the orchard cautiously and inspected the trees. No fruit was left – every single piece had been picked from the trees, and likewise nothing remained on the ground. But he knew where it all had gone.

He swung wide around the orchard and spiraled into the clearing, hiding behind dense scrub brush. He crept between two large crates holding generator equipment, and from there he could see the whole settlement.

He inhaled sharply when he saw how much of the camp had been dismantled. Everything was gone – the electronics, pots and pans, tools, even the equipment shed – all packed up and ready to move. Only a few remaining crates lay in the clearing awaiting departure. The four wheelers had been equipped with small trailers, and these were being loaded with the last of the crates – his only remaining cover.

Five meters ahead lay the large fruit crates. Several were closed already, but two remained open.

Now was his only chance.

Ducking low, Yeh Xin moved into position, then darted between two large bales of hay before diving toward the two open fruit crates. He raised his head – the area seemed clear. He stood slowly and peered into the crates. One was full and covered with canvas, the other was partially empty. But the contents of both were well out of reach from the ground. Carefully he reached up for the rim of the full crate and vaulted over the top, landing on the canvas. He peeled back the cloth and ducked below the rim of the crate as he filled his cargo pants with fruit.

But a moment later voices approached, and he froze. With nowhere to escape, Yeh Xin pulled the canvas over himself and lay still. The voices grew louder, and soon they were almost directly over him. He stopped breathing as he heard several men dumping fruit into the crate next to him.

Then...*silence*. He didn't dare move.

The sun had crept over the valley rim now, and he could feel the sunlight warm the canvas. But suddenly it grew dark again. He heard – *and felt* – a thud directly above him, and the walls of his crate shuddered.

Then he cringed as he heard nails being driven into the lid of his crate. He breathed slowly, trying his best not to panic. The crate next to him was sealed as well, and soon after the hammering ceased he felt his crate rise and sway. And as scared as he was, he marveled at the fact that this heavy crate he lay in was being lifted and carried by *human hands*.

Check that – *superhuman hands*.

The crate jolted as it was dropped onto a springy platform – presumably one of the trailers – and he could hear straps being ratcheted in place to secure the large box. The rough wooden slats left openings in the crate large enough for dim light to filter through, but the canvas was stifling. Soon Yeh Xin found the edge of the cloth and pulled it back, pressing it against the lid as he moved it with his hands and feet until it was bunched up to one side. Now air could circulate over him and he could breathe. He shoved and squirmed, settling into the fruit until he had made a divot under his body. As frustrated and scared as he was, for the moment he remained safe and hidden. But when the crate was opened...

He lay back and sighed as the four-wheeler began to pull the trailer, chanting a sutra softly to himself as the trailer tilted. They were likely climbing the lava tube, the start of what he assumed would be a long ride. Finally his hunger got the best of him, and with just enough clearance above his body, he snatched up a fruit, raised it to his mouth and began to eat.

Chapter Eighteen

"**A**re you hearing me, Major?" Colonel Frank Anderson snapped. "We don't have the troops to spare, and I sure as hell ain't pulling the men out of Uganda – I'll tell you that *right now*. We've already shifted troops from Afghanistan, Saudi Arabia and Ethiopia to the Transit Center at Manas. The Kyrgyzstanis kicked us out of there long ago, and now they want us back? Every country in a thousand-mile radius is screaming for more support for the Uyghur while my men are scrambling around at Manas, trying to erect enough shelters to house all the troops *and* stay hidden at the same time. And you want to dump *more* men in there? How long do you think before the Russians or the Chinese find out about this?"

Major Tom Shenley, acting Kyrgyzstani military liaison, shrunk back to hide behind the top brass sitting near him at the Pentagon conference room table, but Anderson transfixed Shenley's gaze inescapably, forcing a reply. "We're undermanned, Sir," Shenley answered weakly. "With the Turks following the '-stan' countries in raising their military alert levels, we can't keep up with the logistics of coordinating the influx of troops and equipment."

"Well, *find* a way, Major. We're not increasing our visibility any further." Frank turned his attention to a civilian woman sitting across the table. "Mrs. Colton, kindly fill us in as to why our presence is so vital in Kyrgyzstan, and why Secretary Rosemark sees the need for us to spread our Middle Eastern and African troops so thin."

The Under Secretary for Political Affairs leaned forward to speak. "We've been over this before, Frank. With things heating up in western China, we need a nearby air base. The Kyrgyzstani Transit Center at Manas was once a strategic position for us, but we got ourselves kicked out. This is a golden opportunity to reestablish a foothold in Central Asia *and* support our allies."

Frank scowled, the answer grating on his nerves. "Just how much support are we willing to give the -stans in this matter, anyway? If Turkey and its allies move troops into Xinjiang to support the Uyghur, what will our military stance be when the Chinese resist?"

"Secretary Rosemark is prepared to consider escalation if the situation worsens, but not until then. We need plans for military support, Colonel. Already we've publicly denounced Chinese treatment of the Uyghur and other ethnic Muslim groups in Urumqi *and* accused the Chinese of holding our missing soldier, Sergeant David Harel. Likewise the Chinese military thinks we've taken their soldier, this..." She paused to shuffle some papers, searching for a name. "...Wu Yue – their missing soldier. So we're kinda on each other's shit lists at the moment. But there've been further developments recently." The Under Secretary turned to her analyst, Andrea Blaine. "Andrea?" she inquired, prompting Andrea to begin her brief.

Andrea rose with a stack of papers and hurried to the podium, which stood in front of a large screen. "It is an honor to be here. Thank you," she started.

Turning to the screen, she pulled up a CNN image of a smoldering military vehicle in the foreground. Nearby, Chinese soldiers led several men away, their hands cuffed behind their backs. The scroll bar across the bottom read, "Chinese militia detain alleged saboteurs in the Xinjiang city of Urumqi".

Andrea paused the clip. "As you can see, Chinese military presence has ramped up considerably in the past few days. The troops that had amassed outside the city have moved in, and parts of Urumqi are now secured under martial law." She paused for emphasis. "Many of the Uyghur residents have been taken into custody along with other ethnic Muslim groups that are viewed as sympathizers. The Chinese claim that the Uyghur are responsible for terrorist acts of sabotage, most notably the destruction of an ammunition dump on the outskirts of the city. The Uyghur deny this, but resistance groups are forming. Soon there may be open fighting in the streets."

The briefing continued, after which the questions began. As the answers became increasingly repetitive, Frank stole out of the room to make a phone call.

"NSA – Lambard here," the voice in the receiver replied.

"Ed – it's Frank. Listen, whatever happened with the Meg girl? Did any more data surface on her?"

"I was going to ask you the same thing, Frank. We gave you everything we had on her."

“Well, I’ll let you know if we find anything. We’ve already deployed a search team to the site to look for Harel and for whatever drove the Chinese to visit the area. If Meg turns up there we’ll let you know, although somehow I get the feeling NSA will know what we find even before I do…”

Lambard ignored the glib comment. “Frank, what’s so important about this girl? You already have the location of the ‘hot lead’ the Chinese were investigating – don’t you think you’ll find what you’re looking for there?”

“Maybe,” Frank replied, “but if not, she’s our last viable link to the fruit.”

Chapter Nineteen

Andrew stared up at the ridge as the afternoon sun rose. This time of day was his favorite – sunrise in the valley, when shafts of light burst through the vegetation like glorious pillars from the heavens. The signal of a new day of growth for the fruit.

But no longer.

Stripped of their bounty, the trees in the orchard looked skeletal – symbols of immortality now sentenced to death by the tribe's complete harvest, bereft of the salvation they once bore.

Andrew knew that the harvested fruit was safely on its way to the tribe's Mombasa port facility, along with the equipment and most of the members of the tribe. But as he surveyed the barren clearing that he had come to call his new home he felt a tight lump swelling in his throat. It was here that he had found family and a renewed faith, but now his new home would be stripped away once more. He had caused this – his callous plans to capitalize on the fruit, and his support of Martin's greedy ambitions. All a catalyst to the displacement of a tribe that had called Eden its home for over a hundred and fifty years.

Andrew stood with Kabilito, waiting silently for the end while Meg, Harel and Wu Yue sat on a nearby log under the watchful eyes of Subira. Kabilito had wanted the little group to drive to Mombasa together rather than fly with the tribe and the cargo. Andrew guessed that Kabilito wanted time alone with the newcomers on the long drive so that they would open up and begin the process of acceptance. It was fine with him – maybe the drive would distract him from the infernal sounds in his head. So in the end only a handful of them remained behind to finish the work.

After a few moments Akiiki emerged from the remains of the orchard carrying empty gasoline cans. "It is finished," he announced somberly. Then he dropped the empty cans on the ground and took a deep breath. "We need to hurry. The search parties will be here soon."

Kabilito stooped and picked up a torch with a gasoline-soaked rag. He lit the cloth and held the torch aloft. "Forgive us," he murmured. Then he threw the torch at the orchard, and it flew, farther than any mortal could throw it, streaking toward the intended target.

And the trees of the orchard erupted in flame.

Andrew stood staring at the inferno as it grew and engulfed the valley floor, quickly propagating from each source of fuel to the next – an eradication plan made by the tribe long ago in case of imminent evacuation. He felt a hand on his shoulder. Turning, he found Kabilito comforting him as the others climbed onto the remaining four-wheelers.

"We must go, Andrew," Kabilito said softly.

But the fire had dredged up the lasting memory of his home in New York, where flames had engulfed the farmhouse *and* his friend, Martin. It was suddenly overwhelming, and his eyes welled up as he shuffled off to the waiting four-wheelers. Reluctantly he took his seat behind Kabilito.

As they reached the lava tube entrance he turned back toward the valley. He could hear the growing rhythmic beat of approaching helicopter blades over the roar of the flames. They would escape just in time – but because of him, Eden was now a fiery Hell.

Chapter Twenty

Jelani felt the car slow as he rode in silence. He was sweating under the hood covering his head, and the coarse material scratched his face. His wrists were bound behind his back with crude, rough rope.

Finally the car stopped. He heard a door open, and he was wrenched suddenly from the back seat. He stood on cramped, wobbly legs. Sunlight filtered through pinholes in the weave of his hood, though he could see nothing beyond the fabric. He felt strong hands gripping him harshly, and he was shoved through an opening – *a doorway, perhaps*?

The hood was ripped from his head. He gasped and inhaled sharply, squinting in the sudden illumination. Bright, vertical lines resolved into sunlight pouring through cracks in rough plank walls that formed a tiny wooden shack.

Time for Act II, he thought. As his eyes adjusted he became aware of the purpose of the tiny structure. Except for a thin border around the walls, the floor was nothing but a pit. A *deep* pit – one for holding captives.

He could sense several men in the room behind him. Rough hands held him tightly, teetering on the edge of the pit. Feet shuffled, and he felt breath on the back of his neck. Unable to turn, he heard the sudden, sharp click of a switchblade extending. He let his face show panic, though that was an emotion he no longer comprehended.

With a violent tug the blade severed his bonds, and he drew his arms from behind his back, rubbing his wrists in a show of pain.

Hands shoved him forward suddenly, and he lost his balance, falling forward toward the gaping pit. He flailed his arms and cried out for effect, but someone grabbed the back of his shirt and steadied him at the last second. Laughter erupted from the men in the shack behind him.

He was tossed onto his back and a rope was looped under his arms. He stared up into unfamiliar faces that sneered back at him. Struggling and cursing, they lowered him into the pit. When he reached the bottom they dropped the rope in after him. Then he heard the door of the shack slam shut.

Once alone, he sat on the floor and rocked himself back and forth, cackling. He reached into his pants pocket and felt the remains of a maisha fruit, pulverized from harsh treatment at the hands of his captors. But the fruit fragments were still tasty, and he shoved the pieces greedily into his mouth, seeds and all. He curled up and slept on the floor of the pit until a loud crash awakened him – the sound of shack door slamming open.

It was dark now. He must have slept the afternoon away. He stretched and scratched his ribs, aware of several voices above him. A ladder was thrust down into the pit, and he had to jump back to avoid being hit.

He climbed until he neared the top and felt the grip of several hands on his shirt, and he was hauled up the remaining distance and shoved out the door of the shack.

A crowd surrounded him, jeering and spitting in his face. He estimated close to a hundred men and a few women, some carrying torches, some with rifles. The crowd parted to let him through, though they didn't hesitate to trip and slap him as he was dragged and shoved along.

Through the crowd Jelani could make out grassland and plains, but few structures. The group did not appear to be permanently settled here but were probably using the spot solely as an assembly point. From what he knew of them they kept a low profile, moving frequently to avoid capture from the local government. They might be on the run, their numbers waning, but their loyalty was undeniable. He could sense a brutal and savage strength in these people.

They approached a decrepit cinderblock structure, likely a tiny house at one time. Only three walls remained. The fourth was reduced to rubble but had been replaced with logs and mud stucco. The men dragging him kicked open the door to the one-room house and shoved him through. They threw him to the floor, and he heard the door slam shut behind him. Raising his head, he saw a table and a two chairs. A bearded man sat in the far chair, leaning so far back it looked as though he could topple at any moment. The man wore loose-fitting robes common to the region – a nondescript look that clearly allowed him to blend in. He smoked a cigarette. His relaxed posture told Jelani that he was the leader.

Four other men stood in the room, flanking him. Dressed

in robes similar to the leader, they all towered over Jelani, nearly hitting their heads on the rafters, each with a long machete on his belt. The leader nodded to them casually with a dark look in his eyes. The men surrounded Jelani, hauling his lithe frame up to the empty chair to sit facing the leader. Two of the men grabbed him by the wrists and pulled him forward, pinning his outstretched arms to the table roughly. The other two unsheathed their machetes and held them above his forearms.

The leader leaned forward, his composure betrayed by the intensity of his visage. "And who the hell do you think you are?" he growled softly in Swahili.

Jelani could contain himself no longer. First a cackle slipped from his lips, but when he tried to suppress it, he instead burst out laughing. His body shook hysterically while his forearms were held motionless, still splayed on the table, held firmly in place by the two burly henchmen.

Surprisingly, the leader suddenly laughed with him, and their peals of mirth joined in misplaced song. The leader wiped his eyes, still laughing, and asked the question again as he composed himself. "No, seriously, who are you?" he managed in between his lingering chuckles.

Jelani's hilarity tapered down as well. He sighed contentedly as one does at the end of a good laugh before clearing his throat to reply. "I'm your new leader," he answered. Then he stared hard into the eyes of the man before him.

A dark rage passed across the other man's face, as if he had been suddenly slapped. Jelani continued in a determined tone. "You think I'm joking? I'll give you one chance to kneel before me. If not, I'll slaughter you and every man in this room – except for one."

The henchmen stared at each other in confusion. Leaning back in his chair once more, the leader regarded his gaze while replying casually, "And why not kill us all?"

"Because I need a witness," Jelani answered.

Without breaking his stare the leader slowly reached up to form the sign of the cross, from forehead to sternum to shoulders.

Then he nodded once more.

The machetes were a blur as they streaked downward, terminating suddenly on the table with a sickening, wet thud, severing Jelani's forearms cleanly.

He pitched back his head and screamed at the ceiling as blood spurted from the gory stumps. Burying what remained of his arms in his chest, he doubled over while his severed hands opened and closed reflexively on the table before him, pumping out what little blood remained in the vessels.

At first he sobbed, but lament soon turned back into laughter. With tears streaking down his cheeks, he held his stumps aloft so the five men could bear witness to the healing. The bleeding stopped first, then bone, tissue and sinew ran a gruesome race of regeneration, each knitting and splicing ahead of the other until wrists reformed. Palms sprouted from wrists, then fingers burst from flesh like sprouts from soil, lengthening and thickening while skin wrapped around tissue and tendon.

The henchmen gasped, and the leader's face froze in terror. And as the last bit of flesh reformed, Jelani rotated his newly-formed hands around and around in the dim light for all to see.

He turned to the men and shrugged. "Your choice," he announced.

Then he attacked.

With his open palm he struck the sternum of the closest henchman while still sitting. The force of the blow was so great that it crushed the bony plate, driving it straight through the man's spine and out his back. Blood sprayed across the table, and Jelani lifted the dripping, impaled body and hurled it through the thick air to crash against the cinderblock wall.

The other men screamed. Jelani calmly picked up the fallen man's machete and stood. With a single swing he drove the blade cleanly through the next man's skull, slicing him open all the way down to the base of his neck. He pulled the blade free, blood spattering the packed-earth floor as the body dropped to the ground.

Turning the machete sideways, he swung the blade in a wide arc, decapitating another henchman. The remaining man bolted for the door, but Jelani kicked out at his leg, breaking his femur. The man screamed and crumpled to the ground, his upper leg bending like limp, overcooked pasta.

He then turned his attention to the leader. Wetness stained the crotch of the man's pants, and he finally fell over backward in his chair. Jelani was on him in a second, brutally hacking the body into pieces as the screams became increasingly choked with blood. With one last blow he chopped the man's head from his neck, sending it rolling across the floor to rest against a table leg.

He methodically severed and collected heads while the remaining man screamed. Then, grasping the heads by the hair, he gathered them all up in one hand and lifted the screaming man by his neck with the other. He kicked the door open and shoved the man outside to crumple at the feet of the shocked and silent crowd.

Gibbering, the man dragged himself along the ground,

crawling toward the safety of the crowd as Jelani raised the severed heads high above his own.

"From now on, you follow *me,*" he yelled brutally into the cool night air.

The crowd fell silent. Staring at the gruesome display and the gibbering man crawling from the shack, they knelt, one by one, pressing their bodies against the ground in homage to their new leader.

Chapter Twenty-One

Captain Gao unclipped himself from the hoist and signaled he was clear. The smoke was shifting again, and the drop site was no longer upwind. Crouching, he circled the clearing in a wide arc as the chopper mirrored his movements in the sky to avoid the smoke.

The fire had burned away large sections of the tree canopy, exposing areas that were previously too dense for the chopper to deploy the troops. Blackened grass crunched underfoot as soldier after soldier unclipped and cleared the drop area for the next man. Soon all the members of the team had dropped, and Gao led them as they fanned out across the outskirts of the valley. The fire was still raging in the center, and even upwind the smoke obscured vision. They circled the inferno at a safe distance, searching for any sign of their missing man, Wu Yue.

The valley floor became rockier, with blocks of black

basalt jutting up from the ground. Through the smoke Gao could make out a cliff face, rising up to form one wall of the valley. As they approached the wall he saw a wide, gaping hole – an almost perfect circle leading up through the cliff.

This must have been the entrance to the valley they missed. He winced in regret. How could he have missed such a tunnel?

But his self-deprecation was stripped away suddenly when a form appeared through the haze. Gao halted his group with a raised fist and squinted into the tunnel opening. A man in fatigues with a rifle crouched and entered the valley from the tunnel shaft. Then another soldier came through, then one more.

Gao's team was completely exposed. He frantically signaled his men to cover, but it was too late. One of the soldiers from the tube shaft caught sight of them and began yelling to his men. *In English*.

Of course - *the Americans*. Gao had been briefed this morning – they had lost a man in the skirmish as well. He raised his rifle threateningly and his men followed suit, yelling back at the newcomers. They outnumbered the Americans, at least the ones that had exited the tunnel. He had no idea how many remained hidden.

The US soldiers began to retreat back up to the cover of the tube as Gao scrambled for his radio. He guessed that the US communications technology wouldn't work under all that rock, but he imagined one of them would be sent back up the tunnel. They'd need to radio for instructions from their commanders now that there was engagement.

He did the same. The directive that crackled from the static of his handset was clear – his command wanted him to stay put, secure the valley and guard the exit of the tunnel.

There was to be no engagement – no rounds fired unless they were fired upon. In reality, if the Americans chose to waltz out of the tunnel, he was to let them do so. But it didn't mean he had to make it *look* that way.

Gao chose six soldiers and set them, under partial cover, guarding the tunnel. He positioned them so that their cover was credible, but also he made sure that they were visible from the entrance. If fired upon, they could return the favor with enough protection to drive off whatever came through the rocky opening.

Gao and the rest of his men fanned out and began searching. He guessed that he didn't have much time before the Americans returned with greater numbers, but for now the valley was his.

Chapter Twenty-Two

They followed the mountain paths out of the Rwenzoris and around the nearby town of Kasese. Andrew and Kabilito were in one jeep, followed by Akiiki, Meg and Sergeant David Harel in another. Subira and Sergeant Wu Yue trailed behind in the last vehicle.

Skirting Kasese to avoid traffic, they eventually crossed the Nyamwamba River, then pushed on to the north through the smaller settled regions of Rukoki and Mubuku. Away from the shadow of the mountains, only brush and farmlands separated the small towns.

Rather than cut east across the dirt jeep paths of the plains, the caravan continued north, staying on the main road until they reached Fort Portal. From there they turned east and drove the Mubende-Fort Portal Road, through farmland and forest and over the never-ending plains, interrupted only by the occasional nondescript settlement.

They paused in the Mubende district to buy supplies for their trip. There they enjoyed a lunch of fresh cassava, sweet potatoes and goat. Subira rationed a maisha fruit to each of them from a satchel, which they ate raw before climbing back into the jeeps and continuing east.

To Andrew it seemed as if the buzzing sounds and pressure in his head subsided somewhat as they drove. He thought it might be because it had been awhile since he had touched the newfound fount of power.

The drive also gave him time with Kabilito – time to talk through the loss of the valley. At first he just couldn't bear the thought of another home stripped away, but Kabilito reminded him that his place was with the tribe, and that they would rebuild. Over many miles and with Kabilito's guidance, Andrew came to understand that a house is just a structure, but a home is defined by those around you. Although they had lost the valley, they had preserved both family *and* fruit, and that was all that really mattered.

They switched passengers several times between Mubende and the larger town of Mityana, which gave Andrew time with Meg and Harel, and finally with Wu Yue. Since his outburst before leaving the valley, he found that his sudden understanding of Mandarin had stuck. It was easy to converse with the Chinese special ops soldier, although hearing himself speak a new language was frightening.

During the drive Subira shared with them some of the history of the tribe, and he told them of the fruit and the prophecy that demanded its protection. Andrew sensed that the newcomers had begun to accept that the tribe could not release them, though they were still bitter over their captivity. Frustration bubbled over in their conversation, but each of them admitted they were amazed by the fruit and the strength and healing they were gaining from it. They also seemed to understand the tribe's responsibility to control that power. They understood it, but they didn't like it.

Andrew found Harel to be the most accepting and open. He was young and relatively carefree, having joined the military for adventure, only to later learn that it was hard work fraught with responsibility. It was almost as if he was partly enjoying his newfound freedom, at least for the moment.

It took a while for Andrew to engage Meg in a meaningful conversation, and likewise Wu Yue was reluctant to speak at first. Their cool demeanors eventually warmed, though, as they passed through the beautiful countryside, and they began asking questions about the tribe, the fruit, and later about Andrew's past. Soon he found himself sharing his own story with them.

As he recounted his own story about Martin, the fruit, and the search in the Rwenzoris that led him to the tribe, he began wondering if Kabilito and the tribe would have ever allowed him to leave. Or if, in reality, he was their prisoner, too.

Well, not exactly a prisoner – he wanted nothing more than to stay with the tribe. But when he finished his story he trailed off, wondering if it had ever truly been up to him. Or maybe Kabilito knew all along that Andrew would stay with the tribe and had simply given him the illusion of choice. A sliver of doubt entered Andrew's mind, but he suppressed it, at least for now. He was where he felt he belonged, no matter how he had arrived.

From Mubende they drove several hours until they reached the modern city of Kampala, the sprawling capital of Uganda. Andrew wished they could have spent time exploring the city, but to save time they took the Northern Bypass to avoid the traffic jams common in the densely populated metropolis. Still, from the highway he was able to catch glimpses of the high-rises forming the skyline to the south interspersed with the ramshackle houses on the outskirts of the city. A short while later the city gave way to a more rural feel, and Andrew guessed that this was an older part of town.

Soon they reached their destination on the shores of Murchison Bay, a northern inlet of the massive Lake Victoria. They pulled off the road and parked in a long driveway. Through the trees Andrew could see the waters of the lake as they unloaded the jeeps. Each of them carried bedding and light supplies up the driveway to the small, historic home where they had stopped for the night. Andrew walked alongside Kabilito, marveling at the immaculate preservation of the old saltbox house. The clapboard siding and brass lights were in perfect condition, and the sprawling yard rolled down toward a small dock on the bay.

"Where are we, Kabilito?" he asked.

"We've spoken of this place, Andrew, when we first met. You should recognize it from the story. Did you not notice the town's name on the sign as we left the main road?"

"It was a port name – Port Bell, I thought it read," he answered, slowing as he reached back into his memory. Finally he recalled their discussion from his first trip to Uganda, and he stopped dead in his tracks. "This isn't, this can't be...," he stammered, looking at Kabilito in surprise.

Kabilito shook his head solemnly. "It is indeed. The Lake Captain's house, and our first exposure to the new world so many years ago – the home of Captain John Evans and his daughter Beatrix – our little Bea. When Bea died she willed the house to us along with the shipping business, and we've kept it preserved all these years."

"This is incredible," Andrew replied excitedly, drunk with nostalgia. He recalled the story of the tribe's first trip out of the valley of Eden over a hundred and fifty years ago, sparked by their curiosity upon seeing an airplane flying over the mountains. On their way east they had camped in their ancestral home – the Kilembe valley, long before the region had been mined. Although not a trace of their old home had remained, the sacred valley did impart a dream to Akiiki. He had a vision of a prophecy that the fruit was to be preserved as a secret, until a sign appeared. The tribe was to watch for a shift in the people of the world – the signal that humanity was ready for the power of the fruit from the Tree of Life. More than that they could not glean from Akiiki's dream, but it had been clear that they needed a presence outside of Eden to watch for such a sign.

That presence was realized through meeting John Evans, a lake captain in Port Bell who took them on as longshoremen. Later, with the strength of the tribe and his own business acumen, Captain Evans rapidly expanded his Lake Victoria cargo trade into an international shipping company based in Mombasa, Kenya, on the Indian Ocean.

But it was the captain's daughter, Bea, who solidified the tribe's relationship with the outside world forever. When she was still a little girl she had fallen deathly ill, and the lake captain was desperate. As a last resort he had accepted the tribe's offer of help, and they had healed her with a maisha draught that they carried to the captain's house in an earthen cup. He was forever in their debt, and he agreed to take on Kabilito as the manager of his growing Port Mombasa shipping business. The tribe now had their window to the world.

Bea took over the company once her father died, and she worked tirelessly to grow it into one of the largest on the Indian Ocean. She never married, nor did she ever have children, so upon her death she willed the business to the people to whom she felt the closest – the people of the tribe. On her deathbed she revealed that she had kept the earthen cup from the time when they had saved her life, and she lovingly passed it and the shipping company into their stewardship along with her father's saltbox house on the lake.

As Kabilito fiddled with the lock on the door Andrew gazed across the rolling lawn to the lake. The Captain's steamboat, once converted from a ship of war as Andrew recalled, was nowhere to be found. It was replaced by a modern powerboat tied to a dock on the lake shore. Nonetheless, the view was gorgeous, and the setting sun cast golden ripples across the bay as brilliant white lake birds swooped low over the marshes, seeking a final morsel before settling down for the night.

Once inside, the little group unrolled their bedding, then gathered outside on the lawn. With the help of Harel and Wu Yue, Subira carried wood from the shed and set a fire in a small pit in the yard. Akiiki brought grilling tools from the kitchen, and they cooked dinner from the supplies they had bought in Mubende. They grilled salted goat, plantains and maisha over the fire while they stared out over the lake.

As they ate, Akiiki and Subira took turns relaying the tribe's story of their time in Port Bell and Mombasa at the conclusion of World War I. Meg and Harel sat mesmerized by the tale, told to them by historians who had actually lived through the events themselves. And although Andrew was disturbed by his new abilities, he tried his best to compartmentalize his fear while he translated the story for Wu Yue.

The story was lengthened, however, when Sergeant David Harel began interrupting. Curious to a fault, he peppered Akiiki and Subira with so many questions it became almost comical, and even Meg stifled a smirk.

"How did the tribe find Captain Evans?" he asked. "What disease did Bea have? If animals ate the fruit, would they be immortal? If you eat too much fruit do you get diarrhea?"

After the story wound down and the others were finishing their meals, Kabilito and Andrew stole off to talk, walking down the lawn toward the lake as yet another volley of Harel's incessant questions began.

Andrew chuckled softly. "He's a curious one, that Harel," he noted.

Kabilito shared in the laugh. "Well, at least he's interested," he replied. "I had a good talk with Meg and David earlier, but Wu Yue and I don't speak the same language. Strangely, I feel as if I can almost understand what he's saying, though it seems like there's something blocking my comprehension of it – like static over a bad phone line."

They reached the dock at the lake's edge and sat on the wooden planks, staring down the mouth of the bay at the tiny lights twinkling from the archipelagos in the distance.

"What did *you* learn from your time with the others?" Kabilito asked.

"Well, Wu Yue seems to be willing to help out – making crates in the valley, loading the trailers, and even making the fire tonight. He's a bit hard to read, but he says he's glad to have escaped cleanly from an oppressive military unit. He says they'll assume he's missing in action – killed or captured in the battle with the US soldiers. Otherwise he would fear for his family back home. The government doesn't handle desertion well, especially by soldiers as highly trained as him. His parents would be disgraced, or worse yet, punished on his behalf. He isn't married and has no children, so no obligations there."

"And Harel?" Kabilito asked.

"Likewise no wife or kids. He's young and idealistic, and seems smitten with the tribe's mission. He wants to be part of something bigger than the military – something more important. And he's *definitely* curious about the fruit's power. He's concerned for his parents, too, but more for their grief. Similar to the Chinese, the US will likely believe him killed or captured when they can't find him, and eventually they'll inform his parents. He doesn't want his mom and dad grieving for him."

"Hmmm – maybe there's something we can do about that. But isn't Wu Yue concerned that his parents will worry, too?" Kabilito asked.

"He must be, but he didn't mention it," Andrew replied.

Kabilito squinted across the bay and considered this for a moment. "There's more to him than meets the eye," he said, straightening. "I know we're demanding a lot of them, but there's no other way. They'll have to adapt."

Andrew regarded Kabilito before speaking. "You know I wasn't a fan of taking them in, Kabilito. How long do you really think this can last before they completely shut down or revolt? You can't reasonably expect these strangers to leave their former lives – everything they held dear, everything they trained and worked for – just to follow the tribe."

"The power of the fruit and the prophecy are compelling, Andrew. Many choose to be a part of something greater –

something that can benefit mankind, something ordained by God. Even you gave up on bringing maisha back to New York once you learned of the prophecy, the tribe's history, and the evil the power could cause in the wrong hands. You yourself chose the tribe over prosperity and fame."

Andrew sighed. "I did, and I was healed. The fruit healed my wounds, and the tribe, with God's help, healed my spirit." He shifted uncomfortably on the dock. "I'm grateful for everything, but now it feels like the power is growing uncontrollably. The drive out here helped clear my mind somewhat, but I still feel something inside that won't go away. I try to block it out, but it's always there. It gives me a headache, like a constant swarm of bees in my mind. And the fruit's healing and strength powers seem so *magnified* now, and not just in me. I saw Meg get a splinter the size of a meat skewer when we were loading crates – she just ripped it out and healed in less than a minute. And she's only been around for a few weeks..."

Kabilito nodded solemnly. "I don't understand it any more than you do. And you're right, they've gained power quickly. We'll need to test them sooner than we normally would have – perhaps once we arrive in Mombasa, assuming they continue gaining strength at this rate. As of yet I've seen no signs of them turning, though."

Andrew shuddered. "And what of me showing signs of turning? Do I need to be re-tested? I feel like I'm a threat, like I might lose control at times."

"We will look after you, Andrew. Keep an open mind, and continue sharing your thoughts with us. Together we'll get through this."

They watched the sun dip below the horizon, painting the clouds with a brilliant glow as sounds from the campfire filtered down to the water's edge. Finally Andrew broke their silence. "And what of me, Kabilito? Did I ever really have a choice in the matter, or would I have been kept by the tribe, as they've been?" he asked, motioning up the lawn to the group's newcomers.

Kabilito stood and brushed the dust from his clothes. "Come with me. I want to show you something. In fact, please gather the group and meet me in the sitting room of the Captain's house so all can see."

Andrew did as asked, and soon they had assembled in the little room. Kabilito motioned them forward to stand around a carved wooden cabinet in the corner. Carefully he turned a key in the latch and lifted something from one of the shelves. He placed it gently into Andrew's hands.

It was a simple, earthen goblet, bereft of decoration, and it was ancient. With wide eyes Andrew recognized it from Kabilito's story, and he inhaled sharply.

It was Bea's cup, passed from the tribe to Bea, then back to the tribe from her deathbed. The cup in which they had carried the lifesaving draught to her bedside. The cup that bound them to Bea and she to them, and the vessel that opened a window to the outside world from which to watch for the foretold sign.

With Andrew translating for Wu Yue, Kabilito spoke, underscoring the gravity of the relic Andrew now held in his hands. "You're holding a symbol of dreadful choices that were once made. A father choosing to trust an unknown cure, a people choosing to accept a prophecy, a man choosing separation from his family to watch for a sign from God, and a woman choosing to pass on that which she held most dear to those closest to her. This cup is a link to the past, and the promise of a future – a future that needs us to protect the maisha until its time has come."

The words hung heavily in the air as Andrew passed the cup along through the group, each holding it briefly, each reaching through time to contact the past as palpably as the touch of Bea's hand on the vessel so long ago.

The moment passed, and the little group finally bedded down for the night – Andrew, Wu Yue and Akiiki upstairs, while Meg, Harel and Kabilito were on the first floor. Though trust in the newcomers had grown that night, Andrew noted that Subira stood watch outside the little house, draped across a wooden bench right outside the front door.

But as he blocked out his headache and forced himself to sleep Andrew realized something more – that Kabilito never really did answer his question.

A finger brushed lightly against her cheek. It was the touch of an unseen hand gently caressing her skin. It was the hand of God, or perhaps of Kabilito, the tall, powerfully handsome Ugandan with the mesmerizing, ancient eyes. But the nails of the hand suddenly grew sharp and grotesque, pinching her hard and tearing at her flesh. Tearing, biting...

Meg bolted upright from her bedroll and swatted at her cheek, dislodging the ugly horsefly. It buzzed away angrily in the darkened house as she caught her breath from the disturbing dream. Her chest heaved and she pulled at the sweat-soaked shirt sticking to her body. As she calmed herself she scanned the room. It was the middle of the night. In the darkness she could make out Kabilito's slumbering form, and behind him, Harel's.

Motion from the sitting room caught her eye. She turned to find that the window had swallowed Wu Yue's legs, leaving his arms free to lift a bulging sack that now dangled absently from one hand. His body was frozen in mid-motion, and in the darkness his eyes materialized, staring directly back into Meg's.

Their eyes locked – the Chinese soldier's watching, gauging, Meg's startled and uncertain. Her mouth dropped open, and with her gaze riveted to his she began turning slowly to wake Kabilito. Panic flashed across Wu Yue's face, and suddenly he held up the palm of his free hand, arresting her. Beads of sweat burst from his brow, and his eyes darted around the room, coming to rest back on Meg's. He stared at her imploringly, then frantically motioned for her to come with him.

Several moments passed. Meg's heart pounded in her chest as she wrestled with the decision. Finally she rose silently in the dark, her feet padding softly against the old plank flooring as Wue Yue continued waving her forward. When she reached the window he slipped out of the open frame, pulling the bulging sack outside with him. Dropping to the ground silently, he quickly scanned the yard, then looked back up at Meg and waved her along once more.

"Meg?" Kabilito called sleepily from the room behind her. She froze, her hands on the windowsill, eyes staring into Wu Yue's as she struggled internally. Time slowed. She felt opportunity draining away with each passing second.

At last she exhaled, resigned to her fate. "Just a draft, Kabilito," she replied, reaching up for the sash. Slowly she slid the window down. Her eyes never left Wu Yue's even as the glass pane closed to separate them, simultaneously releasing him and binding her to the tribe.

As she walked slowly back to her bedroll, she reflected on her decision. Maybe she had been driven by defiance, or maybe with the fruit out there she really did have a better chance at getting some of her own. *But something about it didn't feel quite right...*

A cry from upstairs suddenly tore through the night. "Wake up! Wu Yue is gone!"

Footsteps pounded down the stairs as Kabilito shot up from his sleeping bag. A shout sounded outside, and for an instant she felt Kabilito's penetrating gaze accusing her. A moment later Akiiki and Andrew flew down the steps and into the common room. She ripped her eyes from him and bolted after Andrew through the front door and into the cool night air.

Outside a form streaked across the front lawn toward the dock. The man carried a sack that swung wildly in his clenched fist. Another man raced after him – Subira, returning from patrolling the back yard.

Wu Yue was running incredibly fast, and Meg marveled at his speed as he gained the dock and leapt into the small motorboat. But Subira was faster still, his body a blur, racing down the lawn toward the pier. She heard the boat engine roar to life, and she caught a glimpse of Wu Yue kicking at the stern cleat. It snapped off in response, dock lines and all, and he spun to tear the spring line from the mid-ship cleat. Free from the pier, the little boat jerked forward as Wu Yue slammed the clutch into drive and punched the throttle full open. Subira reached the dock just as the boat tore off into the open waters of the black lake, and the four of them – Meg, Kabilito, Andrew and Harel – slowed to a halt, far too distant to help yet mesmerized by the action.

As the boat sped away, Subira jumped from the pier – an incredible leap arcing high into the night air. For a moment Meg thought his momentum would carry him over the boat's wake and into the cockpit, but even Subira's amazing strength and speed were no match for the powerful motor. He splashed into the black waters with outstretched arms, a mere body length from the boat's gunwale.

The little boat disappeared into the darkness. Subira spat out lake water, treading to stay afloat as he stared out toward the receding sound of the boat's engine. Defeated, he finally turned and began swimming back to the pier.

Chapter Twenty-Three

Jelani walked through the orchard, gently caressing the leaves of his new maisha plants. He stepped carefully around the miniature canvas tents that would later shield each sapling from the brutal Ugandan sun. The plants could only withstand sunlight for a few hours each day, as he knew all too well from his stay in the valley.

The terror group had bent to his will almost immediately. The sole survivor of the slaughter in the shack spread the word of his power, and only a few, minor displays of strength and healing were needed after that. They fell into line quickly, and it then became easy – pleasurable, in fact – to set his plans in motion. He leveraged their religion, posing as a messenger from God, and that was enough for them. When needed, his displays of justice were swift and terrible, and he reveled in their recognition and fear of his power. He would accept nothing less.

Cultivation had begun in earnest. For the time being his people covered each plant by hand, but the large structural frame they were erecting would soon provide shade for all. The canvas roof panels they had planned would open to expose the entire orchard, and they could scale-up operations by building more of the structures as they expanded. But even the limited space they had cultivated so far was productive. Rich Ugandan soil nourished the plants in the fledgling orchard, and they had ample water from the many tributaries of nearby Lake Albert. The saplings were already flourishing, providing fruit at an astonishing rate.

The location was perfect for growing maisha *and* for raising an army. It was a hidden place with little access, about eighty kilometers west of Gulu in the wilds of the Amuru district. This was the site of the original group's training camp, where initiates began learning the trade of terror – a secret site nestled between slopes carved by streams that fed the river system. Everything he needed to create a new paradise was here – he just needed more followers, *and more fruit.*

As he walked through the camp he dreamed of expansion. He smiled at his people, and they in turn cowered in fear. At first he had put them to work digging irrigation channels for his orchard. When the channels were complete, he set them to planting. Luckily the fruit trees grew quickly. He had nearly exhausted the group's emergency food stores, but the encampment had swiftly transformed from terrorist training ground to farmland, and the fruit production was now nearly enough to sustain them.

Even so, he frequented the town of Gulu regularly with several followers that he deemed worthy. They would make the long trip across the grasslands and earthen roads for supplemental food and supplies, as well as to collect payments. Their money came primarily from the churches and congregations of Gulu. Protection payments the group had established years ago to fund their activities. And although he now joined them on collection visits, Jelani was careful to remain largely unknown to Gulu. The weary shop owners and ministers saw him only as a new face among the many thugs that had always shaken them down for coin.

But today's trip to Gulu was spent mainly in the marketplace. In addition to the basic staples they always bought, this time they loaded their off-road vehicles with bushels of fresh fruits and vegetables, goat, spices, pork and fish – all in preparation for a great feast.

Upon their return, his people had completed the work as he had commanded. Great pots of maisha were waiting to be stewed, and plates had been set on makeshift banquet tables. He rode into the camp flush with generosity, and his followers swiftly unloaded the bounty from the Gulu markets to prepare it for the feast.

The food was plain but hearty, and Jelani's tribe gorged themselves as he sat at the center of the head table, surrounded by his chosen few. He surveyed the tribe from his vantage point – mostly Ugandan, Sudanese and Ethiopian, and even some Europeans who had abandoned their families and culture to join the "holy war" as was fashionable these days. He smiled warmly at the Westerners in particular. Although they had initially left their decadent countries to join the Christian extremist group, they were now *his*. They had become part of something much greater and more ambitious than they could have ever imagined.

Jelani finished his meal quickly and bowed his head in anticipation. At the right moment he stood, and the crowd silenced themselves.

"My people," he addressed them in a powerful voice, "you came together in the name of Christ, but your leaders failed you. Today I tell you that I was sent by God himself to lead you in their stead!"

The cheers were deafening, and they rattled their cups noisily against the rough plank tables. He let the exuberance die down before continuing in their native Swahili.

"We prepare now for the holy war – the great battle against the infidels. But first our numbers must grow. And so I will leave for a time, and when I return I will bring new soldiers to help in our war."

His countenance grew dark, and his voice deepened. "But let it be known that any man that deserts or seeks to disrupt what I have grown here will suffer the same fate as your previous misguided leaders."

He waved his hand at the spears surrounding the little shack in which he had once been held captive – spears that each bore the head of a former leader. They had desiccated in the heat, and for a time the flies and smell surrounding them were unbearable. But they served their purpose, striking fear into the hearts of the men and women of the new tribe, even as his followers grew in strength.

The power they gained was like a drug, each craving it more than the next. And the more maisha Jelani fed them, the more his dominance became inescapable. Just as he had planned, his was a terror group driven by terror – the fear of an idealistic, motivated and highly-trained leader, swift to dole out justice ordered by God himself. But along with the fear came reward, *and addiction*. Each could feel his own strength growing, and collectively their hunger for the new power grew.

"The world has grown complacent, and the Lord is angry," he bellowed. "Follow me, eat of the fruit of God, and gain the power that he meant for you. Become strong, and together we shall cleanse the world of this disease. Follow me, and become immortal!"

A wave of impassioned screams washed over him, and he smiled. Drunk with dreams of power, the crowd turned their attention back to the feast, and with that Jelani took his leave.

The waiting car near the shack was already running. Gwandoya, the man Jelani had spared that night in the shack, stood holding the rear door open for him eagerly. He was fast becoming Jelani's right-hand man. Having witnessed Jelani's fury and the carnage he had unleashed, Gwandoya was now beyond loyal. He was fanatical.

Jelani ducked into the back seat and closed the door as Gwandoya slipped into the driver's side. "To Entebbe, Gwandoya," he said softly, scratching his ribs and stretching his legs in anticipation of the long ride to the airport. He reached into his back pocket, pulled out his international airline tickets and set them aside with his passport as he settled back in his seat.

Gwandoya adjusted the off-road vehicle's mirror until he could see Jelani's eyes. Then he wished he hadn't. They made him uncomfortable. "To where will you travel from there, Master?" he asked nervously.

Jelani stared out the window at his tribe as they pulled away. "To the east, Gwandoya," he answered absently. "Conflict breeds idealism, and I require both."

Chapter Twenty-Four

The boat engine drowned out Wu Yue's hysterical laughter as he steered around Lake Victoria's Northwestern peninsula toward Entebbe. He reached out and gently rested his hand on his prize – a sack full of the miraculous fruit the tribe had called "maisha."

He was free, finally. For days he had played their game, trying his best to control himself as he felt stronger and stronger each day. The amount of power that surged through his veins was incredible. And when he brought it back to his commanders, he would be a hero. He'd also be rich – he could live anywhere, do anything he wanted. And he'd sure as hell keep some of the fruit for himself, too...

He rounded Ntabwe, the southernmost peninsula before Entebbe, then blew past Kasenyi. But he throttled back before he reached the airport. The boat's wash caught up to him as he considered his options, and he was tossed about momentarily, floundering in his own wake.

Finally he turned northwest and headed just north of Entebbe. *Better to play this safe and call in help.* He scanned the shoreline until he found what he wanted – a sparsely populated, largely uncontrolled landing site close to the airport where he could approach Entebbe unseen. It was a golf course, with good tree cover, open spaces and plenty of hiding places if needed. He gunned the engine as he neared a sandy beach at the foot of the course and reached for his satchel. He'd need a head start to break through the tree line. The beaching would be a good distraction, and anyone watching would be drawn to the sight of the boat.

A moment before the boat rammed itself on the beach he stood up on the bow and crouched, grasping the bag tightly. As soon as the boat began to lurch forward he lunged, leaping high and far from the bow. The engine stalled as the propeller dug into sand, and Wu Yue was launched into the air.

He soared up and over the beach, crashing down in the trees at the edge of the fairway. He grunted as he tumbled, and he felt several ribs crack. Pain shot up his outstretched arm, and he was sure that his radius or ulna had split. Or both...

He sat up amidst the trees, laughing hysterically. The pain didn't bother him – he knew it was temporary. As he ran deeper into the cover of the trees he felt the bones of his arm pull back into place. His ribs rejoined, bones knitting. Bruises formed, then disappeared just as fast.

He jogged lightly with the satchel until he found what he needed – two golf carts, parked conveniently near the tree line while the golfers examined the green twenty meters away. Wu Yue's training and stealth served him well as he crawled along the brush cover to the vehicles. He reached into the cart's storage compartment to retrieve his prize, then turned and sprinted into the forest, holding down the power button on the stolen device. The exclusive club near Entebbe prohibited mobile phone use, so most were left behind in the cart during play. As the phone lit up and came to life, Wu Yue slowed and punched in the secure, untraceable number of his commander's line. He leaned back against the tree and smiled. Once they sent reinforcements to pick him up by chopper at Entebbe he could relax. As the phone connected he pulled a fruit from the sack and bit into it, cackling and savoring both the maisha and the moment.

Chapter Twenty-Five

Andrew buried his face in his hands as the jeep tore down the road toward Entebbe. They had packed the vehicles hastily and set off to the airport immediately following the escape, and although they were all tired and frustrated with the turn of events, he was beside himself with guilt.

Kabilito was driving as he finished a phone conversation with the corporate pilot, Brittney. The private jet would be ready, but not until they had searched the international airport for Wu Yue as thoroughly as security would allow. It was the logical place for him to have gone, and they were ultimately headed there anyway. But everyone acknowledged that the chances of locating the Chinese soldier were slim.

Andrew was dimly aware that the phone conversation had ended, and he raised his head when he felt Kabilito's strong hand on his shoulder. "This is not your fault, Andrew,"

Kabilito intoned.

"It is!" Andrew snapped back. "I'm the only one who talks to him. I thought he was on board with us. I shouldn't have talked him up so much. He duped me..."

"Listen," Kabilito interrupted, "the last time the fruit was unleashed it resurfaced, and we recovered, as you well know. The power of maisha cannot stay hidden for long in the wrong hands. It will reveal itself wherever he carries it, and we will reclaim it once more. But for now we must stick with the plan and reestablish a home for the tribe regardless of whether or not we find Wu Yue at Entebbe."

Andrew stared out the window as dawn's glow broke over the outskirts of Kampala. "If only I had been thinking clearly. If only I could rid myself of this pressure in my brain, maybe I would have seen it." He shook his head. "I've been so distracted with everything – this voice that comes out of me, the new languages, the buzzing sounds in my head, the sudden strength – all of it." He turned to his friend. "I don't know who I am anymore."

"This is new to all of us, Andrew. In fact, this was more my fault. I should have known your judgment would be affected by your struggles. I was overconfident in my ability to convert the others to our ways. I should have realized that not everyone is compelled equally by the prophecy, or by our history. The retelling of a tale pales in comparison to having lived it, even if relics survive as proof."

"I was moved by the cup, Kabilito. I know Meg and Harel were, too. But even though I could speak with Wu Yue, reading him is a different matter. Maybe it's a cultural thing." Andrew stared at the road ahead as the streetlights extinguished themselves at the command of the rising sun. "I can't believe how strong...and *how fast* he was..."

"That's another problem," Kabilito replied. "I largely dismissed their desire and ability to escape. We let our guard down, and Subira's watch became simply a ritual."

"So what about Meg and Harel?" Andrew asked.

Kabilito glanced in the rear view mirror at the caravan behind them. In the middle were Subira and Meg, while Akiiki and David Harel drove together in the last jeep. "We'll need to tighten our watch," Kabilito answered. "I do believe they'll come around, but we can't rush it. One of the benefits of having the largest shipping company on the Indian Ocean is that we have use of the corporate jet. We can move about freely on the flight to Mombasa, pull each aside and talk to them privately. Akiiki is perceptive and persuasive, and with God's will he'll be able to discern their true feelings."

They drove in silence after that, and Andrew pretended not to notice Kabilito's knuckles whiten with pressure as he gripped the steering wheel.

Chapter Twenty-Six

"We're late already, Major. What *is* it?" Frank hissed at Mackenzie outside the closed doors. Major Graham Mackenzie shuffled through a stack of papers, dropping folders on the floor and swearing as they fell from his hands. Raised voices from inside the room reached a crescendo, and Frank rolled his eyes impatiently.

"Here it is, sir," Mackenzie said, relieved. He slid a photo out of an envelope and showed it to the Colonel.

Frank squinted, looking at the grainy picture. A smoke column rose from a charred, blackened valley, and he could see a small structure or tent that had been erected in the ruined vegetation. He could make out some people, too, but from the picture it was unclear who they were or what they were doing.

"And this is...?" he trailed off expectantly.

"It's the valley, sir. *The* valley. And those are the Chinese troops, setting up a base camp of sorts. But they've brought some equipment from what we can tell – some electronics to analyze something – maybe soil samples, maybe water. It's unclear."

Frank frowned, still staring at the picture. "And they burned down the valley? Where the hell were the people who lived there? Where was the fruit?"

"The Chinese didn't burn down the valley, sir. The tribe did, as far as we can tell. And there's no sign of the fruit. That's why we think they torched it – to eradicate the fruit so no one could lay hands on it."

"But if they didn't do a good enough job..." Frank paused.

Mackenzie picked up where the Colonel left off. "Then yes, the Chinese will find it."

Frank handed the photo back to the major. "And why aren't our guys in there?" he asked sternly.

"We were, sir, but the Chinese got a drop directly into the valley and we came down a tunnel we found. The chopper maneuver was risky on their part with the smoke and all, but it paid off. They had the advantage of position and we were holed up in a tunnel with only one way out. They covered the exit pretty well."

"Any shots fired?" Frank asked, concerned.

"None. After the last encounter we weren't about to risk it," Mackenzie replied as he retrieved the folders from the floor.

"Do we still have the green light from the Ugandan Government?" Frank questioned.

Mackenzie stood, his folders secured haphazardly. "They're bitching and moaning, but we're good to go."

"All right Major, then get back in there, grab a patch of real estate and start sifting through the ashes. They don't own that spot, and they sure as hell aren't going to shoot at us anytime soon. Don't engage them, but don't back down, either."

"Will do, sir," Mackenzie confirmed.

As Frank reached for the door handle Mackenzie fumbled for his phone to relay the orders, dropping several more folders in the process.

"Crap," the major exclaimed, bending to the floor again.

Frank would have smiled at the misfortune, but he was already opening the door into a shit storm of his own. Inside, Secretary of State Bryce Rosemark was pointing a finger and bellowing at Major Tom Shenley, acting Kyrgyzstani military liaison, about troop visibility at the Kyrgyzstani Manas Transit Center Base. Rosemark stopped in mid-sentence and glowered as Frank sat at the table.

"Nice of you to join us, Colonel," Secretary Rosemark retorted.

"Sorry – dealing with a little situation, sir," Frank replied, noting that Shenley had disappeared into the crowd of cabinet members.

Rosemark waved his hand impatiently at Andrea Blaine, the analyst working the case. "Andrea's got more information on the Xinjiang issue. We were waiting for you to begin." He turned to Andrea. "Now that the Colonel is here, please proceed."

"Thank you, Mr. Secretary," Andrea began, clicking to the first slide of her presentation. "Conditions in the outskirts of the Xinjiang city of Urumqi are deteriorating rapidly. The Chinese have ramped up their troop numbers considerably in the past few weeks, and they've taken control of the northeastern city district. They're imprisoning the Uyghur and other ethnic Muslim protestors, and many have fled to live in the wilderness. The refugees have been driven east into the foothills of the Bogda Shan mountain range in the eastern Tien Shan Mountains. We estimate five thousand have fled, but this number is growing daily."

Andrea paused, glancing at those gathered.

"As you know, Xinjiang is an Uyghur Autonomous Region. It's a huge area, mostly rural, but the urban centers have grown rapidly over the past several decades. The Uyghur Turks, Kazakhs, Tajiks, Kyrgyzstanis and Mongol Muslims vastly outnumber the Chinese in the rural areas, but they're the minority in the cities. They've garnered support in their respective homelands, and now protestors are using the media to turn attention to their mistreatment in Urumqi. The Uyghur in particular have rallied around claims of genocide. They assert that their people are being displaced from their rightful land so that China can take control of the cities – the power centers in Xinjiang. Once their presence is diminished in the metropolitan areas, it will be only a matter of time before the entire region slips from the grasp of the Uyghur and into Chinese control. So what began as an Uyghur protest of Chinese negligence and unsafe conditions in Uganda's Kilembe mines has now grown into a global situation. Even the Hui, the Chinese Muslim population in Xinjiang, are against their homeland in this matter."

Andrea paused and advanced to the next slide as she sipped water from a glass with a shaking hand. "As you know, Turkey, Kazakhstan, Tajikistan, Kyrgyzstan and Mongolia are supporting the refugees with our help from the Transit Center at Manas. At first we were helping with the administration and logistics for emergency food and supplies for those displaced to the foothills of the Bogda Shan Mountains. But the cargo we're moving now consists more and more of weapons and armor to arm the refugees."

"Thank you, Andrea," Secretary Rosemark interrupted. "So you see, ladies and gentlemen, we have a choice to make. We've stayed largely under the radar until now, but we can't possibly expect that to continue – it *will* leak. So either we refuse to run weapons through Manas, pull out, and lose the foothold we've regained there, or we help arm the refugees and risk the wrath of the Chinese, as well as others that may not take so kindly to the US importing weapons into the region...such as the Russians, for instance."

One of the representatives on the cabinet raised a hand. "Has any progress been made with respect to the missing US soldier? Or China's missing man?"

"None," Rosemark answered. "Relations are strained, to say the least." Secretary Rosemark turned to Frank. "Colonel Anderson, could you give us a status report of the troops at Manas?"

But as Frank began rattling off the latest troop tallies and equipment reports from his men in Kyrgyzstan, all he could think of was the valley, burned to a crisp, and the men he had just sent there.

Hurry up, Major, he thought. *Find that fruit before the Chinese do...*

Chapter Twenty-Seven

Andrew stared out the window of the jet as they approached Kilimanjaro. The mountain was breathtaking, but he wished he had seen it before the mighty glaciers that once adorned the crown had melted away.

He had slept a bit since takeoff, but he was still exhausted. Last night's sleep was interrupted by Wu Yue's escape, and the morning had seen little rest as the group fanned out and scoured the airport for the missing Chinese soldier. After several hours they finally conceded and made their way to the private hangers, allowing their pilot Brittney to usher them onto the corporate jet.

Andrew turned away from the window to find Meg asleep in one of the plush recliners. The jet was luxurious, with mahogany veneer table tops in between the seats. At first Meg had played cards with Harel, but soon sleeplessness took its toll and she drifted off, leaving the Special Ops

Sergeant alone to tinker with one of the tribe's broken satellite radios.

Kabilito caught Andrew's eye and then motioned to Akkiki. Together the three of them relocated to the seats around Harel's table. Andrew absently picked up the cards, shuffling them nervously. Harel looked up from his work as they sat. The radio had been dismantled, and he was touching the connections with the probes of a voltage meter. "I think this one's fried, Kabilito – it got smashed in the back of the jeep when we bolted out of Port Bell. I can fix it if we can get a replacement speaker in Mombasa."

"Thank you, David, we'll do that," Kabilito said. "We appreciate all of your help."

Andrew saw Kabilito look up at Akiiki. Taking the cue, Akiiki began. "Could we speak with you for a few moments, David?"

Harel set the radio down, suddenly aware that they weren't there to play cards. He grinned. "Yes, in fact, there're a few things I'd like to talk to you about, too."

"Of course – I'm sure a lot of questions will arise," Akiiki replied. "You'll find that we are quite transparent. But first let me ask you, how is it that you are so willing to leave your unit and join us? I know we've given you little choice in the matter, but you seem to have taken to the notion quite well, certainly better than our missing Chinese friend."

Andrew studied Harel's face, but all he saw there was genuine shock.

"Are you kidding me?" Harel asked, incredulous. "I was as good as dead – shot, bleeding, concussed, with a shattered shoulder and an arm full of shrapnel – the whole nine yards. I was stumbling around, lost in the Rwenzoris, days away from rescue, and the Chinese were crawling all over the place. I was a goner. And then, after I shot up your guys, you healed me – *overnight.* It was miraculous – *I am living proof of a miracle*. That sort of changes things. My parents are very religious. I'd say I'm somewhat religious, too – maybe more spiritual. And trust me, there were no miracles in the army for a Jew from Brooklyn. Then you tell me that this magical fruit is tied to a prophecy that will change the world, and then you ask me if I want a part of it? *Seriously?*"

Andrew couldn't help but smile. There was nothing complicated about the diminutive soldier, and his enthusiasm was comical and infectious. Andrew found himself genuinely liking Harel. He was smart, funny, and a team player with a good attitude.

"And plus," the soldier continued, "I have the perfect alibi – I'm MIA, baby!" He clapped his hands and whooped.

Out of the corner of his eye Andrew saw Meg jump at the sound. He could have sworn he saw her eyes open briefly, only to snap shut a moment later. Andrew smiled again as Harel continued.

"And you guys are like the friggin' Avengers! You've got super powers, an international company and your own jet...not to mention that *I* get to eat the fruit, too. So I get to be super strong, with instant healing powers, and maybe, just maybe, I get to help save the world. *Sign me up!*"

Kabilito and Akiiki looked at each other quizzically. Andrew guessed they hadn't expected this reaction from him. Akiiki recovered quickly, though. "And what was it that you wanted to ask of us, David?" he said.

Harel sighed. "Well, the one problem is my parents – they'll be worried sick. The military might have already informed them that I'm missing, and knowing them, they'll assume the worst." Harel looked straight into Akiiki's eyes. "I need them to know that I'm okay."

It was Kabilito who answered, however. "Well, maybe that's something we can fix," he replied. He stood and motioned for Harel to follow, and with Akiiki and Andrew in tow, he led them to the back of the jet. Kabilito opened a small panel and withdrew a satellite phone receiver. He held it out to Harel, who looked uncertain.

"Go on – take it, David. Call your parents. Let them know you're fine. If the military has already told them you've gone missing in action, tell them that it's part of a cover, that you've been selected for a secret mission, and that the government needed it to look as real as possible. If the military hasn't come yet, tell them they will, but that this is all classified, and that even your commanders don't know. But you need to swear them to secrecy – they can't tell anyone that you've been selected. Do you think you can do this?"

Harel accepted the receiver and grinned wickedly. "Hell, yeah!"

"It's okay, Mom. It's perfectly safe – I won't even be in the field. I can't tell you any more than that, but you don't have to worry," Harel was saying loudly into the satellite phone. Through the earpiece Andrew could hear the squeal of delight, and he held his hand over his mouth to keep from laughing.

Harel covered the receiver with his palm and narrated the conversation. "She's saying she's proud – super proud of me...oh, now she's telling me–wait, she's talking about the neighbor's *foot infection*. Now Dad is yelling from the next room, 'Why does he care about the foot infection?' and she's yelling back at him..." Harel rolled his eyes and suppressed a laugh. "They're still going at it. He's saying, 'Why would he care when he's a big secret agent'... Oh, this is *classic* Harel household stuff."

Finally Harel had to interject to end the one-sided conversation. "Okay, Mom, Dad, I gotta go now. But remember, this mission is mostly desk work, so don't worry."

"*MOSTLY?*" Andrew heard Harel's mother shriek through the earpiece. He chuckled.

"Yes – *mostly*, Mom. The rest is just training. You guys take care – love you both!"

And with that Harel hung up the phone, shaking his head and grinning broadly. Then he turned and pointed to Kabilito's forearm and the symbol emblazoned there – a sword of fire wreathed in flame, ink sported by all the tribe members, signifying their commitment to guarding Eden's secret.

"Hey, when do I get my cool tattoo?" he asked casually.

Chapter Twenty-Eight

"**A**nderson," Frank intoned into the receiver.

"Mackenzie here, sir. Just got a call from the valley. Captain Maxwell tried a drop into the sector, but the Chinese brought in backup support and they're crawling all over the zone. They set up a temporary base and they're combing through the soil. They have so many men in there we couldn't even get close, sir – we couldn't penetrate the perimeter."

"You couldn't simply walk past them?" Frank asked.

"They formed a wall around the tunnel exit and the scorched portions of the valley. I mean, a *human wall*. We'd have to *engage* them to push past, sir."

Frank chewed his lip. "All right, Major, just sit tight and observe for now – we'll get some help." And with that the call ended. He tried calling the Ugandan ambassador next, with the intent of gaining control of the region for "security" reasons, but that accomplished little. The ambassador promised that he'd speak with the ministry but cautioned Frank against expecting support soon. Even simple requests were often met with diplomatic red tape, and with the Chinese pressuring them to oust the US from the Kilembe region, the Ugandan government was unlikely to comply with Frank's demands.

He hung up the phone and slammed his fist on the desk angrily, rattling the receiver in the cradle. Strangely, the phone immediately rang, as if his blow had delivered a caller. He frowned, then picked up the phone.

"Anderson," he barked.

"Frank, it's Ed Lambard."

Frank sat back in his chair. "Hey, Ed – let me guess, the bug in my phone stopped working and NSA wants me to install a new one for them?" he asked sarcastically.

"Nah, don't worry – we'll do it when you're not there. All kidding aside, how'd your men do in the valley?"

Frank relayed the details, and Ed offered some satellite surveillance support that he gladly accepted. *If we can't be there, at least we can keep imaging the area*, he thought. They'd already lost several drones – shot down by the Chinese, though they denied it.

"At least there's one saving grace," Frank offered. "Since the Chinese are still combing through the valley, it means they don't have the fruit yet."

"Unless they do, and they're trying to make sure we don't get it," Ed replied. "Maybe they're removing any trace of it before they pull out. What's the plan, Frank?"

"Get more men in there, ASAP," he replied.

"You got permission from the Ugandans?" Ed asked.

"Working on it, Ed. Working on it."

Chapter Twenty-Nine

Kabilito unlocked the door to the Mombasa warehouse complex and led the group through the offices. The rest of the tribe had already settled into the little-used building well before Kabilito, Akiiki, Subira, Meg, Harel and Andrew arrived. He greeted several of them warmly as they bustled about the office, setting up laptops and organizing inventory lists of all the supplies taken from the valley.

"We developed this facility in secret years ago as a contingency plan," Kabilito said as he led them past the office cubicles. "To our employees it's just another of our buildings here at the port, but in actuality it can house all of us indefinitely while we look to relocate."

He opened the door to the main warehouse building and stepped aside to let the group into the massive space. There on the warehouse floor were all of the crates they had hauled out of the valley – some unpacked, some still closed. They were stacked in neat rows, and he led them through the maze of cargo to a set of stairs on the far side of the building.

Upstairs he showed them the living areas. Spacious bedrooms stretched the full length of the warehouse, some with several beds to accommodate the families in the tribe, others just single quarters. Each bedroom had its own bathroom and living area, similar to a hotel suite.

There was a well-appointed industrial kitchen big enough to service a large restaurant, and a common dining area that brought back memories of the valley, with beautiful hardwood benches and tables made of massive wooden planks.

He pointed out the artwork decorating the living areas – breathtaking pictures, paintings and sculptures depicting the Rwenzori Mountains and the valley, including images of the orchard, huts and even the lava tube, all arranged artfully to create an ambiance that felt like home. Kabilito grew solemn looking upon the pictures of the old fire pit, and more than once he saw Andrew lean in close and shake his head dejectedly as he surveyed the beautiful works of the lost valley.

"Many have become quite adept at expressing our love of the valley through art," he said, picking up a gorgeous sculpture of a maisha fruit from a display. He examined it before passing it around the little group. "We'll always treasure the memory of Eden, but God beckons us to carry on and regroup."

Andrew remained silent throughout the tour. Kabilito wondered if he was dealing with the pressure and sound in his head again. He made note of it as he walked them back through the warehouse to the first floor offices. Finally he led them downstairs to a basement under the main floor. He breathed deeply of the moist air on the way down the slick steps. The temperature increased as they descended into utter blackness.

Upon reaching the bottom Kabilito paused in the darkness to peer at a small glowing screen on the wall. He smiled when someone behind him – probably Harel – bumped into one of the others as they stopped abruptly.

Kabilito looked at the timer on the screen as it ticked down, his face illuminated by the glow. "Just a few more moments. Gather around me here," he instructed.

Suddenly a burst of brightness blinded them as the warehouse basement was bathed in a warm light. His eyes adjusted as he stared across the vast expanse. "Whoa," someone breathed behind him.

He smiled at the reaction. It was impressive even to him, though he had initiated the project himself. Stretching from wall to wall were hundreds of maisha trees, all laid out in a grid, all reaching up toward the lamps positioned on the low ceiling. Hydroponic growth media ran in giant troughs across the floor, fed by an automatic batching system against the far wall. Timers and sensors controlled the lighting, the mixing of the hydroponic food and water, the humidity and temperature levels – everything. He heard the familiar, gentle whirring of the pumps as they started, pushing nutrient-rich water through the trough system.

Impressed, Andrew whistled softly at the sight. "This makes my greenhouse back in New York look like a window planter," he said.

Kabilito looked at Akiiki and both grinned, sharing a private joke. "Akiiki thought this was blasphemous, at first – growing the Tree of Life in an artificial environment," he said. "That was until I reminded him that this was simply an extension of our orchard back in the valley. If God meant for us to protect the fruit, then we'd better have a backup plan. And honestly, what's the difference between cultivating rows of trees in the orchard and this? It's only a small step."

"If the Pope can drive around in a protected golf cart, I guess a little technology isn't so bad," Akiiki joked. "We were given brains to invent and create."

The remainder of the day was spent unloading essential and perishable items from the crates and storing them where they belonged. The fruit, of course, could remain in the crates indefinitely, being immortal like the powers it endowed.

Reunited, the tribe feasted that night to celebrate – maisha medallions fried in garlic and butter, fresh fish from the Indian Ocean, wild goat from the Kenyan plains and crisp, lightly-steamed Nakati leaves. They stayed up late, planning, talking and enjoying the company they had missed.

That night Kabilito went to bed with the door to his room left open. He lay awake, restless, in the room across the hall from Meg. Although several of the tribe were awake and keeping watch downstairs, he remained suspicious, the memory of Wu Yue's escape still fresh in his mind.

Sure enough, near midnight Meg's door slowly swung open, and he watched as she padded out of her room and moved down the hall. Silently Kabilito rose and followed her. She crept to the other side of the building to the darkened common room on the second floor. Kabilito watched from the doorway as she approached the large picture window. The window didn't open, and situated above the high first floor of the warehouse a jump to the outside pavement would certainly disable her if she decided to smash the glass. *But not for long...*

Instead he watched as she sighed, placing her elbows on

the windowsill. She stared listlessly across the busy Mombasa port and out to the Indian Ocean beyond. He waited for a few moments before walking across the room to join her at the window.

She looked up as he approached. "Oh, hi, Kabilito. Couldn't sleep either, huh?"

He ignored her question as he stared out into the night. "The port never sleeps – always the cargo must move, the shipping must continue. It is a restless, bustling thing, this port. I remember when sails and steam were the engines of trade – when the port was much smaller. But that was a long, long time ago."

He pointed out the cranes that their company owned, their tops lit up by flashing caution lamps and spotlights. The giant frames swiveled over the ships and dropped their cables to clutch at the containers, grasping, lifting, and rotating around to place the big boxes on rail cars in an endless cycle.

"Bea and I practically built this port – at least our section of it, which is the largest by far. Back then we toiled to grow the company, as she knew her father would want her to do. It became her life, and she was obsessed with it. She had no time for relationships, no time for children. But she had time for us, and her efforts supported the tribe in endless ways both then and now."

"Did she know the tribe's purpose, Kabilito?" Meg asked. "Did she know about the fruit?"

"I believe she suspected at first, and then as time progressed and I didn't age, she must have known something was different. But that sort of realization is not made overnight, and she never mentioned it. In the end, I think that's partly why she willed the company to us. She knew we were here to do something good, and she knew we'd endure." He paused, reflecting. "I stayed close by, always – partly to learn the business, but mostly to watch for the prophesized sign. We spent much time together, and I became her only true confidant. But as focused as she was on the business, those were good times for her and for me. To build such a thing as this, to create these jobs – it is a satisfying thing."

"What about your family?" Meg inquired in a wistful tone.

"I was separated from my family–from the whole tribe and from the valley. I did visit them, and occasionally they stayed here with us. Bea missed them, too. We were all friends by the time they left Port Bell to return to the valley after our first excursion east. But I was tasked with establishing an outpost in this foreign place, far away from home and far from those I loved most."

"That must have been difficult," Meg noted, "leaving your home and family to create a new life in a strange land."

Kabilito studied her with his penetrating gaze. "At times, all alone in Mombasa, away from the valley and my tribe, I simply wanted to...*escape*."

Meg stiffened, then hung her head. "I let him go, Kabilito," she said, regret in her tone. "I watched him run away. And I would have gone with him, too. I was obsessed with the fruit, obsessed with bringing it back to Regentex. But listening to Harel on the jet and thinking it through on my own, I realize now that this is a chance to be part of something much bigger, much better than profit margins. I've succeeded in my career. I think what I've accomplished would make my mother proud. But this fruit, it represents something even more – the possibility to really change the world, to make a difference. To act with humanity's best interests in mind, not those of our shareholders."

Kabilito continued to listen as she shuddered unexpectedly.

"Trust me, I appreciate that you saved me from the attack in the mountains," she said. "I was as good as dead. In a way I feel like an ingrate – you saved me, but I betrayed you. And although you can't let me leave, I do understand why. But I felt compelled to let Wu Yue escape. Maybe it was defiance, maybe just comradery between captives, but whatever it was I'm truly sorry about it. I jeopardized the mission. If Akiiki's dream is true – if the prophecy is real, that's much more important than what I was doing. I was only making money for shareholders. God knows I'm not leaving much behind there at Regentex, or even in the States for that matter. I know that now."

Meg trailed off, and Kabilito put a hand on her shoulder warmly. "You mentioned God, Meg. Do you have a religion?"

"No, not really. The closest I've ever come to one is the Hinduism my Yoga instructor taught me. I practice meditation, mainly to release stress from work. I guess work was my religion, but it was really nothing more than a diversion – a meaningless one at that, and unfortunately I was blindly devoted to it. I had no business being in that mountain range. My ambition took me *way* outside my skill set."

Kabilito paused as Meg shifted her weight and turned to face him.

"Look, it's not easy for me to believe in prophecies or religions," she continued, "but the power of the fruit is undeniable – it's unlike anything I've ever seen. It's a miracle, and if ever there was a possibility that I'd believe, now's the time." She reached out and squeezed Kabilito's upper arm. "Thank you for saving me. I know it would have been easier to let me die."

He smiled at her. "Seldom is the right path the easy one," he replied.

The silence of the sleeping warehouse enveloped them like a warm blanket as they stared down at the harbor. The Indian Ocean washed endlessly against the piers of the bustling port, and together they drank in the harbor lights as they rippled over the waves.

Suddenly a gunshot tore through the stillness, and they both jumped. Then another rang out. By the third Meg and Kabilito were already out the door and racing through the corridor, down the long flight of stairs to the warehouse below.

Others joined them as they ran down to the first floor in time to witness the top of a large maisha crate fly off and skitter across the warehouse floor, its hinges torn out by the blasts. Tendrils of gunsmoke rose lazily from the crate as the tribe approached. Kabilito held up a hand to stop their advance as he continued forward alone.

Suddenly a man leapt from inside the crate brandishing a pistol. He leveled the gun at the tribe as Kabilito and Meg bound forward to tackle him. Together they drove him to the floor. Kabilito wrestled the gun from his hand but the attacker tossed Meg aside easily. Finally Andrew, Subira and several tribe members dove at him together, overwhelming him and pinning him to the floor.

The sounds of the scuffle echoed across the bare walls of the expansive warehouse as the struggle subsided and the man was restrained. Kabilito rose, brushing the dust from his clothes as the man was dragged to his feet by the others.

He's strong from eating the fruit, Kabilito thought, breathing heavily from the effort. He calculated the number of days since they had sealed the crate as they left the valley. It had only been a week or so...

Too soon – the power gain continues to accelerate. He studied the man. He was Chinese – combat-trained and probably military, but he wasn't dressed in government-issue fatigues.

How did he get into the crate? He must have been hiding in there when the crate was sealed. So he was watching us in secret...an operative, maybe?

A feeling of dread washed over Kabilito. It seemed so long ago that Martin and Andrew had started this chain of events that turned the valley into a revolving door. How many others had found their way to Eden without their knowledge? Their once airtight protection of the fruit and its secrets had been blown wide open, like this crate. They might as well be handing out maisha on a street corner these days.

Kabilito shook his head and motioned for Andrew, who left the intruder in the custody of the tribe to join him. Andrew looked over his shoulder at the man and wiped the sweat from his brow before turning back to Kabilito.

"What are we gonna do with *this* guy? He must be a spy," he said, mirroring Kabilito's own thoughts. "We can't assimilate him, too, Kabilito, we just *can't...*"

"We must," Kabilito interrupted, freezing the look of dismay on Andrew's face. "And you must learn from him all that he knows – were there others, did they steal fruit..."

"What's the point?" Andrew hissed, incredulous. "Wu Yue already ran off with it. Either he was mad and he's building his own sick empire somewhere, or he's bringing it back to China where they'll happily begin making super soldier drugs. Either way, the fruit's gone – it's out of our hands. And we just let him go..."

"Enough," Kabilito chided. "What were we to do? Fan out and search the city with six people, two of whom were flight-risks, too? As I told you, we must have faith. The fruit will resurface. God would not have entrusted us with the burden of protecting this wonder without the means to do so."

Andrew rolled his eyes in exasperation. "This isn't some fantasy land, Kabilito – the good guys don't always win. It's not like the Chinese are going to be stupid enough to broadcast a network television show about the fruit," he argued in a sarcastic whisper.

Kabilito stiffened and squinted, staring directly into Andrew's eyes. "I thought you believed, Andrew. I thought you had faith, but now I see that you must be shown." He straightened. "No matter how you feel about it, you *must* agree that we need to do all that we can to understand the extent of this breach. If you won't help, then you are no longer aligned with us," he replied sternly.

Andrew sighed and dropped his shoulders. "Look, I..." He trailed off, speechless. "Of course, Kabilito. And I didn't mean to..."

Kabilito held up a hand and stopped Andrew, then pointed to the man wordlessly. Andrew reluctantly walked over to the captive, who was being held to the floor in a sitting position by Subira and Akiiki. The man looked up at Andrew as he crouched to talk. Kabilito listened as Andrew began to speak to him in Mandarin, then in Swahili, then in English, all to no avail – the man was trained to remain silent.

Harel strode forward, squaring his shoulders and cupping his fist with his hand. "Kabilito, you want me to..."

But Kabilito held him back and stood still, watching the interrogation. "No, David, but thank you," he answered, his eyes boring in Andrew's back.

Andrew looked over helplessly, but Kabilito squinted back at him, jerking his head angrily toward the Chinese man. He saw fear in Andrew's eyes, but he kept his countenance steadfast until Andrew shuddered, took a deep breath and turned back to the man once more.

The sheet metal walls of the warehouse reverberated deafeningly as the voice issued from Andrew's mouth. It wasn't clear to Kabilito what language was being spoken or even what words Andrew used, but one thing was obvious – a command had been summoned, one that could not be denied.

Words began spilling from the man's mouth, and though Kabilito didn't hear every word, it seemed to him that he understood parts of the narration. Maybe it was a combination of the man's facial expressions, his body language and gesticulations, and the intonation in his voice. Maybe his observation of all these things together allowed him to glean what was being said from the exchange, but soon he ceased caring and simply listened.

As Andrew continued compelling the man to speak Kabilito learned several things. He heard the man's name: Yeh Xin. He gathered that Yeh Xin was an operative for the Chinese government on a mission to find the fruit. He was hiding in the valley when he saw Harel shoot at the tribe, then he saw them heal. He had witnessed Andrew using the voice on Wu Yue. Later he'd been forced to hide under the canvas in the crate, but the tribe had sealed the lid, and he was trapped.

The strange conference continued. Irresistible

commands flew from Andrew's mouth and Yeh Xin continued answering. It seemed as if the forced interrogation reached a fever pitch until suddenly Andrew stood and spun around to face Kabilito, his face twisted in shock.

"What is it? What did he say?" Kabilito asked.

"It's Jelani," Andrew breathed, his voice barely a whisper. "He saw Jelani in the valley."

Kabilito's jaw dropped open as Andrew turned back and began rapid-firing questions in earnest, his voice charging the air with electrifying power. In between answers he stopped to relay information.

"He saw Jelani hiding in a...a hole, or hollow hidden in the brush...he was living in there, and he was..." Andrew turned back and asked a question before continuing. "He was gibbering and talking to himself, laughing crazily, scratching himself and acting strangely."

An icy grip clutched Kabilito's spine. His mind scanned his memory of the valley in vain, searching for a hollow they never found, in a valley they burned to the ground.

Andrew continued. "He says he hid from Jelani in a tree. Jelani left after Harel and Wu Yue arrived. He says Jelani took a whole sack of fruit with him, then disappeared. But after Jelani left he climbed down and tried to secure some of the fruit to bring back to his commanders. That's when he hid in this crate."

Andrew reached up and wiped the sweat from his brow. His face was white and he was shaking. He pressed his fingers against his temples, clearly in pain, but Kabilito knew they needed more.

"Ask him about his mission," he said softly to Andrew. "Find out all you can."

Andrew drew a deep breath and turned back to his work.

"He says his commanders knew about the fruit from data infiltration into the emails of a pharmaceutical company, *Regentex*..." Andrew looked up at Meg, who raised a hand to her mouth, stunned.

"We were hacked," she told the group, "but I thought it was just corporate espionage. If *he* knows about that, it proves the Chinese government was involved. We had been working with the cyber division of the NSA..." Light dawned in her eyes as she looked over at Kabilito. "Oh, no, Kabilito, we were working with the NSA on this. They were tracking the cyber-attacks and had access to all of our emails, all our files..." She trailed off.

Kabilito swallowed. "This means both Chinese and US intelligence know of the fruit."

Meg nodded slowly.

Yeh Xin hung his head and muttered something under his breath. Andrew turned and spoke to him, this time without using the voice. Yeh Xin was shaking his head, his voice a whisper, as Andrew relayed the information to the tribe.

"Wait...he's saying something about his mother. He says they'll kill her now. He says they'll think he deserted them and abandoned his mission..."

Kabilito cocked his head and frowned. "Andrew, ask him about his mother, why she's being held, and why they would kill her."

Andrew began speaking to Yeh Xin in soft tones, but the spy wouldn't answer. Andrew raised his voice, agitated, but still Yeh Xin resisted, shaking his head. Tension rose as the struggle continued in a war of wills until finally Andrew cracked visibly. He bellowed, using the voice, and Kabilito felt his hair blown back by the force of the command as Andrew's booming voice echoed and rippled the very air around him.

Yeh Xin blurted out sentence after sentence as Andrew translated. “He says they took her, they took her and beat him when he was young. They imprisoned her for dissidence, for speaking out against the government when his father died in a state-run chemical plant explosion. They forced him into service, told him they’d kill his mother if he didn’t become a spy, if he didn’t succeed...”

Broken, Yeh Xin trailed off. Andrew asked another question, again without the voice. Yeh Xin answered, and Andrew slowly lifted his head. He was shaking as he stood, perspiration dripping from his brow. “This was to be his last mission, Kabilito,” he said feebly. “His last mission – to find the fruit and bring it back. If he did that, she’d go free. If not...”

Andrew’s knees buckled, the power of the voice having taken its toll. Kabilito bolted forward to catch him, slipping an arm under Andrew’s form as he fell. He cradled his head as Andrew’s eyes blinked erratically.

“Andrew,” Kabilito spoke softly at first, then more forcefully. “Andrew!”

Andrew’s eyes fluttered open. “Talk to him yourself, Kabilito,” Andrew replied weakly. “He speaks English and Swahili, too.” Then he passed out in Kabilito’s arms.

Kabilito turned from the bed, a look of concern on his face. He started for the door.

“Kabilito,” he heard Andrew intone weakly.

He spun around and hurried back to the bed to sit with Andrew. “Just rest,” he replied. “You passed out using the power on Yeh Xin.”

Andrew swallowed, then continued in a whisper, his eyes half-closed, fluttering. "It's as if I'm fighting another force inside. I'm afraid that I'll lose control permanently and turn. And it seems to be getting worse as the voice gets stronger. Each time I concede a little more control. Each time the buzzing grows louder, and the pressure in my head increases."

Kabilito considered this. "I know this sounds insensitive, but it's the truth: either you will turn, or you won't, but you cannot continue with this imbalance – this fighting and struggling against the power. Clearly it's growing, but you need to embrace it – not fight it – and learn what happens. The struggle alone might make you go mad."

He paused for a moment, studying Andrew's face. His eyelids were closed, but his mouth opened slightly to speak. "I can't do that, Kabilito. I can't just...give myself up."

"But what if that's how it's supposed to work? Maybe it manifests when you are under duress because that's when you let your guard down. Maybe then you are able to embrace the power a little more easily."

"Either way, I can't continue like this," Andrew replied. "My resistance is eroding, and I'm losing my identity." He sighed and rolled over to face the wall. "I just need to rest."

Kabilito laid his hand on Andrew's shoulder before leaving the room. Meg and David approached down the corridor as Kabilito closed the door quietly.

"How is he?" Meg asked.

"I think he'll manage for now," Kabilito answered. "The power of command seems to deplete him greatly, which is a departure from the other powers granted by maisha. He's sleeping now. We'll check in on him later."

They began to walk down the corridor to the common

room. "How's our guest?" Kabilito asked.

"He's all right," Harel replied. "He's eating something now."

Kabilito thought back to his discussions with Yeh Xin. After it was clear Andrew was safe, Kabilito and the others had spoken with the operative, this time in English. They found him willing to talk, now that Andrew had forced him to divulge any information of interest to them. They had searched him thoroughly. They already had his gun, and they had taken away a hidden knife as well. They had found a worn booklet of Buddhist sutras, which Kabilito found curious, filing it away in his mind for later. Yeh Xin had no communication device, though, which they found implausible. When questioned, he said that he had lost it climbing into the crate. But that seemed strange to them – they would have found it on the ground when they loaded the trailers. Sure enough, though, once they removed the maisha they found a small satellite radio, turned off, at the bottom of his crate. They guessed that it had been torn from his belt, only to fall deep into the maisha where it lay out of reach.

Kabilito, Meg and Harel walked to the kitchens where they found Akiiki and Subira feeding the operative a hot meal. That was Subira's way of gaining trust. And having eaten nothing but raw maisha for days, Yeh Xin was more than accepting.

As Yeh Xin ate, Akiiki began to tell him about the tribe, the fruit, and the healing powers Yeh Xin had witnessed in the valley. Kabilito guessed Akiiki wanted to dispel some of the mystery surrounding the tribe, hoping that it would make them seem less threatening. He knew they were dealing with a highly-trained spy, but he was human, nonetheless. Yeh Xin asked a few questions, and they answered them as best they could.

Later Kabilito and Subira steered the conversation to Yeh Xin's mother. He described the day she had been taken from him, his forced enrollment in the military and his eventual rise as an operative. Kabilito asked about the booklet of Buddhist sutras they had found in his hidden pocket. Yeh Xin only turned away.

But Kabilito pressed him on it. "I know something of this religion, Yeh Xin. I know how you must have struggled reconciling pacifism with your missions, the devotion to save your mother with the tenets of purging desire, and the resolution of the hatred toward your mother's jailers with the need to perform."

Kabilito leaned forward, and Yeh Xin's jaw froze in mid-chew, his interest piqued. "I think our interests may be aligned, Yeh Xin," he told the spy. "What would you say if I told you we could free your mother and help you both escape to better lives – to something more worthwhile – a mission more in line with your tenets?"

"My concern is more with execution, less with ability," Yeh Xin replied, resting his fork on the plate. "I've seen the power of the fruit, and having eaten it I feel stronger myself – not enough to have ripped the lid from the crate bare-handed, but enough to appreciate what it must be like for you. But even if the strength of your entire group was behind me, freeing her is complicated and risky, and it might not work. You don't know these people. They have the full backing of all the resources of the Chinese Government. Even superhuman strength and healing might not be enough."

"What's the alternative?" Kabilito asked. "Do you really think they would *ever* let her go free, even if you completed your mission? You think they'd accept the risk that you'd eventually defect, or talk to the press?"

"I've thought on this," he replied, "but I have no alternative."

"Well, now you have us," Kabilito said. "You need your mother broken out of jail, and deep down you know we're your best shot at that. We need help tracking Jelani from someone trained in the art, and we have to know if the Chinese soldier, Wu Yue, has brought back the fruit or if he's still at large."

"And how am I going to help with that?" Yeh Xin asked.

Kabilito smiled and held up Yeh Xin's satellite radio. "You'll need to report in, anyway..."

Harel caught on. "Hey – yeah, man! If I can sell my mom on some line of shit, I'm sure a super-spy like you can come up with something."

Yeh Xin frowned. "I'm not sure what you're talking about, but what choice do I have? I know of Andrew from my briefings – he's the man who interrogated me, is he not? Even if I refuse he can just compel me to act."

Harel shrugged. "Your choice."

Chapter Thirty

Mehmut Akhun peered warily around the corner of the low-rise building in the northeast outskirts of Urumqi in Xinjiang. He was careful to hold his robes tightly against his gaunt frame so they wouldn't fall into view. Down the street he saw the roadblock – the same three Chinese soldiers as yesterday, standing guard in front of a barbed wire barrier.

Beyond the roadblock the snow-capped Bogda Shan Mountain range dominated the landscape. A great plume of smoke rose from the horizon, evidence of the ongoing battles in the foothills between the Chinese and the displaced Uyghur. Those were his people out there, branded as rebels and forced out of the city, hunted by his own countrymen. Far better than this place, though.

Mehmut had been in contact with his brother, who had made it out of the city with his own family. There was safe passage to the north of the contested areas, and his Uyghur brethren would help guide them to the refugee camps. Staying in the city meant capture and imprisonment. The Bogda Shan foothills were a harsh alternative, with near-freezing temperatures this time of year, little food, and the constant threat of attack. But they would be free, along with thousands of their Uyghur blood.

Yesterday the Chinese soldiers at the checkpoint were at least somewhat alert, but as they day wore on they discovered that holding down an abandoned road in a remote section of the city was not the least bit stimulating. Today Mehmut witnessed outright lethargy. One man sat on the hood of the military vehicle while the other two stood smoking cigarettes, staring out at the mountains and the rising plumes of smoke.

It's now or never.

Hunched over, he scurried from his cover and crossed the street. Hiding behind an abandoned building, he ducked his head back into the open road. The soldiers were still smoking, still staring out at the landscape.

Mehmut wiped the sweat from his brow, took one last look down the street, and turned back to the corner he had just left, frantically waving his family along. From a burned-out doorframe his wife's eyes were barely visible under her shawl, and Mehmut saw the frightened faces of his two daughters enveloped in her robes. Once again he beckoned them, glancing again down the street at the soldiers. Finally they came, his older daughter first, then his wife, dragging the younger one. His younger daughter was scared out of her wits and resisting her mother. But before she could cry out, his wife lifted and carried her across the street, half-jogging, half-sprinting across the rubble-strewn pavement.

Mehmut breathed a sigh of relief as they joined him at

the corner. A few quick words spoken harshly to the younger child underscored the gravity of their flight, and with their interests realigned they continued weaving their way across the city.

Stealthily they traversed the outskirts of the district, hiding in the shells of the former shops and homes of their friends. Mehmut's own shop, far behind them, had been their hiding place until now. Everything they owned was in the shop – it was their livelihood and their home. He could not leave it to these savages, but he could no longer risk his family's freedom remaining hidden under the floorboards of their shop. They were among the last to leave, and their dwindling food supplies would no longer sustain them all. They had begged and pleaded with him to join them, but his own father had instilled stewardship within him, and, like several of his friends, he would stay to protect his property, or die trying.

At least he would see his family to safety this day. He checked his watch – he was already late, but his brother would wait for them. Ahead, Mehmut could see the barricades that stretched around this section of the city, hastily erected by the Chinese to keep the "Uyghur rebels" from returning and stirring more unrest in the city. He knew he was close now.

Taking his daughter from his wife's arms, he ran the remaining distance, through the alleys, ducking below the scaffolding and awnings that lined the streets. Finally he reached the barricade fence and the small, secret hole that had been cut at the bottom of the chain link mesh. Through the open weave of the fabric draped over the tall barricade he could see his brother on the other side. His form turned at Mehmut's approaching sounds.

"Mehmut?" the shadow whispered desperately, "is it you?"

"Here," Mehmut replied softly. The fabric rolled back and Mehmut stared into his brother's worried eyes. "How is it there, my brother?"

"It is getting worse – they must come now, else we won't be able to avoid the fighting. Hurry..."

His older daughter went first, but not before he hugged her tightly one last time. She was a brave girl despite her tears. He smiled confidently at her and kissed her forehead before she crawled under the flaps of the severed chain link fence.

Next came the younger, but she would not budge. She turned and grasped at his robes, sobbing. He held her tightly to say goodbye, but from the corner of his eye he saw motion down the street. A patrol of Chinese soldiers was sauntering lazily down the abandoned street, smoking and kicking at the rubble as they joked and talked. They were still a good distance away, but Mehmut knew they would not be distracted for long.

He looked desperately into his wife's eyes. Gently she pulled his daughter from him, wiping the tears from her dust-streaked cheeks. After he whispered words of encouragement in his wife's ear, she managed to persuade the little girl to slip through the hole and into the waiting arms of her uncle.

Wife and husband shared a momentary hug before she, too, began to crawl under the fence. But the delays added up, and Mehmut winced as the inevitable shout came from behind.

He rose slowly to buy his family some time. He heard them scurrying behind the fence as they climbed the embankment on the other side. He lifted his arms high in the air in surrender, listening in satisfaction at the pounding of their footfall against the packed earth as they fled. The soldiers were still two blocks away, running directly toward him when finally Memhut could no longer hear the sounds of his family's escape. He took a deep breath, then spun and sprinted along the fence.

"Halt!" came the cry in Mandarin above the pounding of his heart. He leapt over a deep pothole, the remnant of some past explosion, and dove behind the decrepit shell of a rusty car. Gunfire erupted from down the street, pockmarking the pavement around him and pinging from the sheet metal of his cover.

They were almost on him when he tore his robe off and bundled it in half. Reaching far to the back of the car, he flung the robe up and over the trunk, letting it open and flutter over the rear bumper. It worked – the ploy momentarily distracted them as he slipped out from the cover of the car and sprinted to the nearby street corner. Bullets ripped into the robe and ricocheted off the car bumper as Mehmut ran down the side street undetected.

Chapter Thirty-One

The Chinese military assistant ran headlong down the corridor and into the office of his superior, breathlessly panting out a name.

"Yeh Xin!"

Gao Jun, commander of the African Special Operations forces, bolted up from his chair, swearing. He grabbed the boy and hustled down the corridor. "Yeh Xin? Where the hell has he been? Hurry up, boy!" he bellowed.

The boy led him to the communications room. He burst in, barking the same question as he pushed two soldiers aside. "Where the hell are you, Yeh Xin?"

The speaker on the desk crackled with digital interference, the telltale sign of the encrypted connection. "Kenya, sir. Did Wu Yue bring the package home?" came Yeh Xin's voice.

Thrown off, Gao Jun muted the phone. "What have you

told him?" he demanded of the men in the room. "Does he know?"

"No, sir," stammered one of the communications personnel. "We've only just gone through the identification protocol – it's him all right, sir."

Gao Jun punched the mute button again. "I'll ask the questions, Yeh Xin. Report on your mission."

"I've been tracking the tribe, sir. Some of them were returning to the valley. They got behind me before Pixiu could reach the rendezvous point. I had to shut off the radio and descend to the target location to avoid detection. I heard the gunshots up on the ridge. One of the American soldiers found his way into the valley, followed by Wu Yue. Both were badly injured. The American shot some of the tribe members, but they healed instantly. Then they healed both soldiers with the fruit. The tribe packed everything up and burned down the valley. I hid but managed to track them all the way from the Rwenzoris to Port Bell, where Wu Yue escaped. They kept a close eye on Wu Yue before he fled. I couldn't make contact with him without being detected, but I created a distraction that helped him escape in the boat."

Gao Jun glanced over at the communications officer, who nodded – it all checked out. "What's your location now?" he demanded.

"The foothills of Mount Kenya, sir. After Wu Yue escaped they left Port Bell and met up with the rest of the tribe with the supplies. They've started another orchard here, sir."

Several of Gao Jun's aides entered the room, listening on headsets. They quietly closed the door and removed the earpieces to listen through the speaker.

"And you couldn't report in until now?" Gao Jun asked, skeptically.

There was a pause on the line. “I’ve been a bit…boxed-in, sir,” Yeh Xin replied.

“Hold the line, Yeh Xin,” Gao Jun said, muting the line once more and turning to his aides. “What’s the possibility he’s compromised?” he said, addressing them bluntly.

“Pretty high, Sir,” one of them answered. “His story checks out. He even knew of the boat Wu Yue took, but that doesn’t mean he couldn’t have been captured after Wu Yue’s escape.”

Another aide spoke. “It’s possible they’re using this new command power on him that Wu Yue reported, sir. We can’t assume he’s still with us, but there’s nothing to suggest otherwise either. He’s still valuable as I see it.”

“But it makes no sense to feed intelligence back to them if he is compromised,” Gao Jun concluded. “All right – we’ll keep him in the field in case he’s still ours.”

Gao Jun pushed the mute button. “Yeh Xin, we need you to stay in the field. Keep watch on them, and transmit your coordinates.”

“So you have the fruit, then – Wu Yue made it back?” came the question.

It was Gao Jun’s turn to pause, but he recovered quickly. “No, he isn’t here. He may have gone rogue with the prize. Your orders are to stick with the tribe.”

“You mean until I recover the prize, Sir?” asked Yeh Xin hesitantly.

Gao Jun paused again, a little too long for comfort. One of the aides frantically scribbled a word on a scrap of paper and held it up. It read “Xinjiang.”

“No, there’s been another related development,” Gao Jun finally replied. “We need to know if any of the tribe have left recently, specifically to the Xinjiang region.”

The speaker remained silent for a few moments before crackling to life. "They come and go, sir, but why Xinjiang? What's the situation?"

"Rebels have been attacking the militia there after the riots broke out. But there have been sightings of a man dressed in robes who destroys ammunitions depots, incapacitates troops, and then runs off. Several of our soldiers have reported shooting him dead, but he gets up instantly and runs off, unharmed. Sounds to us like the prize at work."

"Could it be Wu Yue?" Yeh Xin asked.

"Unlikely," the commander replied. "We think it's someone from the tribe, helping the rebels. They've been forced into the mountains, where they continue to attack our search parties. Apparently this terrorist is a hero to the Uyghur – he comes and goes, disrupting our militia then fleeing into the mountains. He's even helped in some of the skirmishes in the foothills, disabling our forces before disappearing."

"But if I can bring back the prize, sir, isn't this irrelevant? That's my mission – bring back the prize, then you release my mother..."

"No prize, no release, Yeh Xin," Gao Jun told him, "but you're to stay there and monitor activity for now. And transmit your coordinates as soon as this call has ended. You're already in position to take the prize when we pull the trigger. Xinjiang is too important at the moment. Your mother is safe, for now. "

"You're changing the game, commander – this wasn't the..."

"I make the rules – you follow them. Remember that, Yeh Xin," Gao Jun replied ominously.

Still wrapped in a blanket, Andrew sat shivering, struggling to listen to the exchange, translating when he could for Kabilito, Subira and Akiiki until Yeh Xin disconnected the line.

"Well, we need to come up with some bogus coordinates," Yeh Xin said, setting down the radio.

"But won't the Chinese search there?" Andrew asked.

"I doubt it," Kabilito replied. "We'll pick a location that has good tree cover. They'll search by satellite, but getting clearance from the Kenyan government to deploy a military mission will be nearly impossible, especially since they cannot divulge any reasonable intent. And they won't give away the location of interest without tipping off Kenya that something is going on there. They know the Kenyans would search the site before they ever gave permission." Kabilito turned to Yeh Xin. "You did well."

"I'm not sure how much of it is true, though," Yeh Xin replied. "It's possible they're lying about Wu Yue. There were a lot of pauses on the line – plenty of time for them to confer and reply to my questions." He shifted in his chair. "There's a good chance they believe I'm compromised, because it should have been more important for me to bring back the fruit if they didn't already have it."

"Where would they have taken Wu Yue if he had returned with the maisha?" Kabilito asked.

"Beijing," Yeh Xin replied. "To the top security, military weapon research and development complex laboratories. That was the plan at least. They would analyze the fruit there – try and synthesize and exploit it. Same thing with Wu Yue, if he returned. He's already ahead of the curve with his powers. They'd study him like a lab rat, though he may not be aware of that, given his low level security clearance."

Andrew frowned, agitated. "How do we know what to believe? Maybe they actually have Wu Yue and they're lying about these supernatural sightings in Xinjiang. Or maybe the man helping the rebels *is* Wu Yue."

"He wouldn't heal that quickly, not yet, at least," Subira pointed out. "They said he jumped right up after being shot..."

"I don't know, Subira," Andrew said. "Look at how fast Meg and Harel have progressed. The power is accelerating."

"True enough," Kabilito replied, "but there would be no reason for Wu Yue to go to Xinjiang. He's not from there. What would his motivation be? And why wear robes?"

"Maybe there's no rationale. Maybe he's turned and gone crazy," Andrew offered.

"He didn't seem crazy," Harel said.

Yeh Xin chewed his lip. "I agree with Kabilito – there's no reason for Wu Yue to head to Urumqi or the Bogda Shan region. Either he's corrupt and he's keeping the power to himself, or he'd contact his superiors and they'd pick him up and bring him to the lab in Beijing. Furthermore, there's no reason for my commanders to make up such a story."

"Unless they're trying to drive us to Xinjiang," Subira said, ominously.

"I'm confused," Meg admitted. "Why would they want us there?"

"Because we're an unknown threat to them," Subira answered. "They have an idea of our power, but the extent of it is unclear to them. So they might try to lure us into a trap."

"But if the sightings are true," Akiiki said, "and if it's not Wu Yue, there's only one other person it could be."

A pall fell over the group. "Jelani," Kabilito said, voicing the answer on everyone's mind.

Subira broke the silence. "No matter who it is, he has the fruit, and we need to go to Xinjiang and find him."

"Wait," Harel interjected, "why would Jelani benefit from going to Xinjiang any more than Wu Yue would?"

Kabilito answered him. "From Yeh Xin's description, it sounds like he's turned, which would amplify his evil nature. He's already killed hundreds in the mine battles and in his earlier terrorist exploits. He could be looking to kill more, but on a mass scale. He could be looking to raise an army."

"But again, why in Xinjinag?" Harel asked.

"The unrest," Subira answered. "It's been widely reported. Thousands of rebels forced from the city, amassing in the mountains. They're desperate, oppressed, and ostracized from their homeland – an easy target for a messianic leader right in the middle of a political tinderbox."

"So it's settled," Kabilito said. "We go to Xinjiang..."

"On the way to rescuing my mother," Yeh Xin interrupted. "That was the deal."

"Yes," Subira confirmed, "first Xinjiang, then your mother...who is being held where, by the way?"

"Beijing," Yeh Xin answered.

"Which is also where the military research laboratories are," Meg pointed out. "In a way it's perfect. We can recue your mother *and* retrieve the fruit from the lab in Beijing, unless it truly is Wu Yue stirring up trouble in Xinjiang."

Subira turned to Yeh Xin. "Are you sure your commanders were telling the truth about your mother – that she's still safe?"

Yeh Xin nodded. "If I had remained radio-silent much longer, they might have assumed me compromised, or dead.

But now that I've resurfaced with a credible story they'll want to retain their leverage. She's safe as long as I'm active."

"And if we're walking into a trap?" Andrew asked.

"Then we spring the trap," Subira answered.

Silent assent passed through the room, determination reflected on every face.

"I'm in," Yeh Xin voiced first.

"Wait," Andrew said, "*You* can't go. How will you get through Chinese immigration without the government knowing?"

Yeh Xin shrugged. "I have aliases the government doesn't know about, and I've made passports before. It's not that hard."

"But...," Andrew protested.

"I'm *going*," Yeh Xin asserted. "It's *my* mother, and you need me to find both the prison *and* the lab complex."

Andrew looked at Kabilito, desperation in his eyes, but Kabilito nodded toward Yeh Xin. "We don't have a choice," he said.

"The passports aren't even the real problem," Yeh Xin continued. "Neither is the prison. I can find my way around that place. But the laboratory complex is huge, with security and guards everywhere. Even if we make it inside we'll need to be able to somehow identify if the fruit is there, and if so, we'd need to find where the research is being carried out. I'm no scientist – I wouldn't know a flask from a beaker. No, we need to coax the information from someone at the facility..."

Andrew felt everyone's eyes on him, and he lifted his eyebrows in protest. "Did you all see what happened last time? The power is less and less controllable – more unpredictable each time." He shook his head to clear it, but the sound and pressure were worse than ever. "We can't rely on the voice to get us through this. It's just too risky."

Meg chimed in. "I worked at a pharmaceutical company – I'd know where to look. And if Andrew or Yeh Xin translates for me I could locate the research facilities from their files, or even from the titles on the doors."

Andrew felt his jaw drop, and he swung his head back to Kabilito. "They haven't even been tested yet, Kabilito! We've talked about this – how fast the power is growing, how it's accelerating... I'm not the only one that presents a risk here."

"But if we can't rely on your power," Meg said, "there's no one else to guide us."

Andrew started to object, but Kabilito silenced him with a raised hand. "We've also talked about faith and trust, Andrew. And in this case there's simply no alternative."

Harel interjected. "I'm in, too."

"No – no way," Andrew heard himself say.

"Look," Harel replied, "you're headed into a combat zone in Xinjiang. Anyone here experienced in warfare?" Andrew looked on incredulously as Harel made a show of surveying the room. "No one? Good – it's settled then. I'm in, too."

Andrew slammed his hand on the table as he rose. "This is stupid. I can't believe we're even considering this. But why ask me? What the hell do I know? I'm probably crazy, anyway."

Then he turned and stormed out of the room.

Chapter Thirty-Two

Standing behind the Secretary of State, Colonel Frank Anderson watched the President of the United States sit back on the oval office couch and rub his temples. "So we got caught with our hand in the cookie jar, eh?" the President said, sighing.

Secretary Rosemark leaned in from the sofa facing the Commander-in-Chief. "Mr. President, it's only an accusation at this point, but they know that weapons are coming out of Kazakhstan and showing up in Xinjiang, and that we're there providing logistical support. Of course we'll still deny it, but it was really only a matter of time. They're threatening to pull personnel out of their embassy, as usual. It's a bluff, of course, but with the skirmish in the valley, the missing soldiers, and now the support for Turkey, Kyrgyzstan and the Uyghur...it's all starting to pile up."

"And what of this situation in Uganda?" the President

asked.

Frank stiffened as Rosemark half-turned in his seat to stare at him. He cleared his throat and tugged at his dress uniform uncomfortably before answering. "Basically, we're being kicked out, sir," he began, quickly adding, "but so are the Chinese. Yincang, the quasi-government company running the Kilembe mines, has reneged on their contractual production commitments. They've lost all interest in the mine, claiming that the Ugandan Economic Development Ministry misrepresented the remaining mineral resources." *In reality,* he thought, *they probably found what they needed in the valley, and now they have no need to stick around.*

He continued aloud. "So Uganda is pulling the plug on them, too, and expelling the Chinese Special Ops troops as part of the package. But they don't want to damage trade relations with either of us, so they're making an effort to effectuate the perception of fairness. They're giving both of us the boot."

The President took a long draw from his water glass as he thought. "What a mess," he commented. "But we're not about to back down from our support of Turkey. I'd trade a military presence in Uganda for one in Kazakhstan any day." He set the glass down. "We're staying at Manas."

Frank clenched his teeth. *Well, Mr. President, if you only knew about the fruit you might want to stay in Uganda instead,* he thought. *But the Techno-warfare division insists on keeping this secret, even from you...*

Chapter Thirty-Three

The private jet touched down at Urumqi Diwopu International Airport in Xinjiang, and the passengers were ushered to the immigration lines, sleepy from their all-day flight.

Andrew watched nervously as Yeh Xin nonchalantly handed over his newly-fabricated Ugandan passport, but the officials let him through without a second glance. *Helps if you're a spy, I guess,* Andrew thought, anxiously fingering his own entry documents.

Kabilito's status as the CEO of a major shipping corporation had certainly helped smooth the entry process. Although parts of Urumqi were in upheaval and civil unrest, business continued in the remainder of the commercial hub, and trade was an important part of the local economy. Kabilito's application for the group's visas had been granted without delay. Yeh Xin, meanwhile, had proven to be a master forger, creating fake passports not only for himself but for Andrew, Harel and Meg – all of whom needed to remain missing.

Preparing for customs, however, was a bit more difficult. Aside from clothes and personal items, their backpacks were stuffed with snacks, each containing a high concentration of maisha. Kabilito's old trick of resealing commercial potato chip bags filled with fried maisha slices could only get them so far. So they had created other treats with the miracle fruit: cookies, crackers and chocolate pirouette wafers, all resealed in the original packaging. The gluttonous amount of food they carried raised eyebrows in the customs line, and for a tense moment the officials debated amongst themselves as they stared down at twenty bags of chips. They opened one and stared questioningly into the sack, then looked up at Harel who simply patted his belly and licked his lips. Frowning, the officials rolled the top of the opened chip bag, handed it back hesitantly to Harel, and let them through.

A short trip with the pre-arranged limousine service took them to the outskirts of Urumqi near the Eastern Shuimogou District in the afternoon. As they rode along the border of the Uyghur section they saw barricades and checkpoints allowing only those with proper credentials into the sector. Andrew stared out the window at the low-rise buildings, many with wooden planks boarding up the windows of the shops that lined the streets. Smoke rose from somewhere in the center of the region, and the few residents who wandered the streets looked to Andrew like zombies in the apocalypse. Not all of the commercial enterprises in the district were run by Muslim Uygur, however, and business continued in the secular portions of the city sector regardless of the oppressive militia.

As they moved west and away from the restricted zone Andrew was overwhelmed with the size of Urumqi. After a while he shook his head in bewilderment. "Where do we even begin?" he asked aloud to no one in particular.

"The hotel," Kabilito answered as they turned off the main highway and into the parking lot of the modern inn, and soon they had checked into their rooms. They met to discuss plans and strategy while they were eating dinner.

In the end they decided there was little they could do except to dive into the district and begin asking around for any sightings of the mysterious, immortal robed man – the man the Uyghur had come to call a hero. Yeh Xin's commanders had revealed that he bounced between the mountains and the city district, coming and going at will. When in the city, he'd reportedly destroy Chinese military equipment, weakening the militia's grip on the sector. Andrew hoped they'd locate him quickly, because the alternative was scouring the foothills of the Bogda Shan Mountains to the east while being shelled by Chinese troops.

Andrew's sleep was fitful that night, and he dreamed that he was surrounded by hundreds of strangers, high on a cliff overlooking the ocean. His father sailed a boat far below on the waves, beckoning Andrew to join him. He was pushed by the strangers, driven toward the cliff, hands from those around him shoving him and forcing him forward until at last he stood at the edge. Kabilito was there, bound tightly with rope. Yeh Xin stood beside him in handcuffs. Andrew reached out to Kabilito, but he simply turned to Yeh Xin, a flurry of unintelligible words spilling out of his mouth. Yeh Xin turned to Andrew and suddenly lashed out with a foot, kicking him over the edge. Shocked, he fell toward the rocks below, the frothy ocean rising to meet him. Just before he was dashed on the boulders in the violent surf he saw his father rise in the boat, reaching out to him, desperately calling out his name. He awoke in a sweat and padded off to the bathroom, dashing cold water on his face and staring in the mirror for several minutes before attempting sleep once more.

Early the next morning the group ate a small breakfast before staring on foot toward the restricted zone. Kabilito carried a small backpack, and Andrew suspected it contained some maisha. He recalled their trip to Long Island, seemingly so long ago, when Kabilito had brought fried maisha hidden in a potato chip bag. Back then, the hope was that they could make a draught to save Martin – to restore what little remained of his sanity and start him down the path of healing. But now, he could only guess at Kabilito's intentions.

Ahhh, Martin...your ghost still haunts me, even so far from home...

They wove their way across the city streets heading east. The thick air was laden with particulates and it was difficult to breathe. Andrew's eyes stung at first, but through the haze he saw signs of rapid development throughout the city. He was amazed at the construction. It seemed that everywhere a new high-rise was sprouting up, primarily urban residential with shops lining the street-level floors. Cranes turned and spun in every direction as far as the eye could see. In some sections the buildings all looked the same to him, with drab architecture repeated over and over. In other areas attractive parkland split up the cityscape, with large water features and beautiful bridges. But these improvements were awkwardly integrated into the manufacturing and commercial zones only a few blocks away. Nearby, Hui mosques and Han Buddhist temples competed for space with hotels and shopping malls amidst confusing patches of concrete and pavement. To Andrew's eyes the whole urban design of Urumqi was disjointed and frenetic.

They reached the first checkpoint on the eastern district outskirts, and Andrew waited anxiously as the soldiers sternly examined their papers. Kabilito smoothly provided reasons for their visit and answered their questions with Yeh Xin's acting as translator. They were here from a shipping company in Mombasa, he explained, visiting business clients in the district. They squinted at Yeh Xin and his passport the longest, but they eventually waved them through.

Andrew felt eyes boring into his back as they left the barricades. They walked the streets, some strewn with rubble, others pockmarked with potholes and divots, remnants of past explosions from the riots and violence. Patrols marched by now and then, keeping a close watch on the group. He stared idly into the broken windows of the storefronts as he trudged along. It was clear that the Han and Hui shops remained open, while the Uyghur-owned were closed. What wasn't clear to him was the tribe's strategy. *Are we just going to stop into one of the few open shops and speak with someone at random?* It was almost as if Kabilito was relying on fate, or something else to guide them.

He finally was compelled to ask. "Kabilito," he queried, "what's the plan? We're just wandering around, aimlessly..." He trailed off as Kabilito paused and stared at him with a disappointed look on his face.

"Such little faith, Andrew," he replied, his eyes boring into Andrew's soul. "When you believe in the prophecy – that God has a plan for us and in fact has issued an *order* -- then you will truly see what guides us. But until then, just follow."

Kabilito continued walking, leaving Andrew standing in the road dejectedly. He felt a palpable rift growing between them, and he dwelled on it for several moments before he turned and caught up with the group.

They were just about to pass the corner of a building and cross the street ahead when suddenly shouts echoed down the avenue one block to the left. Andrew ducked back behind the cover of the building and peered around the corner. Kabilito and Harel did the same. A hooded man in a robe sprinted into view, running down the avenue the next block over, disappearing behind the building across the street. Shouting, a small patrol of Chinese soldiers ran after him.

Jelani is here, Andrew thought as he pressed himself against the cool bricks, pulse racing. They retreated to the cover of the adjacent abandoned shop, hiding in the building's shadow. A few moments later the hooded man reappeared far ahead, now on the same avenue as them, running at full tilt. He had rounded the far corner of the building across the street, sprinting now toward them, his head held low. Distracted by his flight from the Chinese, the man seemingly hadn't yet detected them.

"Quickly," Kabilito hissed, pulling them all into an alcove. They backed into the small, sheltered space as the hooded man slowed a block away. Andrew peered out from the recess and saw the man fiddle with a lock before throwing a door open to duck inside. As the door shut behind him, the avenue was empty once more.

"Come on," Andrew said, stepping out from the alcove into the street to apprehend the fugitive. He bolted for the next block.

"Wait," called Yeh Xin and Harel at the same time. He stopped on the sidewalk, froze and closed his eyes, kicking himself mentally. *Too late*, he thought – *I'm an idiot*.

The Chinese troops appeared around the far corner,

running up the avenue past the door the hooded man had entered. He heard a groan from behind as the soldiers crossed the street toward him before the rest of his group intervened from the cover of the alcove.

"Halt, stop right there!" one of the soldiers cried. Chests heaving, they slowed and circled the little group.

"What can we help you with, Officers?" Andrew heard Yeh Xin ask in Mandarin.

"Where are you coming from?" the team commander demanded, panting. "Did you see which way he ran?"

Andrew kept his eyes locked on Yeh Xin's face. The spy was utterly convincing in his confusion. "He...who? We just came from our hotel. I haven't seen anyone since the checkpoint back there," he said, pointing in the direction of the city.

"You didn't see anyone?" Andrew heard the commander ask. "A man in robes – his face hooded, running down the street?"

Andrew did his best to look confused, turning back to Kabilito and Akiiki. Subira stared straight ahead at the other soldiers, gauging them. Meg ran her fingers across the bricks of the alcove, attempting to appear casual. Harel simply shrugged and cocked his head.

"No one ran by," Yeh Xin said slowly. "We were just talking about our friend who owned the store here." He motioned to the abandoned shop beyond the alcove. "Do you know what happened to him? It looks like he closed up his shop..."

The commander rolled his eyes as one of the soldiers behind him tugged his sleeve and pointed down the opposite street. He swung a finger in the air and pointed, signaling his men to deploy in that direction. As they jogged away he turned back to Yeh Xin, but before the commander could speak Yeh Xin, feigning nervousness, answered his unspoken demand. “If we see anyone meeting that description, we’ll tell one of the patrolmen right away.”

The commander eyed him sternly. “See that you do,” he replied, then turned and ran off after his team.

Once the soldiers had left Andrew addressed the group. “Sorry, I didn’t think they’d circle back...”

“They were following the man. Of course they would,” Yeh Xin said, frowning. He started off down the avenue toward the hooded man’s hiding place. The group followed him, and Andrew filed in at the rear, shaking his head. *I’m just a liability at this point*, he thought, swatting at a buzzing noise near his ear. But no insect was around him, and so he shook his head to clear it and continued, unnerved.

They reached the door through which the hooded man had disappeared. It was a large, wooden plank door with faded paint and a worn brass handle. Beside it the windows were boarded shut, and rusty chains hung from empty sign supports jutting out from the side of the building. It looked as though the shop had been abandoned for months. Kabilito grasped the door handle and depressed the lever. The door creaked open on ancient hinges. In his haste the man must have left it unlocked.

Andrew followed the group into the store. Inside he saw empty shelves laden with cobwebs and dust. What little merchandise remained lay strewn about the floor in disarray, littering the hardwood planks – spray bottles, packages of cloth, cans, and boxes of household items. Sand and dust crunched underfoot, and footprints crisscrossed the grimy floor.

The shop itself was small – clearly some type of grocery

and hardware store, with a back room separated from the front by a curtain. Andrew walked across a worn, hand-knotted Oriental rug and around a checkout counter to the back room curtain and pulled it aside. Behind it was a small kitchen and living area, along with additional rooms sectioned off by hanging curtains. He thought he saw an empty bed inside one of the rooms through the fabric. He reached forward to pull the curtain aside, but suddenly he heard someone call out from the shop front and he hurried back.

Yeh Xin, Harel and Subira were on their knees on the plank floor, staring down into a pit. A hinged hatch lay open beside them, and the rug Andrew had walked across was folded under the hatch door, apparently attached to the top. He crossed the room as Kabilito, Meg and Akiiki rushed over to join him.

A pair of eyes looked up at him from the pit, partially shrouded by a hood. It was clearly the fugitive, but something bothered Andrew about him. The man looked scared.

"That's not Jelani, is it?" he asked through the rising pressure and buzzing in his skull.

"He's not the man I saw in the valley," Yeh Xin replied.

As his eyes adjusted to the darkness Andrew saw empty cans of food and water bottles lying in the bottom of the hiding place, as well as a bedroll, a small prayer rug, and some personal items. It looked as though the man had been living there for quite some time.

Yeh Xin reached down and removed the man's hood. A flurry of Turkish spewed from the fugitive's mouth, and Andrew wondered how he even recognized the language the man spoke. Words formed and understanding coalesced, and suddenly he realized he could perceive meaning. And then it was as if he had spoken the language all along.

"My shop is all I have left," he heard the man tell them in a desperate voice. "Leave me." His cheeks were gaunt, and from the drape of the grimy robes hanging from his arms it was clear his last meal had been eaten long ago.

"We're not going to hurt you. What is your name?" Yeh Xin said in broken Turkish, crude-sounding and heavily-accented to Andrew's ears.

"Mehmut," the man responded apprehensively, "Mehmut Akhun."

"Let me try," Andrew said, then asked Mehmut in perfect Turkish, "Why were you running from the soldiers?"

He was dimly aware of Yeh Xin staring at him with an astonished look on his face.

"All Uyghur are hunted now in this part of the city," Mehmut replied. "We did nothing – my family is innocent. Yet they capture everyone and throw my people in jail. They say we are terrorists, and that we destroy their equipment and supplies, but it is not true." Andrew heard Yeh Xin struggling to translate Mehmut's words to the rest of their group.

"Where is your family?" Andrew asked.

"They escaped to the mountains – they are safe, with my people," Mehmut replied. "I stayed behind to protect the last of what we have left – our livelihood, our home." His hands were shaking as he licked his dry, cracked lips. "I was going to join them myself if things got worse. They did get worse, but the Chinese increased the patrols and security along the border, and now it is impossible to escape." He waved his hands at the empty cans of food. "And now I'm reduced to thievery. All I can do is raid the stores of my people for any scrap of food I may find, hiding from the soldiers under the floor like a trapped rat." He shuddered, staring at the pack on Kabilito's back. "Please," he begged, licking his lips again with a dry tongue, "please may I have some water – something to eat? I starve..."

Kabilito rummaged in his pack and handed Andrew a water bottle. Andrew cracked open the cap and handed it to Mehmut, who gulped it all down thirstily, crumpling the bottle to drain every drop. Kabilito then handed Andrew a bag of maisha chips.

The buzzing noise swelled in his head as Andrew waved off the fruit. "No, no," he whispered to Kabilito in English. "We can't keep..."

He trailed off as Yeh Xin snatched the bag angrily and handed it to Mehmut. "What's the matter with you? The man is starving," he snapped. Mehmut tore open the bag's fake seal and gobbled down handfuls of the chips.

Shocked, Andrew turned back to Kabilito, who simply nodded toward Mehmut. "Ask him about this man they've been hunting," he told Andrew. Frowning, he focused on Mehmut once more and asked him about the immortal saboteur.

"Yes," the man said between swallows, "we have all seen him. At first we heralded him as a hero – this hooded man who runs like the wind. It was said he could not be hurt. He was shot fatally several times, only to rise from the ground and run away, back to the mountains. Each time he would come and destroy their weapons, blow up their stores of ammunition, incapacitate their vehicles. Each time we would cheer at the misfortune of the soldiers – taunting the men against whom we protested. But cheering was foolish, and served only to implicate us in crimes we did not commit. Soon we were blamed for the vandalism. We were hunted and beaten, and our families were dragged off to jail. This man we had once cheered we now scorned, wishing he would stop. Eventually he did, but it was too late."

"Where is this man now?" Andrew pressed, squinting in pain at the headache roaring in his skull.

"Gone," Mehmut replied. "He fled back to the mountains. He was last seen in the foothills. Our camps are there, in a hidden place. My family, my brother – all there, and I am trapped here..."

"Where was he headed?" Andrew asked. "Where is this hidden place where the camps are? We need to speak with them, find out which direction he was traveling..."

Mehmut looked up, his pleading eyes hungry, filled with an opportunity he recognized. "I can take you there!" he said excitedly. "You must take me with you – please! I will show you..."

A feeling of dread crept up Andrew's spine as Yeh Xin translated for the group. Turning slowly back to Kabilito and Subira, he could tell from the look on their faces which position they would take regarding Mehmut's request.

"You can't be serious!" he blurted out. "There's no way we can take him with us." He turned back to Yeh Xin, desperately seeking another opinion.

Yeh Xin answered without taking his eyes from Andrew's. "Yes, Mehmut, we will take you there," he finished in broken Turkish, intoning the obvious will of the group.

Furious, Andrew rose and turned back to Kabilito, but he saw no recourse in the eyes of the man he had come to know as friend. "You're letting *him* decide?" he demanded incredulously. "You never even tested him!"

He stood, grabbing Harel by the jacket and lifting him from the floor easily. The buzzing noise in his head was now intolerable.

"Or him!" Andrew cried. He spun, searching for Meg, his hand lashing out to grab her shoulder as he located her. "Or her!"

But Harel swatted his hand down before he touched Meg, then broke free of Andrew's grasp and dropped catlike to the floor. "Watch it, pal," he said dangerously.

All Andrew could do was stare into the kaleidoscopes that were Kabilito's ancient eyes. But Kabilito looked right through him. "There's been a shift in the power," he said, slowly. "The old rules no longer apply, Andrew. We need this man to help guide us into the mountains. Yeh Xin is right."

A dark realization crept in, seeping into Andrew's thoughts like a thick, black oil. *They're going to let this total stranger into the group despite what I say. They don't listen to me, yet they heed Yeh Xin, because he's worth more to them*. His head throbbed, clouding his thoughts. *I've been betrayed – cast aside...*

In a daze he staggered away from the pit, dimly aware that the others were calling his name. *They're manipulating me – using me*, he thought as he started slowly for the door. *I was never given a choice. It may have* seemed *that way at first – the* illusion *of choice, but now I see it for what it is. I'm a prisoner – I was always going to be kept, just like Meg, just like Harel – all so that they can maintain their precious secret...*

He held his head in his hands now, the dizzying buzz reaching a crescendo as he struggled to maintain control. His skull felt like a pressure cooker. *I've lost my home, the valley,* and *the tribe – the last of what I held dear...and I've been replaced, now that I'm losing my mind...I've got to leave before I turn...got to get away before I harm someone...*

Harel reached for him, placing a hand on his shoulder, a look of concern on his face. But Andrew didn't care. He shrugged it off and walked out the door and into the street.

"Let him go," was all he heard Kabilito say as he left.

He walked swiftly down the avenue in the direction they had come. He knew subconsciously he was backtracking, but he didn't know where else to go. Shouts called from behind him, crying out for him to stop. *It must be Harel and Kabilito,* he thought, but the voices sounded strange. He just continued walking ahead, the buzzing sound as loud as a freight train in his head. He was sweating profusely, swatting at the air, scratching at his scalp to rid himself of the noise – that incessant *noise...*

Is this what it feels like to turn? To go mad? He barely registered the sound of approaching footsteps pounding the pavement, running, running...

Go away, Kabilito, go and fool Yeh Xin into doing your bidding now. Go and fool him with promises to save his mother, like you did with me, pretending I'd have a home, a new family. I'm done with you, done with the fruit...

His legs collapsed as someone collided with him, and his face was pressed into the ground. From the corner of his eye he saw the uniforms of Chinese soldiers holding him at gunpoint. He could easily shake free and defeat them. He'd take some shots, no doubt, and of course he'd heal. But he didn't struggle – he didn't resist. And he wasn't about to use the voice – the power that had driven a wedge between him and the tribe, the curse that had driven him mad.

Damn that noise – that infernal buzzing – that pressure in my head...

He let them take him, handcuff him, and haul him to his feet. They shouted questions at him, asking him in Mandarin where the fugitive was, why he didn't stop when they commanded.

He allowed himself to be dragged along the avenue in a daze, not bothering to stay upright. Reaching the sentry point at the edge of the controlled zone, they shoved him into a makeshift prison – an abandoned building made of solid concrete. He heard them call their superiors on a radio, heard the reply that he was to be held there until the change of guard that night. He slid down the wall and sat hard on the cold floor, placing his head in his hands. They stood outside, guarding the only exit, talking about the American spy that just stood there and let them take him. They'd drag him into headquarters at the end of their shift and turn him over to an interrogator. They laughed in anticipation.

But he no longer cared. He'd already lost everything.

Chapter Thirty-Four

His dark eyes stared down at the refugee camp high in the Bogda Shan Mountains as he pulled his hood over his head to shade his face. Concern etched his features as he surveyed the small shelters and tents set under the many cliff outcroppings and overhangs common to the region.

He counted over one hundred Uyghur. Some performed chores to keep the encampment tidy. Children played near parents who kept a close eye on them. Several of the men were armed. He observed that the guns and rifles were a random mix of weaponry, likely cobbled together from whatever could be found or smuggled to them. A few of the armed men stood sentry, scanning the horizon and the pathways leading to their small settlement.

A muffled thud in the distance drew his attention, and a plume of smoke rose slowly from the foothills below. *They were shelling again, this time closer.*

From the path below he saw a new family arrive – a mother with her two girls. She carried the smaller one while the older girl walked, carrying a large pack. They looked exhausted, and several of the Uyghur rushed over to help as they entered the encampment. Behind them came a man bearing several sacks. He dropped the sacks near a clearing to help them set up a tent.

Soon afterward a group of six men arrived, each wearing military fatigues. They lugged a heavy crate into the settlement, and many in the camp crowded around the wooden box to help open it. A cheer rose as the lid was pried off. The man craned his neck from his hiding place to see inside. Rifles, guns and rocket launchers lay amidst packaging fluff in the open crate. Several smaller boxes were hauled up the path, and the man guessed that each contained ammunition for the weapons. He crawled back from the ledge, leaned his head against the cliff face and drew a deep breath.

Soon he was climbing back up a hidden path, brambles tearing at his robes as he ascended. Reaching a clearing, he paused and composed himself, then strode forward to where another stood waiting, back turned, similarly robed and hooded.

"There are more now," he revealed in a thick accent, "over one hundred women and men. More small arms smuggled in, too, with a few rocket launchers."

The hooded man remained motionless at first as he stared at the ground. Then he straightened and nodded slowly in acknowledgement.

Chapter Thirty-Five

Harel shifted the pack on his back and tightened the straps. He walked tirelessly, his maisha-fueled legs powering him forward with long strides along the sandy stream bed leading to the Bogda Shan. He turned to check on Mehmut, who was eating more of the fruit chips as he struggled to keep up. Sometimes they carried him to maintain their pace and to let him rest. Other times Mehmut simply walked and bore the strain by himself, and Harel thought that he could almost see the man strengthening, impossible as it seemed given so little time with the fruit.

After Andrew had left the little store Kabilito had pulled a change of clothes and a baseball cap from his pack, and they had disguised Mehmut as one of them. With one less person in the group, the addition of Mehmut had replenished their numbers in case they ran into the same patrol.

They had searched for Andrew with Mehmut leading

them through the district. Harel and Yeh Xin had found some tracks – drag marks in the dusty road that led to a heavily guarded abandoned shop. Harel had argued that Andrew could be in there, and that they needed to rescue him. But Kabilito stopped him. Even if Andrew was indeed held captive, he reasoned, it was by his own choice. Andrew could have easily escaped by using the voice or by simply overpowering the troops. And freeing him – if that was even what he wanted – would draw attention to the group. It would likely reveal Mehmut as well, who they needed desperately to guide them to the Bogda Shan settlement and, hopefully, to Jelani. No, Harel reflected, getting Mehmut safely out of the district had been more important.

Eventually they had found a smaller sentry point – only two guards standing by a barricade along a lesser-traveled street leading out of the controlled zone. The group had remained hidden around a building corner while Harel and Yeh Xin approached the guards unseen. Striking simultaneously, they had incapacitated their targets and knocked them out cold, and the group had passed unchallenged.

They had gathered their belongings from the hotel and taken taxis northeast to the sparsely-populated Aha'adecun region of Urumqi, far from the controlled zone and with easy access to the foothills of the Bogda Shan, which they now approached.

As he walked toward the foothills Harel thought of Andrew, left alone in the lock-down district. *By now the sentries would have reported that they had been attacked,* Harel thought. *Reinforcements would be called in, and all checkpoints would be on high alert. That would make entry into the area nearly impossible.* He shook his head, ashamed at leaving one of their own behind.

As Kabilito caught up with him while they walked, Harel felt a hand on his shoulder. "His story has yet to unfold, David," he told him, as if reading his thoughts. Harel pondered this during their hike, marveling at Kabilito's steadfast will and wisdom. *He* is *more than a hundred years older than me*, he thought.

They hiked for an hour along the streambed, following the meandering path south and east as they breathed the cold, arid air. Using the snowy mountain peaks as their guide, they crossed grassland, orchards, and industrial farms that lay in wide strips along the slopes. Hay bales taller than men dotted the land, wrapped in white plastic and floating in the brown cropland like marshmallows in hot chocolate.

The landscape soon gave way to foothills, and they found themselves climbing steep inclines to cross over roadways that capped the hilly crests, only to hike back down once more. They continued the endless cycle of climbing up and scrambling back down until the peaks became too steep for roadways, and the land too harsh for settlement or commercial use.

Eventually Mehmut pointed southeast to a footpath along another dry streambed. The path rose into the steep hills surrounding the Bogda Shan. They followed it upward, snacking on maisha as they climbed.

The old stream had dried up from the construction of irrigation channels serving glacial melt to Urumqi, but not before it had formed a deep channel in the mountainside. Harel stared up anxiously at the steep walls of the canyon they now climbed. *It's a poor military position*, he thought. *Snipers could be anywhere along the ridge.*

"Watch for mines on the ground," he cautioned the

group. "This path might not be so secret anymore. Don't step in any ground cover – tall grasses, low-lying shrubs, dirt that looks recently disturbed – anything that might conceal a mine."

The canyon walls soon opened and the gorge widened. Parallel hills ran rampant across the landscape as they continued to climb, providing more than ample hiding for troops from either side.

Sure enough, something soon whistled overhead, cresting the ridge to their left and exploding against the far hill. Another followed. Then, on the opposite hill, men appeared at the crest. Gunfire echoed across the foothills, sporadic at first, then in earnest. It tore through the afternoon air, accompanying the explosions of the mortar rounds. Shots erupted from both sides of the canyon.

We're in trouble here, Harel thought. He scanned the features of the terrain, searching for cover. He found it in a channel that ran perpendicular to the riverbed canyon, forming a ridge that would protect them from both sides.

"Over here!" he yelled, picking up Mehmut and sprinting up the hill. The group followed as bullets pockmarked the ground around them. He felt something tear into his calf and he stumbled, clutching at his leg. Subira appeared beside him, effortlessly lifting Mehmut from his shoulders as he healed. Blood dripped from his leg for several meters as he ran, but the wound soon closed. He followed Subira up the hill, with Mehmut screaming and covering his ears as he stared back down the slope with wide eyes.

Akiiki was not so lucky. A bullet drove into his back and through his abdomen as he ran alongside Subira. He was thrown to the ground, bashing his head against a boulder as he fell. His leg bent awkwardly and snapped as his body skidded to a stop. Temporarily unconscious, his body began to roll back down the hill. Harel changed his angle and started after his limp form, but Kabilito was faster, sprinting past him and scooping up Akiiki's body as he ran. He winced as he saw Akiiki's stomach. A bloody crater marked the exit point of the high-caliber round. But the wound closed a second later, leaving nothing but torn, crimson-stained tatters as evidence of the attack. Akiiki's leg twisted into place of its own accord as he awakened, and he tapped Kabilito's shoulder as he leapt from his back, twisting in the air. He began running before his feet touched the ground. Landing fully healed, he sprinted ahead of Kabilito and into the shadows of the ridge.

Witnessing the marvel of their instant healing, Mehmut began to scream again. There was nothing Subira could do, so he doubled his speed and dove after Akiiki. Harel slowed to let Meg pass, then ran with Yeh Xin the remaining distance to the overhang he had found. They lay, panting, against the cold rocky ridge face as mortars soared over their position to slam into the far hill.

A robed man appeared on the crest of the hill across the canyon, but he was immediately shot down. His body rolled down the far hill, leaving bloodstains along the rocky slope as it tumbled. Arms and legs flailed lifelessly all the way to the bottom until the corpse came to rest in the dry streambed only twenty meters from where they now hid. The man's head rolled to one side as his body slid to a stop, and his wide, dead eyes stared at them, horror frozen on his face.

Mehmut cried out, spouting what sounded like gibberish to Harel's ears. He pointed to the man as a flurry of Turkish spilled from his lips.

"He says that he knows this man, that he recognizes him from town. He says they're killing his people," Yeh Xin translated for them.

The battle intensified. Rockets that were launched appeared in a puff from the Uyghur side of the canyon, and soon Chinese bodies rolled to the bottom of the canyon to join their dead enemies. Mortar shells launched in puffs of smoke from both hills as the rebels struggled to retain their position. They were clearly outnumbered and outgunned. *And we're caught in the middle,* Harel thought. *At least we're under cover for now, as long as one side doesn't overrun the other...*

Mehmut continued to scream in horror at each of his brethren that fell. Several times the group ducked as shells exploded around their position. Apparently both the Chinese and the Uyghur rebels had concluded that they were enemy combatants, shooting at them when there was no visible target above the crest of the respective hills.

As the killing continued it became clear the Chinese were winning. Mehmut grabbed the collar of Yeh Xin's jacket, yelling into his face. Yeh Xin translated for the group once more. "He's saying we can't just let his people die – he's seen what we are, what we can do. He's saying that we must help."

Harel looked over to Kabilito, who shook his head. "We're caught between them," Kabilito answered. "This isn't like the mine battle, when we could incapacitate a few soldiers one by one under the cover of night."

Harel wracked his brain as Mehmut continued yelling desperately in Turkish. *We can't stop them – there're too many, and we have no weapons except for our hands and feet,* Harel thought. *We'd heal from bullet wounds, but we'd get blown to bits by grenades and mortar fire trying to engage in melee combat. If only the power allowed us to subdue many of them at once...*

Light dawned as he reflected. Amidst the shelling and gunfire, he turned and grabbed Kabilito's shoulder, spinning him around. "I have an idea, Kabilito," he yelled over the explosions and gunfire. "Do you trust me?"

Kabilito cocked his head curiously but nodded. "Yes, David," he yelled back.

"Stay under cover – I'm getting help."

Harel jumped up and ran as fast as he could from their position, back down the canyon toward the city below. A flurry of gunfire followed, bullets pinging off the rocks around him. So fast was his departure that his quickness and speed fooled the combatants, and their mortar fire and bullets danced harmlessly behind him as he sprinted full speed down the dry riverbed away from the skirmish.

The cold air blew through his short hair as he sped down the mountainside. He had never run so fast. It was an incredible feeling – a rush of power pulsing through his body, bursting into his limbs. He was a blur. He was the wind, and he had never felt so alive.

In only twenty minutes he had run the nearly fifteen miles toward the outskirts of the restricted zone. Reaching the sheet metal wall surrounding the district, he leapt to the top of an abandoned car, crushing the hood and leaving a dent that sunk to the engine. He launched himself from the car up and over the barricade, heedless of what lay beyond.

He soared over the wall and onto a low rooftop. He rolled, then dove to the roof of an adjacent building. With no other roof in sight, he dropped three stories to the street.

As his body collapsed in a sickening crunch, he was sure he had broken his legs. He rolled to his back, breathing, waiting...

A shout broke the stillness of the abandoned alleyway.

As he felt his left femur knit together he raised his head. A patrol of Chinese soldiers was heading toward him, guns waving. With the last of the bone connected, he tested his limbs before jumping up and running down the road, backtracking toward Mehmut's store.

The shouts grew dim as he outpaced them. A few shots rang out, ricocheting from the surrounding buildings harmlessly. He tore around the corner past Mehmut's shop and continued down the road to where he had seen the dusty marks in the street. He followed the drag marks until he found the avenue they had passed.

The drag marks terminated at the door to the abandoned shop that lay at the end of the avenue. Guarding the makeshift jail was the same squad they had seen earlier in the day – four soldiers and their commander. Harel paused and stretched his limbs as the troops caught sight of him. They pointed at him and shouted. Here was his chance, he knew. He began to run straight at them.

He picked up speed. At the end of the street one of the soldiers held up a hand and shouted again, but he continued, faster than before. They raised their guns, training on him as he sprinted. Gunfire echoed from the building walls as they shot in the narrow alley, but he continued, legs pumping. A round tore into his shoulder, rotating his torso. Another drove through his thigh. He grimaced in pain, but within seconds the bullet flew out and the wound closed as he kept running. He lowered his head, diving the remaining distance at his attackers with a burst of energy, arms outstretched.

He took the first two out with his initial leap, driving their heads into the pavement and knocking them out despite their helmets. Continuing his forward motion, he rolled onto his feet with amazing speed. The commander, stunned, was now directly in front of him. Harel lashed out with an open hand, clubbing the squad leader in the head. His blow landed on the man's helmet with such force that he felt the bones of his hand splinter, but the strike accomplished its purpose. The man spun around violently, eyes fluttering even before his head slammed into the door of the nearby military vehicle.

Harel flexed his hand as it healed, the bones crackling into place as he sized up the remaining soldiers. With the element of surprise gone, they raised their guns to shoot. Adrenaline pumping, he barely even felt the first round as it slammed into his chest. Through gritted teeth he snarled and dove forward, wrenching the rifle from the man's hands and flipping it around to grasp the barrel. He swung the rifle like a baseball bat, connecting with the first soldier's helmet as the second man fired. The man's helmet flew off from the terrible blow, and he sank to the ground, unconscious.

But the remaining soldier's aim was true. The round shattered Harel's jaw, dislocating the bones. Teeth flew from his mouth in bloody arcs as they pinged against the sheet metal of the military vehicle. Blood ran down the hanging flesh and splintered bone that was once his mandible, and he felt it gush in torrents onto his chest from the open wound.

Staring squarely into the soldier's dumbfounded eyes, he raised his hand and lifted the hanging jaw back into place. As the soldier gaped, too shocked to fire again, teeth sprouted from bone and tissue knitted together. He felt his jaw snap back into its socket and his ligaments rejoin. Fully healed, he wiped the blood from his face while staring at the soldier, who now had dropped his rifle in abject fear. It clattered against the pavement as Harel smiled at him with a deadly stare. Then he lashed out with his foot, landing a kick squarely on the man's chest and sending him flying to the end of the alley over ten meters away. The soldier's body slammed into the sheet metal barrier where he crumpled to the pavement, unmoving.

He stepped over the supine troops and strode to the metal door of the abandoned shop. Still flush with emotion and power, he grasped the handle and pulled, tearing the door from its hinges. Behind it sat Andrew, handcuffed, his back to the wall. He was shaking and muttering, but there was a curious look in his eyes.

After a moment of surprise Harel held out a hand. Andrew accepted it with his both of his, and Harel hauled him to his feet. Grabbing Andrew's wrists he tore the links apart, twisting the metal cuffs until they snapped from Andrew's wrists. Together they walked out into the fading afternoon sun.

Shuddering, Andrew surveyed the unconscious soldiers. "You're a regular fucking Captain America," he commented dryly.

Harel grinned. *There's fight left in him yet,* he thought. "Hey – I *told* you you'd need me here," he replied, clapping Andrew on the shoulder. He held his hand there and looked into Andrew's eyes somberly. "And now we need *you*. We *need* you, Andrew. Whatever you're fighting inside, no matter what demons you're keeping at bay, your friends need you to snap out of it and help. *Now*."

Andrew closed his eyes and drew a deep breath, then nodded. "All right. Take me there."

Harel smiled and slapped him on the arm. "Come on, we need to hurry. They're in a rough spot."

"I won't even ask why you think I can help," Andrew commented, but together they turned, stepped over the soldiers and jogged out of the alley.

Andrew's ears were ringing, but this time not only from the pressure in his head. Shells exploded around them as they sprinted up the old riverbed. A constant barrage of gunfire sounded from all directions as he followed right behind Harel. Suddenly the soldier angled across the canyon toward an overhang carved into the rock face, and together they shot up the slope at an inhuman pace. Andrew could make out the huddled forms of the little group. In a burst of speed they dove for the shelter.

Kabilito smiled broadly at Andrew. "Welcome back, my friend," he said loudly into his ear.

"I didn't think you'd let me leave," Andrew yelled back, his voice competing with the din of explosions. "I thought..."

"You needed time alone. I understand," Kabilito interrupted, his words suddenly too loud against a lull in the battle. He dropped his voice. "It was best that you walked your own path for a time, even if only to see that you were not a prisoner. But you've also been losing control, and it was causing instability within yourself *and* the group. You've been fighting almost every decision since the test back in the valley." Kabilito clasped Andrew on the shoulder. "Your story is not complete, Andrew. Somehow I knew you would be back with us. You weren't in any real danger, and you knew how to reconnect with the tribe. I think you also needed to regain your faith – in both yourself *and* us."

Kabilito looked over at Harel before continuing. "And if I'm correct in discerning David's plan, we need you at this moment."

"But what can *I* do?" Andrew asked. "I haven't gained

any more control over the power. I might use the voice once or twice, but then..." He squinted in pain as the buzzing in his head returned.

"Once or twice might be enough," Harel said.

Andrew buried his face in his hands and shook his head. "I'm barely holding it together. This presence inside me is closing in, taking over – like a voice screaming louder and louder inside my head..."

He trailed off as Meg peered above the rock overhang in bewilderment. Andrew raised his head, suddenly aware of the silence.

"Why have they stopped?" Meg asked.

Her question was immediately answered as five Uyghur resistance fighters crested the hill and began running full speed down the slope, rifles swinging wildly as they rushed the opposite side.

"What the hell?" Harel voiced, astonished.

"They're desperate," Yeh Xin answered, "but doomed."

Mehmut stood, his face twisted in horror. "No!" he screamed at the men rushing down the slope. But it was too late.

A mortar round whistled overhead and tore into the slope, throwing the five men skyward. Limbs flew, bodies were torn apart by the explosion, and gunfire erupted from the Chinese soldiers on the opposite hill.

One of the bodies was tossed clear across the ravine and up the slope, falling right near their position. Both his legs were gone, and blood gushed from the stumps. His left arm was shredded by shrapnel, but still he raised his face to stare hollowly at Mehmut. He reached out with his right arm, an act of desperation by a man in shock not yet aware of his own death.

Recognition replaced the horror in Mehmut's eyes. "Alim?" he whispered, studying the man with disbelief.

Mehmut rose to help, but Harel pulled him down by his robe. Just then a single gunshot ripped through the afternoon air, echoing across the slopes, and suddenly crimson spouted from a hole between the man's eyes. His head fell forward to slam against the rocky slope.

"Alim!" Mehmut screamed as Harel pulled him back down again. Bullets pinged from the rock overhang as the Chinese targeted their cover, and explosions resumed all around them. A rocket was launched from the Uyghur hill in a puff of smoke, slamming into the crest of the Chinese side in an explosion of rock and dust. Screams drifted from the hilltop, and Andrew could hear voices shouting in Mandarin to take cover.

It was too much for Andrew – the translation of languages, the buzzing in his head, the gore, the horror, the explosions and fighting, all reaching an intolerable crescendo in his brain. His eyes rolled back in his head and his lids fluttered as he sank to the ground and lay on the rocky soil. He was dimly aware of Kabilito's face, thrust into his field of vision, yelling something at him. Few words trickled through the confused overload of images and sounds.

"*Embrace the power, Andrew,*" he heard. The words were distorted, as if spoken through a long tunnel. Meg's face joined Kabilito's, concern etched on her brow. The impossibly blue sky framed their faces, rocket trails crisscrossing and spinning above their heads, explosions erupting all around. The buzzing noise now reached a shrill, piercing whine that dominated his thoughts as the world spun and circled above him. Kabilito's lips were moving again, and a distant voice tickled Andrew's mind.

"Embrace it, and share the load..."

Yeh Xin's face joined theirs, hovering over him, spinning around with the others. Akiiki and Subira looked down at him now, speaking softly to each other. Finally Harel stooped over him, yelling something and motioning toward the opposite slope. Andrew's head rolled to the side – a weak effort to see where Harel pointed. But all he could make out was Mehmut, screaming in Turkish and sobbing over his fallen friend's body.

His head rolled back and he looked up at his friends. His mind was a cracked dam behind which floodwaters swelled, rising higher and higher, rivulets streaming and leaking from the faulty wall.

"...Use the voice...stop the fighting..."

The power was amplified, and he knew it was impossible to absorb it all into himself, impossible for him to harness the voice again without losing his mind.

"...Can't resist it any longer, Andrew..."

He felt his consciousness slipping as the faces above him swirled and spun, blending together – Turkish, Chinese, American, African and Anglo. He was astonished at the cultural diversity and stunned that it hadn't sunk in earlier. It was as if he was seeing them all for the first time. He realized now that they didn't simply represent different cultures – they were all different religions as well: Muslim, Buddhist, Jewish, even Meg with her fledgling Hindu faith, all thrown together by fate. The faces swirled around him, each flush with the power of the fruit, the magnified power swelling in each of them now that the power had shifted, intensifying in all of them...

Through the madness he felt a presence, a force pushing him forward, a quiet strength – a hand on a rudder, guiding, steering...

And then it dawned on him.

The prophecy – the shift in humanity, a change in the very people of the world, as dreamed by Akiiki long ago. They came to the tribe one by one – each from a different background, with different cultures, different religions – and the fruit changed them all.

Together we are all a representation of humanity – a unification across race and creed. The power had been gaining strength all along as the newcomers were added, including himself. And it grew faster and faster with each new person, with each new race, with each new religion added to a tribe that was, until recently, *completely homogenous in race and creed.*

The change in humanity promised in the prophecy was the power growing, accelerating in its amplification as the people of the world assembled. Not all were represented, but enough – enough to realize a shift in the power of the fruit and to start down the path.

We *are the sign, personified and realized, at long last*. He knew now that the tribe simply misread Akiiki's dream. It was never meant to be observed on a macro scale – not witnessed in the world as a whole, but instead on a micro scale, in the very people converging around them. It was there all along, and they all had missed it...

Until now.

But why did the new powers manifest in him alone? Did the newcomers not yet have enough fruit in their blood? And maybe the blood of the tribe had been imbued with the power of the fruit for so long that a shift in the power took longer? If only he could clear his mind, stop the turbulent storm and share his thoughts...

Sound filtered in amidst the piercing noise. "*...Share the burden...*"

Was that even Kabilito speaking? And what did it mean? How could he share the burden when the power was walled up inside himself, shut off from the rest of the tribe behind a protective shield? The wall felt both alien and familiar, all at once...

But then he realized something more. *The wall was his own doing*. He had created it that day so long ago in the valley. It was a command spoken when he first touched the power, when he had forced Subira to submit.

The sudden surge of power had scared him – it was something alien, something foreign, overwhelming and irresistible. And he realized now what he had done in that very moment. Reacting to the fear, he had subconsciously reshaped his command, simultaneously forcing Subira to concede while erecting a protective shield – a wall to prevent this new force from spreading any further than himself, to prevent the tribe from being overtaken or controlled.

He had unwittingly commanded them all to block the new power.

But it was meant to be *shared*. The block he had forced upon them had created the wall in his own mind, a wall that suppressed power that couldn't possibly be held by one man alone – *and it was driving him mad*.

A veil lifted from his mind. With utter clarity he suddenly knew what was required. He closed his eyes and dissolved his resistance. The faults in the wall widened as the entire barrier shuddered and finally gave way. The dam exploded and the floodwaters rushed over him, flushing away every thought, drowning his mind.

He reawakened and his eyes flew open. Then he sat

upright and sprung to his feet. His lips parted, and words began to flow. The sound reverberated like a cosmic cello, its strings vibrated by a giant bow. The command burst from Andrew's open mouth, echoing from the hillsides, crashing over the mountains. It slammed into the glacial peaks of the Bogda Shan, where great slabs of ice crashed to the rocks below and snow avalanched down the slopes in great billowing clouds.

He commanded all of them to know the truth of the prophecy revealed – that the power of universal communication and compulsion was theirs to use – and he commanded them to embrace the power themselves.

Their bodies went rigid as it flowed into them. And as they slowly regained their senses, light dawned in their eyes, and Andrew smiled.

He was whole again.

Chapter Thirty-Six

***W**ar.*

The thought of it terrified the President. It temporarily dominated his thoughts as he absently fingered the edge of his desk. The briefing continued, though, and as he was obligated to listen, he forced his mind back into the meeting.

"And the list of evacuated embassies goes on," Secretary Bryce Rosemark was saying. "The Chinese embassy in the Netherlands was attacked this morning by Uyghur activists – they stormed the facility and burned the flag. Riots in Turkey have shut down the Chinese embassy, and they're officially boycotting imports from China, formerly one of their biggest trading partners. Not to mention the demonstrations denouncing Chinese actions in Xinjiang that have been going on here in D.C., in New York, and most recently in Boston and San Francisco."

The president gripped the desk tighter as Rosemark's

aide picked up where the Secretary left off. "Mr. President, as you know, Russia has been sympathetic with the Chinese side, as have North Korea and Brazil. Our intelligence indicates that Russia and China have recently been conducting joint military drills in the Altai Mountain range. These troops are amassing both in Xinjiang and in the Altai Republic of Russia, along the small strip of land just east of Kazakhstan. The Kazakhstanis are infuriated, and they're now mobilizing troops along their eastern border as well. The Russians, of course, deny any involvement in the drills. The net effect is a destabilization of this already volatile region. In Xinjiang, fighting continues in the Bogda Shan between the displaced rebels and the Chinese militia. And now that the cat's out of the bag with our Manas operations in Kyrgyzstan, we're being blamed for the resistance."

Finally Colonel Frank Anderson leaned forward with an update on the African and Middle Eastern activities. "Iran is throwing support behind the Muslim Uyghur, as expected. In Israel, Palestinian shelling has resumed, partly in support of the Muslim Uyghur, partly in reaction to Israel's condemnation of the resistance. This strengthens Israel's ties with China, which were growing rapidly due to increased trade anyway."

Frank paused. "As Secretary Rosemark's office reports, our Manas operations are no longer a secret. There have already been attacks – a shipment was hijacked soon after leaving the base, and it's only a matter of time before equipment is sabotaged at the base itself. There's nothing stopping China from marching into Kyrgyzstan at this point – they've been on the verge of doing so for over a year. Tensions were already high over narcotics trafficking and the rapid Chinese population explosion. The Uyghur are just another flash point. Chinese sympathizers in eastern Kyrgyzstan are rioting, and we have intel indicating that Chinese forces are beginning to amass at the border, staring across at the Kyrgyzstani troops. This is *in addition* to China's joint operations with Russia in the Altai Mountains. Eastern Kyrgyzstan is basically turning into the next Crimea. And if they march while our troops are still positioned in Manas, well..."

The President sat back in his chair and sighed while chewing his pen distractedly. It dawned on him that this wasn't very presidential. He put the pen down and wiped the saliva from his lips. "All right, Bryce – you've convinced me. Increase the alert level, but I'm still not giving up Manas. And gather the Joint Chiefs of Staff for an emergency meeting at the Pentagon. This sounds like it has the potential to fall apart real fast, especially if an invasion challenges our troops in Kyrgyzstan. I want deployment plans together – like, *yesterday*."

Chapter Thirty-Seven

Zhang Li set the tablet down on the bench and rubbed her temples. *I'm the lead pharmaceutics scientist at the Beijing Advanced Warfare Laboratories Facility, dammit – one of the most technologically advanced facilities in the world – and I can't even grow a plant.*

The growth data on the fruit was abysmal. *More like mortality data*, she thought. The seeds germinated well enough, but when placed into the hydroponic media and exposed to artificial sunlight they just...*withered*.

Sighing, she hopped from the padded stool and crossed the lab to the growth chamber, where humidity, temperature and pressure were monitored and controlled. The duration and even the frequency of light could be programmed from the control systems, as well as the concentration and specific chemical composition of the nutrient solution added to the hydroponic media. Several assistants were bent over the control board, and Zhang Li arbitrarily grabbed one by the lab coat lapels, hoisting his head up from the panel. Sweat beaded on his brow as he recognized his assailant.

"Cross reference the sprout growth with the various hydroponic chemistries," she barked into his face, "then see if we overlooked any traces of soil on the remaining fruit skins that we can analyze." She glanced down at the boy's nametag. "*Today*, Li Qiang – not *tomorrow*, not *the next day*, but *today*." She released his coat and he scurried off, breathing heavily.

Stupid military idiots bring back fruit from the field without any soil samples, she thought, irritated. *Am I supposed to* guess *the soil chemistry these things need to thrive?*

She ducked her head into the next room, a large, third generation NME genetics lab. It was here that new molecular entities were made from naturally occurring chemicals, such as from plants, bacteria or animals. At one time new compounds were once replicated chemically; no one wanted to milk them from the organisms themselves. It was nearly impossible to duplicate them perfectly, so they used to try formulation after formulation until they hit on a close surrogate that demonstrated the same beneficial effects they wanted from the original, naturally occurring drug. But this old style of iterative chemical engineering took enormous amounts of time and money.

Enter the new third generation approach practiced in this lab. Here they removed much of the chemical fumbling by genetically altering the original plant, animal or bacteria. The mutated organisms could then synthesize *libraries* of compounds with similar properties to the original one, eventually producing one with a molecular structure that the chemists could mass-produce in drug form.

The scientists in this room conjured up impressive creations – almost God-like, in a way – but they were still her underlings. *And before they could begin genetic alterations they needed an actual plant to work with, dammit.*

"Liu Chang – LIU CHANG!" she called from the doorway. She saw his head jerk up from a group of his peers at one of the meeting tables in the center of the room.

"Yes, ma'am?" he replied obligingly.

"Get that field commander on the phone. Ask him when my soil samples are getting here, and tell him I'd better like the answer or my next call is to his superior officers – *got it*?"

"Yes, ma'am!" Liu Chang called back, pushing away from the meeting table in a hurry.

Zhang Li turned and stormed from her lab down the corridor. Using her key card, she opened a heavy door labeled "Advanced Biologics Operations Research – Security Clearance Required." She nodded at the guard as he quickly removed his feet from the top of his desk to stand at attention. She placed her chin in the plastic cup in the wall and forced herself to relax as the retinal scan system identified her, responding with a soft click as the door before her unlocked.

Inside she disconnected her secure tablet from the charging station and punched in her password. As she strode down the long, narrow room she reviewed the data collected from each subject, noting the most recent results. The dutiful soldiers, each a "volunteer," lay in biometric cots in rows on either side of her. Intravenous lines dripped the latest extractions into their bloodstreams, and several of them were eating a slurry made from the dwindling supply fruit extracts. Each milligram of the compound that went into a soldier made her wince, for she knew all too well that it was irreplaceable. But her government demanded results, and so they had begun trials with what they had. She shuddered as she adjusted the IV drip on one of the subjects, reducing the flow.

Dammit – I need that soil.

Passing the row of subjects, she reached the operating room door at the back of the facility. Another card swipe and she was inside the double door chamber that led to the OR. The first door was designed to close before the second opened, and both doors were soundproofed – a necessary design, for once she was past the second door she was met with a blood-curdling shriek.

She pulled aside a curtain and saw Wu Yue, the Chinese soldier who stole the fruit from the tribe, lying shirtless on a biometric cot. He was hooked up to several monitors, and his hands and feet were strapped down. His chest was covered in blood, some of it dry, some fresh. A team of clinicians and scientists huddled over his bare chest as a surgeon bent to make another incision – this one deep.

Wu Yue screamed and closed his eyes as the scalpel cut. His clavicle and upper anterior ribs were briefly visible before blood welled up and flowed over the skin. A clinician stooped and measured the length of the cut as another recorded vital signs. Zhang Li squinted at the wound, marveling as the blood slowed and stopped while the incision closed itself. *It never gets old witnessing that*, she thought.

Her tablet connected to the secure WiFi, and she downloaded the most recent blunt force trauma data on Wu Yue. "Wait," she said, holding out a hand to arrest the surgeon's next cut. "This shows that the broken femur healed faster than the fractured skull. That's odd, given the relative bone mass. Are you sure this is correct?"

Wu Yue twitched on the cot. His eyes flew open, targeting her. She looked down at him, her interest piqued. He began to cackle madly, but soon broke into outright laughter. Crazed peals of hysterical mirth burst from his open mouth, and he stared wildly into her eyes.

The insane howls continued as she shrugged and noted the observations on her tablet.

Chapter Thirty-Eight

Andrew watched as Kabilito and the rest of the group reeled from their newfound power.

I know what it feels like, he thought.

"Listen," he said, addressing the group. "It's scary – it's a rush of power. I've been there. But you'll find that as you accept it, you're able to speak *with anyone*. Yes, your strength is greater, and you'll find healing is faster, too. But beyond that, you can *compel*. You can fashion words that both communicate with and command *anyone*."

Meg shook her head, recovering from her thoughts. "Andrew, you said the power was turning you, making you go mad. Is that no longer the case?"

"No," he replied. "It was pent up inside, and without knowing it, I blocked it from all of you. It was meant to be shared, to grow in all of us. So it swelled inside me, and I misinterpreted that as turning. But it's manageable now that

I'm not trying to contain all of it."

"But why you?" Harel asked. "Why did the power manifest in you alone?"

Andrew shook his head. "I can only guess. Maybe I was more attuned to change, being newer to the fruit than the original tribe. But I also have a stronger connection than you, Meg and Yeh Xin because I've been around it longer."

Kabilito held up a hand. "Have you noticed something? The bombs – the explosions – they're still all around us, yet we're able to communicate..."

Recognition dawned in Andrew's face, and he finished Kabilito's thought. "...with our minds. We're communicating without speaking, now that the block is lifted."

Astonishment rippled through the group and heads turned side to side as each realized they were hearing the other. Even Mehmut, with such limited exposure to the fruit, was part of the revelation.

"It's like what the apostles experienced in Acts," Kabilito shared, projecting to the group.

"What happened in Acts?" Meg asked.

Andrew heard Akiiki's thoughts as he addressed Meg's question. "In Acts, the apostles were teaching in Jerusalem. Learned men of all nations came to listen to their message, but they all spoke different languages. The apostles were suddenly filled with a power from heaven. Tongues of flame descended upon them, and the Holy Ghost filled the halls. They spoke in tongues that everyone could understand simultaneously, and the foreigners were amazed. In this manner the apostles were able to spread the word of the Lord to all men of all nations."

Andrew absorbed this, stunned. Not only could they speak any language, but their communication now transcended even sound. The enormity of the power and responsibility the maisha endowed was astonishing. *Just as the apostles must have felt in their task to spread the word of the Lord,* he thought.

Subira touched their minds with his. "Enough – it is an amazing tool, but let's find a way to use it, as with the other gifts of the fruit. Andrew has shown us the way of the prophecy, that the world would have need of the fruit's power. Now we must share this power, and instead of observing the world and looking for a sign, we must interact with it in a positive way, so that all may benefit. What better way to begin than for us to stop this battle with our newfound power?"

"Exactly," Andrew added, refocused by Subira's thoughts. "David gave me the answer as we ran back here from Urumqi, although given my instability at the time, I didn't hold out much hope for success. But now that we all share this gift..."

He trailed off as Harel laid out the plan. "Basically, we cut off the head and the snake dies. In this case, the squad leaders control the troops, and they all report into the field commanders, like a chain. We just need to work our way up the chain to the snake's head."

They scattered soon after making their plans. In the end they decided it was best that Mehmut stay behind in the shelter of the overhang. Certainly some of the power's accelerated effects had begun to grow within him, but it was unclear how much healing he had gained with the small amount of maisha he had ingested.

Harel, Andrew, Kabilito and Meg split off to take the Chinese side while Yeh Xin, Subira and Akiiki ran toward the Uyghur. With each other as eyes and ears, avoiding attacks was easier as they sprinted up their respective hills. Harel and Yeh Xin's combat training picked out the likely defensive positions and warned their groups as they fanned out and breached the crests, and both groups were in communication with each other as they turned the assault back on the troops.

Still, it was understood that injuries were unavoidable. Taking the lead as they approached the first squad, Harel was utterly torn apart by machine gun fire. Meg and Andrew split left and right toward separate groups of soldiers as Kabilito jumped high in the air, leaving Harel on the ground to heal. Andrew saw Kabilito land in the midst of Harel's attackers, where he shouted his first command.

A moment later he heard Kabilito in his own mind. "It worked! They dropped their weapons."

Harel healed and was rising from the ground as Andrew heard him communicating with Kabilito. "Great! Now tell the leader to reveal himself and order the others under him to cease fire."

Just then Andrew came within earshot of several entrenched troops, running faster than they could react. It wasn't immediately clear who were the commanders and who were foot soldiers, but with the power of compulsion it mattered little.

Andrew's anxiety rose as he let the power swell within him to compel, but as soon as the command issued from his mouth he was relieved. Gone were the buzzing sounds, the pressure in his head, and the feeling of dread. He no longer struggled to maintain control. His was a mission from God himself, and he wasn't about to fail.

The powerful words seized the troops, and he shaped them as they flowed. Their eyes widened, and their bodies went slack. As if possessed, they dropped their weapons and lay on the ground passively. Compelled to identify himself, their commander stood, dumbfounded.

"Cease fire and retreat to your base," Andrew commanded. "Tell all under your command to do the same. Do not harm another Uyghur this day."

The stunned man immediately picked up his radio to comply. He pressed the mic button and began calling his troops.

In his mind Andrew heard Yeh Xin and his team having similar success across the canyon. But just as the squad commander started to issue orders into his radio, pain suddenly exploded in Andrew's head, and he fell backward.

Then...blackness.

He floated for a while in a cosmic ether. He felt a presence, and a warm light washed over him. Then he was flying through a tunnel of stars, rushing toward the exit. A voice crept into his consciousness, far off in the distance, and he opened his eyes to see Kabilito bent over him.

"Andrew – you were shot through the head," he said.

Andrew sat up and felt the back of his head. Blood dripped from his hair and pooled on the ground, but his skull was intact.

"Whoa – that was intense," he replied, as Kabilito helped him to his feet.

"I shut down another squad," he heard Meg communicate from somewhere nearby.

Andrew and Kabilito stood listening to the growing silence on both sides of the ravine. Only sporadic gunfire remained. The plan was working.

"I've got the field commander here," Harel communicated from a distant location. "He's ordering them all to retreat." Andrew heard him chuckle. "His commanders in Urumqi were going crazy on his radio, so I told him to turn it off. He'll have hell to pay when he gets back there."

"Mission accomplished over here, too," Yeh Xin said from the far crest. "They're headed back to the camp in the mountains. We'll see you back by Mehmut."

Andrew jogged with Kabilito down the slope. Motion across the canyon caught his eye as he saw Yeh Xin, Akiiki and Subira converge on Mehmut's position from different locations.

Reaching the overhang, they all traded stories on how they neutralized the forces. Andrew realized that their ability to counteract many troops by reaching only a few leaders resulted in a powerful force multiplier. They were surprised at how efficient the plan had been, and they congratulated Harel.

Yet everyone had paid a price, Andrew observed. Harel's shirt hung in tatters and blood spattered his chest. Meg's right leg and her entire abdomen were shot through and soaked in crimson. From the pattern of blood Yeh Xin's neck appeared to have been hit, and Akiiki's clothes looked like Swiss cheese. Mehmut stared openly at them as he sat under the rock ledge, absently poking a finger through a hole in Subira's pant leg.

"As much as we've accomplished here," Subira said somberly, "we are far from the end. We may have stopped the fighting this day, but it will resume."

Akiiki nodded. "Clearly this gift was meant for a greater task, though today was a good start. The world will have great need of this in the coming months, I fear. Look at all that is transpiring – the struggles and conflicts of the world seem to be escalating. It can't be coincidence that the sign was realized at this time. If the realization of the prophecy is any indication of what's to come, I fear greatly for mankind. I believe we will have much work to do."

"Who's that?" Meg suddenly asked, pointing down the slope.

Andrew followed her outstretched arm and saw a robed man running from the opposite hill and into the riverbed, following the path up the mountain they had taken earlier that day.

"Maybe he didn't get the memo," Andrew said glibly.

Just then an explosion blasted the ground around the man, and Andrew saw his body fly high into the air. The man's left arm hung loosely from a few strands of flesh, and his leg was split open like an overcooked hot dog. Meg shrieked as the shattered body slammed into the ground near the resulting crater, and the group stared in dismay at the carnage left from the detonation.

"Ugh - a mine," Harel said, sadly. "Poor guy probably forgot where they buried their own..."

He trailed off and squinted at the body, and Andrew soon saw for himself the reason for his hesitation. For as they watched, the man's nearly separated arm...*moved*. It slid across the rocky riverbed toward his shoulder and reattached. His leg closed up, and the man who had been blown apart seconds ago sat up, pulling the hood of his shredded robe over his head as he turned in the direction of Meg's cry.

"What the..." Harel muttered.

The stranger leapt to his feet and sprinted up the riverbed faster than any normal human could run. Seconds later he was almost out of sight as he continued up the path and into the mountains.

"Let's go!" Andrew cried, running after him.

As they gave chase it was clear the man knew the region far better than they. He ducked into crevasses and jumped across ravines unseen to Andrew at first, but they continued nonetheless. He was clearly as fast and strong as they were. There was only one other that could muster such speed and strength. Andrew hoped that their mission to Xinjiang would soon end in his capture.

Eventually Mehmut fell behind, and after some rapid-fire group telepathy Akiiki dropped back slightly so they didn't lose him entirely.

Andrew's feet pounded rhythmically against the ground as he marveled at the man's speed. He jumped from boulder to boulder as he climbed up a steep rock shelf, occasionally twisting his ankles and skinning his legs against the sharp outcroppings. But he soldiered on, ignoring the pain while he healed.

At one point he heard a cry followed by a loud, sickening crack as Subira fell against a boulder ahead.

"I've broken my leg – go on. I'll catch up," he communicated to them as they raced ahead.

For the better part of an hour they gave chase. Subira eventually did catch up, though Mehmut and Akiiki lagged behind. Higher and higher they climbed at astonishing speed, and Andrew felt the air growing colder as the sky dimmed. The snow-capped points of Bogda Peak soon loomed overhead, and the terrain grew rockier. Ledges, overhangs and even small caves appeared all around him as he climbed, always keeping the robed man ahead in his sights.

Andrew could feel Kabilito, Yeh Xin, and Harel right behind him, with Meg and Subira close behind. They reached a crest and climbed over the sharp edge, dropping to the rock floor below. As the others jumped down from the crest to join him Andrew discovered that the terrain had suddenly opened in a wide, semi-circular escarpment with high walls.

It was a dead end. The man they had chased was now only a few meters in front of them. He slowed deliberately, then stopped with his back to the group. Andrew caught his breath with his hands on his knees before rising.

"End of the road, Jelani," he barked.

But something felt wrong. As his eyes adjusted to the darkened area Andrew realized that the escarpment face was riddled with openings, both high and low. Ladders rose to the higher ones, and rough wooden walkways ran along the rock face. Squinting, Andrew slowly realized that they were standing in a ring of caves – caves with trees hidden just inside their mouths. Trees that only now, with the sun at just the right angle, were illuminated with the light of the dying day – only a brief exposure until nightfall.

And each tree bore fruit shaped like an hourglass with red veins crisscrossing the skin.

Dread crept up Andrew's spine as men and women begin materializing from the darkness of the caves, each dressed similarly in rough-spun, hooded robes. More and more appeared – first ten, then twenty. They climbed down the ladders and emerged from the caves to stand next to the robed man. In the end perhaps sixty of them stood surrounding the little band of friends.

Slowly the man in the bloody tatters turned, unwrapping the remains of his hood.

Andrew heard Yeh Xin suck in his breath in shock when the man's face was finally revealed. "That's not Jelani," the spy whispered, forgetting his newfound telepathy.

Dark eyes glinted in the dying light, framed by the man's

youthful face.

"Welcome to Eden," he said in a rich voice.

Chapter Thirty-Nine

It was nighttime in the Ugandan wetlands west of Gulu as Jelani surveyed his army. Their numbers had swelled appreciably with his newest efforts.

They held torches aloft as he stood before them atop a wooden platform. He looked over the faces lit by flames flickering against the black sky – former Christian radicals standing side by side with Muslim militants, the latter freshly recruited from his recent trip to Mogadishu. A handful of Americans and Europeans were scattered throughout the group, social outcasts who felt the pull of adventurous rebellion. He chuckled inwardly at the irony of such a mix of lawless rebels – Muslim, Christian, African, European, even some from Asia and Pakistan, all held together by the might of his hand. They were coming along nicely, each healing and gaining power at an alarming rate.

But none as powerful as him. He waved toward the

orchard, now covered with the structure erected by their own hands, each tree awaiting its brief time in the next day's sun.

"We built this – together!" he shouted, and a roar rose from the acolytes. He smiled, a rush of power surging through his body.

"And together we will fight. We will cleanse the world of the infidels. For we are the chosen ones, and I your leader. And we alone can bring about the day of reckoning – with this, a gift from God!"

He held the fruit aloft to a deafening chorus of cheers. Then he summoned sound from his lips – a terrible sound that reverberated from the slopes and across the grassy plains. It crawled into the minds of his followers, commanding and compelling them to submit.

His army fell to the ground as one and worshipped him with outstretched arms.

ABOUT THE AUTHOR

As a partner and board member of an innovative advertising technology firm, engineer and entrepreneur John Butziger led teams in areas as diverse as environmental engineering programs, medical device research, and product development. He has worked in Manhattan for more than ten years, travelling internationally to deploy new technology and develop business opportunities. He drew upon his extensive experience in international entrepreneurship and science while writing Eden's Revelation.

With a master's degree in engineering and several patents, Butziger publishes in both domestic and international journals. He has lectured on entrepreneurship and engineering at Columbia University in New York City, and the HEC Business School in Paris, France.

Married with three children, Butziger lives in Rhode Island. His passions include travel, fishing, music, writing, and spending time with his family.

Visit his Facebook page for the Order Series

www.facebook.com/theorderseries

You can email him at John@JohnButziger.com

Or tweet him: @JButziger

www.JohnButziger.com

Please Leave a Review!

A lot of work goes into writing a book, and we as authors appreciate your feedback.

Kindly write a review of Eden's Revelation and leave a rating, and if you've read it, on The Second Tree (Book I of The Order Series) as well.

Reviews on Amazon, Goodreads, Barnes and Noble's Nook Press, iTunes, Smashwords or wherever you buy and review books is much appreciated.

Thank you for your support!

COMING SOON
from
John Butziger

Book III of The Order Series continues the story begun in *The Second Tree* and *Eden's Revelation.* The world is descending into chaos and war. Amidst the mortal battles of the world's military powers, superhuman tribes fight for the fate of mankind. Pivoting around sacred ground and biblical prophecies, the lines of cause and effect are blurred: will the power of maisha save the world, or herald its demise?